# *Dark Fantasies*
## *Volume One*

By Samantha Stewart

A collection of Erotic Interludes

*Copyright 2007*

**Dark Fantasies**
By Samantha Stewart

Copyright 2007

ISBN 978-0-6151-5379-7

Published by
*Wooden Paddle Publishing*
*Minnesota, USA*

First Printing February 2007

*Publishers Note*
*This is a work of fiction. Any resemblance to any person, place or occurrences is purely coincidental and is not intended to represent anything other than the author's wild imagination and vivid fantasy.*

www.woodenpaddlepublishing@gmail.com

### For my Husband...

*Peas was nothing extraordinary. Just a simple complex soul in a paranoid world. Someone you would come across and leave you with a smile before you began moving on. Peas was one to take on that world, shaking it to the breaking point. Then with a careless smirk leaving it unbalanced. She was just funny that way.*

*Peas moved along with that simplistic chaos until she crossed that path and stumbled at his feet. Peas was bewildered as she looked up. The sting to her knees ricocheted up her spine.*

*Sir's eyes were beautiful and downcast, almost piercing through her as she stayed put at his feet. Peas felt her gaze divert to the side as he grins.*

*Peas first impulses to run, fly and flee all but completely leave her. She is stunned and finds being there on her knees painfully peaceful. Looking at the treasure that just landed literally at his feet, Sir smiles knowingly.*

*Their eyes meet. Peas catches her breath. Where did he come from? Out of the blue.*

**For the one man who truly understands the woman I am and celebrates it with unconditional love.**

# The Appointment

I hated the idea that I was getting up on my day off to go. I dreaded this day for weeks. I could be going shopping or getting my nails done. Instead I was going to this appointment that I found about as comfortable as having my bikini line plucked hair by hair by a cosmetology student on the second day of her starting the class. Yes, on a scale of one to ten I would rate this a clean zero without any reservations.

My body was fine as far as I was concerned. As for the inside, my philosophy has always been what you can't see can't hurt. Of course with the exception of the infuriating yeast infection that tells you once and for all you are only going to enjoy being the lover boy's bowl for his hot fudge sundae once. All kidding aside, had I kept a better eye on the cherry at the top his sundae and not wrapped my legs around his back and begged for him to fill me with his sweet cream I may not have had to explain to my gynecologist the whole scene when she retrieved a rotten cherry hiding against my cervix two weeks later. After living down the embarrassment at the clinic I had to explain to my amour that he was forever banned from considering my body his serving dish.

I did the typical primping after the shower and focused on the rest of my day would begin if I just got the whole thing over with. Dr. Genesy was a wonderful physician with an open mind and awesome way of making you feel completely normal no matter what the issue is.

This visit was to be a routine check-up. I had it all planned down to minute by minute detail. Five minutes of the how you are conversation followed by hiking up the paper gown and sliding my ass down to the end of the table. Another 30 seconds discussing work as she warms up the hardware she intends to shove between my legs. Then it will be a minute tops where she is sitting between my thighs like an umpire trying to smile as she shoves cotton covered sticks inside swabbing for whatever catches her interest. I lay there looking at the ceiling thinking about whatever could possibly lead a woman to find looking into fifteen or twenty crotches a day interesting enough to make a career out of other than the income. Yes, a total of twenty minutes of mind blowing fun.

After I finish dressing and prepare to get in the car my cell phone rings. I answer while starting the car.

"Could I speak with Kristin, please?" The polite voice asked.

"This is Kristin." I answer.

"Great, Kristin, this is Dr. Genesy's office. Are you on your way to your appointment?" She asks as I back out of the garage and push the button for the door to close.

"Yes, is there a problem?" I ask hoping there is a sudden need for my gynecologist out there and I will have the day free of private probing.

"Not really." She answers in a soothing tone. "Dr. Genesy has been called out of town on a family emergency. She wanted you to still make it to your appointment today. She was afraid you wouldn't remember."

"I remembered. I actually would prefer to wait until she returns if that isn't a problem." I decide as I am moving through the intersection towards the mall.

"Actually she feels it is better if you come in today at the time you are scheduled. She has made sure that you will be fit into the other physician's schedules." The woman sounds assertive and not happy that I am wasting her time trying to bargain my way out of a more than accommodating doctor's intent to provide care. "You won't have to wait."

"Fine. I will be there." I give in instead of fighting about it. The sooner I get it over with the sooner I will be under the nail dryer debating where to meet Abby for her lunch break.

"Thank you, Kristin." The voice says satisfied she can move on to the next call victorious.

I end the call and realize that some stranger is about to put a wrinkle in my plans. How the hell am I suppose to strike up general conversation with a stranger as she sits between my legs digging for something abnormal? I feel my stomach twist in a knot and I look to see in the rearview mirror if *sucker* is stamped on my forehead. I take inventory of any makeup flaws after putting the car in park then brush on my favorite lip color. If you can't be confident at least look like you came to win the game.

"Hi, I am Kristin. I have an appointment for ten with whoever is taking Dr. Genesy's schedule for today." I announced as I stood at the reception area of the large office building.

"Yes, Kristin. We have you seeing Dr. Martinez. Dr. Genesy has an hour slot so that some time could be spent discussing some of your concerns you mentioned at your previous visit." The receptionist smiled clicking on the computer and turning around to retrieve the labels for my papers without giving me eye contact.

"An hour is not really necessary. I think the typical fifteen minutes is more than enough. In and out and no one gets hurt, right?" I laugh hoping she finds it as funny as I do that it just blurted out of my mouth without thinking.

"Uh, the time allotted for your appointment was set by your doctor and if there is a problem with it you are more than welcome to make a follow up appointment to discuss your concerns when she returns." The twenty something auburn haired twit smiled as if she was the deal maker or breaker in my fate behind the door that were to my left.

"That is quite okay. I have a busy schedule." I smile forcefully.

"Don't we all?" The twit agrees with a smirk before looking past me like I barely existed. "Next!"

I pull away from the counter and look for a seat while I imagine her computer malfunctioning and giving her such a shock that her hair twists up into a curly melting mess. That would take care of the attitude.

I barely sit when a nurse enters through the doors and my name is announced. I stand up and follow her through the hallways and towards the very back of the building. Finally after what seemed like a trek into a whole other set of offices I am led into a huge office suite complete with an examining table, beautiful desk and even a small sofa against the opposite far wall. Unusual from the typical sterile room with everything to poke you with in plain site that I was used to.

"Dr. Martinez will be with you shortly, Kristin. Please have a seat." The nurse asks waving a hand toward the chair in front of the desk.

"I am here for a routine gynecology appointment, right?" I ask dumbfounded by the large office and absence of those shiny silver tools they usually display proudly on the walls.

"Yes, you are. Dr. Martinez has come in on his day off at the request of Dr. Genesy to see you so that you don't have a chance to put it off. This Dr. Martinez's office and our regular examining rooms are full." The nurse smiles leaving the room and taking away any chance for me to change my mind.

I look around nervously thinking about making my way back out of the office before the doctor arrived. I know it is pretty pathetic to be so uneasy about any doctor but I have a whole routine set and it is as comfortable as it can get with Dr. Genesy.

Framed certificates lined the walls and I resist getting up and moving closer to read them. I admit the office is refreshing.

Kind of distant from the usual that I almost forget that I am going to have a perfect stranger poking at me in the room.

After ten minutes of waiting impatience takes over and I stand up. I make my way over to a shelf on the wall and find a few small pictures framed. One is of a beautiful woman with black hair posing at her desk. My eyebrows rise at the unusual setting but dismiss the thought as to if she is the one who will be playing with me today. I wait a few more seconds while brushing the bottom of my sundress down and finally look up at the next picture.

I pull it down for a closer look and it is of a wedding party obviously celebrating with champagne flutes in the air. The people and the setting strike me funny. Something is very familiar about both and I look at each person from the right to the left. I think of my stomach hurting from laughing and my head spinning from expensive champagne. It seems oddly familiar that I have seen this picture somewhere before. I study each face towards the left and each seems more familiar.

I look up from the picture for a minute trying to think of where I could have possibly seen it. I try to recall each cousin's wedding and each friend's and come up short. Sure that I recalled all the weddings I attended or was a part of I look back down for some clue as to where I could have seen the photo before. I find my eyes fall on something that should give me a solid clue…my face! I can't believe it, I am in the picture! There next to me is my college room mate and very best friend, Abby, and I finally remember the wedding dance it was taken at.

It was Abby's cousin that was married. Abby's boyfriend was out of town for a football game so she asked me along for an excuse to leave early. One drink led to another and we ended up having more than our share of open bar. I laugh as I remember how wild we were and how much fun it was to have no shame that night. I look at the last two people in the picture and my cheeks burn instantly. Holy shit! The guy that was tending bar there is next to Abby and holding up the champagne bottle that started the whole thing. Putting the photo back quickly, I go back to the chair feeling my palms sweat.

My mind races trying to figure out just who in the hell is going to walk through the door. Abby's last name was Palmer so it can't be her dad or one of her three brothers. I feel the apprehension fill my body from toes up. I swallow hard trying to remember everything I said and did that night intoxicated for the first time…many firsts took place that night.

It starts coming back piece by piece. Dancing alone on the dance floor when someone suggests I dance for the groomsmen. Abby cheering me on with the second shot of tequila didn't help. None of it makes me feel any better when I recall something vaguely about a flight of stairs and the hottest kiss while feeling sharp edges of each step grinding into my back. My heart drops when I remember it beginning on the stairs after he chased me up to retrieve the groom's garter I caught after a wild leap in the air. I told him he was a thief for stealing the kiss and he told me I was a criminal for leaving him with nothing to remember me by except the insatiable need for more.

I never felt more hot and reckless than when I closed that hotel room door shut and locked him out. He was dangerous and uninhibited. His illicit sexual whispers through the crack of the doorframe about what he wanted to do to me almost drove me to the insanity of unlocking it and letting him in. I was so tempted and naïve. I listened to his whispers and felt my body react with each word. I felt the warmth fill between my legs and shivered. So sweet was that kiss that pressed my body painfully to the steps that it takes my breath away even now as I think about it.

I hear a door open and close and realize I forgot to leave. I was sitting in the room and anyone could come through that door and remember me from the wedding. Abby and I made quite a scene. Seven years had passed but what if the person I was scheduled to see was offended enough to remember?

I felt my thighs grow damp and the backs of my knees chill when the breeze of air passed them as the person entered the room behind me. I sat back down and bit my lip as I could hear papers flipping in my chart. Only I could get into such a mess.

I wait for the person to pass and hear no footsteps. I look down to avoid eye contact and that is when I realize it is a man by the scent of his cologne that lingers over the back of my shoulder. Footsteps sound following the scent and I can see dark dress shoes and gray trousers stopping at the shelf. He faced the wall and I try to figure out who he is. He adjusts the photo with my face in the mix of people and I feel my skin prickle in embarrassment. My luck just ran out.

I hear my chart set down on the desk and I decide to stand up and back out of the appointment. The doctor walks back to the door and leaves closing it behind him. I make my move and hurry to the door. I am thinking *only five more steps* when the door opens and I walk right into his chest as he closes the door behind him.

"I am sorry." I apologize backing up. "I had a phone call and I have to leave."

"I doubt that very much, Kristin." The doctor turns my shoulders and faces me towards the chair walking behind me as I ma soon back to the chair.

"Really I should be going…" I make an effort to stand and his hands push firmly back down on my shoulders.

"I don't think so." The doctor says firmly. Leaning down to whisper, his lips brushing my ear. "We have unfinished business."

I must be hearing things. Unfinished business? Okay, maybe I put off appointments and cancel for every reason known to man to avoid being poked and prodded but it is my right. Who in the hell is he to tell me to stay put and finish something? This is not in the plan. There is malpractice written all over his first two comments.

"Put another hand on me and I will…" I say feeling the doctor come around the front of the chair to wait for me to stand.

"Scream?" The doctor laughed before I could look up. "Please tell me that is the case."

I look up and I can't speak. It is him! The bartender. The man with a kiss that could take my breath away. I felt my head swim and buzz. My ears started ringing. I think I am going to faint.

"What are you doing here?" I manage through a weak voice trying to keep from letting my knees buckle.

"I could ask you the same thing seeing as it is you that is standing in my office." He smiles at my shock as if he is finally pleased to have me right where he wanted.

"Your office? Please! I am waiting for the doctor to come in." I gasp moving away from the chair and back stepping towards the door in uncoordinated steps.

"Seems he already did." He walks toward me with a look on his face that said …*baby, you are in so much trouble!*

"Whoa, there!" I am trying to get my plan of action in my head when he gives me that look and I start having the warmth growing between my thighs all over again. "I am sorry but I must leave."

"You must do a lot of things, Kristen." He says looking down at my dress and touches my fingers as I try to cover my stomach in disbelief. "You must work hard, pay your bills, take your required vitamins and you must always finish what you start."

"Okay, I think it has been a little too bizarre to take in just now. I think we can just call it a day right now." I put my hands up to block him from standing any closer.

"Fine with me. I came in just for this appointment." He closed up the remaining space and was pressing his body against me leaving me to try to think straight and breathe at the same time. Two actions that require little effort any other time, but when the man at the center of your most erotic kiss ever pressing up against you seven years after the fact stuns you to say the least. Take my word for it.

"Seven years…" I say trying to push him away.

"Seven years too long with the biggest hard on for you." He whispers brushing his cheek against mine smelling my hair with an aching moan.

"I know this seems hard to believe but this is way too much. It was a wedding dance. It was a kiss. I didn't even know your name." I hear my voice fading, breaking under the sensation of his warm lips finding the pulse at my throat.

"It was a kiss alright. A kiss that I haven't been able to forget and neither have you." He sounds as if this just happened last weekend. "Dr. Martinez. But you can call me Adam."

"You are a bartender." I gasped remembering his talent at wild concoctions with a deliciously hazy sweet bite at your senses.

"Good enough to get me through medical school." Adam grinned leaning back and looking at me.

"I see that. I think I vaguely remember. Thanks again for the hang over from hell." I said once again pushing him away thinking if I push hard enough I can push this whole day out of reality.

"Let me make it up to you and give you a chance to finish what you started and I didn't get to finish." Adam pulled at my hips bringing me in closer than ever.

"Seven years." I manage to say looking into his dark sexy eyes.

"You got married or engaged since your last

appointment, Kristin?" He steps back pulling his hands away suddenly.

"Uh, well, no." I answer watching curiously as he pulls off his lab coat and hangs it up on the rack several steps from where I am standing.

"That makes things look promising." He asks pulling out paper and stretching it over the exam table. "Live-in boyfriend?"

I swallow nervously. "Um, no." Trying to figure out what the hell to do with this guy who seems to have all the credentials required to invade my body and the oral skill to get me beneath him even if he still mixed drinks.

"Then feel free to take a moment to slip into this gown while I get a few things ready." Adam says patting the gown on the table and squeezing my shoulder as he passed me to retrieve a few needs tools for his search of my body.

"You serious? You expect me to undress in front of you and then lay down and spread my legs for an exam." I blurt out in disbelief with my hands on my hips.

"Kristin, I am a doctor not Jack the Ripper." Adam laughed as he opened and closed several drawers in a wall hidden by beautiful wooden cabinets. "Please change into the gown. I am totally objective. Now if I was a dentist and had to focus on your mouth and those lips…"He paused to take a thoughtful breath before he said more than he should.

"Okay, now I know it is a really bad idea." I interrupt feeling my heart beat at the sound of his voice describing my mouth with such a sensual tone. Adam continues to look away and focus on his gathering equipment which seems to grow quite extensive.

"Stop. Get undressed. I am almost done. I finish before you are ready and I guess that means I get to watch. Now there is some incentive for you." He laughs at the sound of me grabbing the gown.

Now why I am in the process of getting undressed instead of taking three steps and moving my ass out the door I will never know. I guess maybe because he is a doctor and I don't want to offend a guy who worked his way through college to achieve the license to practice medicine. I guess I also didn't want to try and explain why I would be asking for my medical records to be transferred out to another physician. Dr. Genesy would really want an explanation. What was I going to say? Adam was as impressed all these years by the kiss that I was.

Ever have one of those moments where that little voice inside that always keeps you out of trouble forbid you to do what your body wanted so badly? Adam was it for me. The whole kiss just lingered in my mind every time a man would kiss me. I couldn't lie to my ex-boyfriend when he finally asked what it took to get me hot. I told him about the kiss and he told me to kiss his ass goodbye. He even took the gourmet ice cream maker we bought together!

"Taking one more look at your chart, Kristin. Then I am going to be ready." Adam informs as he flips through a few pages.

"Okay." I pull my sundress over my head and peel my panties off realizing they were wet just like the space between my legs. "I…" I suddenly stop talking when I realize this means he will discover I was soaking wet and ready for his long thick fingers.

"Great. Let's get started." Adam walks over with the chart open as he approaches where I am sitting on the edge of the exam table. "You have nothing remarkable on your history other than a mishap with a boyfriend and a sundae." He says with a taunting wink as he closes the chart and sets it down on the small table behind him.

"Ex-boyfriend, thank you." I interject trying to save what self-respect I have left.

"I am teasing you, Kristin. You are a healthy, young

woman who is sexually active and that is completely natural. I hope you know that." Adam says with a soft smile meant to reassure me.

"I know that. I didn't need you to give me permission." I snap irritated that the man who bequeathed to me the single most erotic experience of my lifetime was now gaining insight into my limited and clumsy sex play after him. Just what I wanted to have him think I was... a naïve twit. "It takes more than a cherry to get me discouraged."

I feel my cheeks prickle in embarrassment at what blurts out of my mouth while he looks at me in surprise.

"I can imagine." Adam narrows his gaze looking at me with a deciphering focus. His eyebrows rise as he exhales and shakes his head stepping closer to the table and me. I roll my eyes is total disgust at my inability to maintain any sense of ground when it came to him.

Adam takes my vitals without a trace of being unprofessional. "Sounds good. You take care of yourself obviously." He comments listening to my lungs from the front and back.

"I guess." I say hesitating on whom to pay attention to Dr. Martinez or Adam. Both were overwhelming to keep track of. "Are we done now?"

"Very funny, Kristin." Adam leans down next to my legs dangling off the table at the end and pulls out an extension. "You really have a problem with doctors, don't you?"

"You are right, I do. Only those who like to be poked, prodded and even slapped go back for more. I personally wait until they call me. I am proud of the fact that I have to be begged to come in for a regular check-up."

"Are you proud of the fact you can have a person beg or the fact you return for more poking?" Adam laughs bringing my legs up on the extension like a gentleman. "The slapping sounds kind of fun, actually."

I catch my breath at the feel of his bare hands on my legs and his inquiry hanging in the air waiting for a response. Talk about sensory overload. It hit me like a semi-truck.

"The slapping was simply a metaphor." I try to explain my way out of what could be a hint of undiscovered pleasures he assumes I have yet to experience. "I am not into that kind of thing." I sound pitiful after the sentence leaves my mouth.

"There is nothing to explain. If you do you do, Kristin. If you don't then you don't." He smiles like he knows what I may or may not like.

"Thank you, Dr. Ruth, but I keep my kinks to myself and tend not to share them with my gynecologist." I say with my hands fastening tightly to the sides of the exam table.

"And here I thought you were going to divulge your deepest and darkest desires to me. I am disappointed." Adam smirks reaching for my neck.

"Glad we clarified that then." I say with a cool tone hoping he buys the comment.

"Guess I will have to warm up the Tequila and wait in line at the next wedding dance then." He laughs allowing his thumbs to stroke the sides of my face as his long fingers brush at my neck.

Adam reaches slowly up and down my jaw line and feels my neck for any abnormalities. I try not to look into his eyes as he massages the tips of his fingers firmly under the sides of my jaw. He smells so rich and I can't ignore the scent of his hands. I think of using the tip of my tongue to taste the inside of wrist where his warm pulse would be the most sweet. He steps back and reaches behind him to retrieve a hand held contraption to check something else.

"I need you to hold still." He asks as he approaches my face with a tool in his hand.

"Okay." I say as my eyes widen.

"I am going to check your ears." Adam informs me as he

17

places the tip of the light inside my ear and looks in for anything he has or hasn't seen in some medical journal I couldn't begin to pronounce. I think of him finding something gross and I feel my stomach knot up. "Looks good like everything else so far."

"That makes me feel better." I smile as he moves a step away tossing the disposable cover on the tip of his gadget.

"It does?" He asks looking at me with a relaxed smile.

"Could you stop that?' I ask irritated that his smile is making me weaker than I can afford. The closer he gets to my body the less I can resist responding.

"Stop what, Kristin?" He asks softly as he leans on both hands looking into my eyes with such an intense wanton gaze. I feel the content of the world as we know it has been momentarily vacuumed out leaving just him and me.

"That!" I hiss. "You know what you are doing!"

"Lay back." He asks lifting my legs up to rest on the extension on the table. "Please."

"Fine. Anything to get this over with." I sigh looking up at the ceiling folding my arms over my chest.

"Thank you." He laughs softly at my defiance.

Adam slides his hands under the sheet covering my lower body and begins his inventory of what is or isn't there. I roll my eyes and try to look inconvenienced as the touch of his bare hands across my skin sends my nipples to erect points. His fingertips press into my abdomen thoroughly following the usual pattern.

"Do you exam your breasts monthly?" Adam asks as he moves upward in his travel.

"I…" I gasp when his hand is covering my right breast with such heat that my back arches and I gasp in shock at my body's reaction. "Yes…" I squirm in horror that I am reacting to his simple touch in such a hungry manner. "Thank you." I try to move only to find his free hand raise my right arm over my head to rest on the exam table as it should.

"Relax, Kristin." He breathes as I close my eyes in denial while his hand closes and squeezes the mass of my breast expertly.

I catch my breath and think of the Watergate Scandal and my father arguing with my mother on the resignation of Spiro Agnew and the country going to hell. I have no other choice. Except to let my body catch on fire with the next movement of his hand and turn the office into a bonfire waiting to fry all laws of the doctor patient boundaries and public indecency to boot.

Why? You tell me. I have the hottest kisser in my opinion touching my tits seven years later who traded his permit to sell liquor in for a medical license. What more could you want? He is single and made it clear he wanted to take up where we last left off the minute he realized who I was.

"Tell me if this is uncomfortable." Adam instructs as his hands obviously finish with my breast exam and proceed to prompt my feet to lift as he pushes in the extension on the exam table.

"If what is uncomfortable?" I ask as I hold my feet at the same level as if the extension was still in place.

"Not holding your feet up." He laughs placing them into the foot rests that he unfolds from the side of the table giving my calf a reassuring pat.

"Why can't we skip this part?" I sigh covering my face with my hands knowing the minute his hands venture past my naval that anything will be fair game. Don't ask why I lack self-control at my navel but it is a fact he never had the chance to find out.

"Relax." He whispered as he pulled my hips forward as if he intended to adjust me for anything but a professional exam.

Adam smiles as my ass slides down the wax paper to his desired point of reference. I roll my eyes trying to search my memory bank for things like helping Aunt Delyn after her hip surgery to the bathroom. I find the reserve of *so not erotic* memory rapidly dissipating as he places his warm palms on the inside of my thighs.

"Easy for you to say." I puff as I look towards a blank space on his office wall.

"Maybe this will help." He said as his hands lift from my thighs and reappear brushing like a salacious whisper against my skin in-between the most vulnerable spaces known on any woman.

"I think that ..." I try to stall the inevitable which increased his delight.

"You think what?" Adam asks as I bite my lip much to his pleasure as I close my eyes to ignore what my libido cannot.

Of course it is my last ploy left. How else do I contain my reaction to his fingers slipping into the most delicate space tucked silkily between a tightness that has barely been breached thus far by two men? Not that Dr. Feelsgood needs any helpful hints knowing my use thereof after medical school training his skillful hands like female anatomy detectors. A smile appearing across his exquisite face alerts me that his knowledge of my personal space is plentiful. Call me busted and with nowhere to hide.

"I am in trouble." I resolve out loud for the benefit of both of us.

"Depends on what you consider trouble, Kristin." Adam purrs as his fingers flutter their skilled way into my deceiving tunnel within.

I arch my back subconsciously and close my eyes. Anything to detach from Adam's fingers delving within the depths of my juicy passage. Not that I don't want him there, because I so frickin' do. Damn he is good. And keep in mind that is only his educated fingers being professional.

"You..." I curl my fingers tightly around the sides of the exam table.

"Are you sure?" He asks as his thumb takes a smooth swipe at my pink pearly bud hiding pathetically under its protective hood.

"You are so unfair!" I hiss as his thumb passes torturously across the nub of flesh as it peeks out waiting to be stroked again.

"You remember." Adam relishes my position that he now has me in. "I wondered if you would."

"Why…" I cannot continue asking as I catch my breath when another of his fingers joins in the invasion.

"Because last time I remember feeling like you do I was on the receiving end of a closed door praying a cold shower would help." Adam says stepping around to my side never losing the rhythm of his fingers dancing within me.

"Please stop…" I beg with my eyes speaking something completely different.

"After a simple kiss." He requests leaning his beautiful face towards mine. "Prove it wasn't worth seven years of thinking about."

"With you nothing is simple." I manage to interject before his tongue curls upward stroking my top lip seductively.

Previously Adam seemed to have the upper hand due to my lack of experience. I was not prepared for what I started. It was one of those things where the drinks and innuendos all seemed to swirl in a heavenly cloud above my head and by the time I knew what was happening I had no option but to close my hotel door.

Adam's thumb presses and moves in firm circles against my silky pink pearl while his fingers continue tickling the tip of my cervix with deep thrusts of his hand. I part my lips allowing a hot sigh to float across my lips. He captures my bottom lip and sucks painfully hard while keeping his eyes locked on my own.

I feel the gown pull from my body and the cool air nibble

at my bare skin. I gasp at the feeling of Adam's hot tongue trailing its sinful way down my chin and across my jaw as his mouth finds my earlobe.

"You call this a simple kiss?" I breathe out arching my head back while his mouth bites at the tender pulse of my throat.

"With you nothing is simple, Kristen." He pauses to answer fanning his fingers apart inside me until a tight ache begins throbbing.

"Ah..." I exhale loudly at the onset of unexpected pleasure, twisting my hips into his hand.

"You are nice and tight." His lips dance with his words across my open mouth. "So perfectly tight."

"What about the door?" I stumble through the sentence, until his thumb rubs harder.

"Oh, damn!" I moan reaching for his wrist between my legs.

"It's unlocked. Anyone could come in." His words brush across my chin.

I scramble to keep his hand still. "Great, that is why we should to stop!" I hiss at the idea of having to part with the feeling of his skin against mine.

Adam laughs at my nervousness and pulls back to look down at me, savoring what he sees beneath him. He pulls his fingers out of my warm depths and brings them to his mouth. One by one he sucks the juices from each never taking his eyes off me. Clasping my jaw tightly to open in reflex he bends down and kisses me roughly with his tongue dominating my mouth into submission.

The taste of my excitement swirls with each sweep of his tongue. The kiss is anything but simple. He is purposeful, almost demanding as his mouth presses against mine. I breathe in as he exhales trying to find some sort of salvation from something that feels sinfully right. Sensing the sensual chaos within me, Adam pins my wrists above my head to keep from pushing or pulling. He pulls away without warning and looks down at me.

"So, was it worth thinking about?" I ask when his mouth finally lifts from mine.

"Hell yes!" He sighs letting my wrists free and stepping back.

"That is why we should stop." I say rising up to lean on my elbows. "Would you mind giving me back the gown, please?"

"Actually, I do mind." Adam answers irritated over his shoulder as he makes his way to the door. "I really would fucking mind, in fact."

I sit upright to get off the exam table and reach for the gown but Adam has it dangling in his fingers before I have any hope of retrieving it from the floor.

"I don't think so, Kristin." He scolds me with a narrowed glare waving a long finger to tell me no. "I am not going to wait another seven years. That is a promise."

"We really need to think about this." I try to stall him until I can think of a way to suggest going somewhere a little more private than his office without sounding too forward. He doesn't even look back as he locks the door. *What in the hell could sound forward after being blatantly fingered by a doctor during an exam?* I pause to wonder.

"I think we have." Adam decides as he walks over to his desk and picks up the phone dialing the nurse at the back of the clinic building that takes his calls.

"I won't be available for the next two hours. I have a conference call that I will be on and will not be disturbed. Thank you." Adam hangs up the phone and unbuttons his shirt as he walks back towards the table where I am sitting with my mouth open.

"If you think…" I try to protest at having sex with him in

23

his office but he is shirtless and has my face in his hands and his mouth swallowing the rest of my sentence before I can finish.

The heat of his bare skin against mine has my nipples tighten to hard brown fleshy knots brushing against his chest. A hiss of pleasure escapes between us as I wrap my long legs around his hips drawing him in to try and take the lead. Feeling the curves of his muscular ass move under my squeezing hands has me purring out loud and catching his attention.

He raises and eyebrow in surprise. "No, sweetness. That is not how this one is going to play out." His voice confident like a man in control at all times. "Understand?"

"Afraid of assertive women, Adam?" I challenge with a mocking tone. Thinking I am on to something I grow bold and clueless as hell as to what I was about to get myself into. "Afraid I can take you after seven years of practice, Romeo?"

Adam's eyebrows crease to a narrowed fix on mine as he pulls his belt out of his pants instead of unfastening it with the pants and letting it all drop. His jaw clenches like a man who has been called a wimp. I swallow dryly as he walks closer to the end of the table resting down on his tight hands on each side of my lap. His eyes dart back and forth across my face slowly, deliberately. He is assessing what he has before him and what the remark meant if anything at all. He brings his face close to my neck, inhaling the scent of my skin and hair. His lips brush slowly against my ear. A soft hiss sends my heart racing for shelter.

"I want you to bend over like the naughty little girl you are, Kristin, and put your hands under your knees so that all I am going to be looking at is your bare, tight little ass." His words struck my pulse to do double time.

I flash a smile that said he had to be kidding. I look up and roll my eyes to act bored and less than amused.

"Did you hear me?" Adam raises his voice only inches

from my face.

"Huh?" I question as I feel the plastic table pad and the paper bunch up into his tightened fists that were clamping in deep.

"Turn around and bend over." He spoke with forced restraint. "If I have to assist you it will not be pleasant."

"You mean to tell me that you think you are going to expect me to bend over like a dog on this…" I barely stuttered the last word when I felt the room spin and the cool air kiss my sweet bare ass goodbye as I was slammed down face first with breath crushing force into the exam table like a wrestler that lost the big match against Big Bad Leroy Brown. "What the hell do you think you are doing? I tried to assert only to be cut short by something I would never have expected in any of those wild dreams I had of Dr. Feelsgood from the wedding dance.

A loud hiss of air being sliced in half precedes the sound that echoes so sadistically that I wouldn't believe I heard it unless I felt it simultaneously. Which, to my surprise, I had.

"Fucking A!" I yelp swatting my hands in the air trying to cool down the fire set ablaze across my ass. "You son of a fucking bitch!"

"You have a hard time listening, Kristin." Adam growls. "Move your hands!"

"I am so out of here, you prick!" I snap moving up the exam table like a deer spotting on coming headlights.

Another alarming hiss rips through the air before I jump in searing pain at what I now recognize as the belt he had removed seconds earlier. The bastard was whipping me with his belt! I wince and cover my ass with my hands falling flat into the exam table. Tears fill my eyes as I bite back the words I know will only encourage him to strike again.

"Kristin, shall I repeat myself?" Adam asks grabbing at my ankles and pulling me down towards the end of the table. "Bend over and put your hands under your knees. That is your last reminder."

"What the hell did I do?" I bark trying to figure out where it made sense that I was getting whacked with the end of his belt.

"You aren't following a simple direction." He said with a firm tone pinning my ankles down and pulling on the nape of my neck with a firm hold pulling down and back causing my body to fold over exactly as he first expected me to. "Now, was that so hard?"

"I don't…" I caught a cool gasp of air before another slice of leather struck across my ass sending my muscles into spasms.

I release an aching moan and freeze on the exam table afraid to move and all the more wise to the man's intensity of his very word. I stayed bent over trying to think of how long I was going to be in this position. Afraid to ask because I knew the answer depended on me. Eight more bites of leather across my ass answered my question.

I laid there for several minutes waiting for the burn to cool across my bottom. I learned enough about Adam in the previous five minutes to know staying still was a much better idea than trying to pull a reprise of the amateur dominatrix act. Seems like he was a man who enjoyed running the show. I certainly was not in the position to argue the point.

"I bet you would take so much more than what I just gave you." Adam said as he stroked my welted skin.

"I would not." I snapped. "I said I wasn't into that sort of thing. It does nothing for me."

"Is that true, Kristin?" He paused his hands. "Or a weakness in the form of a false denial so that you can get out of the truth revealing itself?"

"Okay, if you think I like having my ass beat to the point it arouses me then you need to go back to school." I asserted moving my hands out from under my knees.

"Really?" His fingers slid into my wetness without warning hooking onto the inside curve of my walls so that he only pulled a little and I naturally went backward to ease the sensation of being hooked to something. "You are very wet for someone who is not aroused, Kristin."

"Are you done now?" I asked, trying to move forward.

"You asked. Now that is a good start. I think we are getting somewhere." He laughed as he wrapped his left arm around the front of my hips and pulled me back by lifting me.

"You are going to get nowhere." I tried to sound like he was imagining the dampness his fingers were swimming in between my legs.

"You are underestimating the situation severely, sweetness." Adam corrected in an assertive tone that gave me goose bumps. "I am going to get everywhere across your body and back."

I felt my knees make contact with the pad of the table and realized I was dangling on the edge. I felt so out of my element that defeat crept close behind as I put my face in my arms to hide out of resignation.

It was the warmth of his tongue as it stroked its way up the back of my thigh that caused me to bolt upright on my knees. I looked back over my shoulder to see the top of his head rise up to kiss his way up the middle of my back until finally surfacing over my shoulder.

"Knowing that your skin is puckered because of me excites you. I can feel it deep inside." He announced softly against the nape of my neck as his fingers delved upward.

I moaned and tossed by head back. "Yes." I admitted without hesitation. I was his for whatever he intended.

Adam pulled my mouth to settle over his while his right hand worked against my swollen bud below with his thumb. His other made its journey to my breasts quickly having them squeezed with the splayed attack of his long large hand. I couldn't find a way to concentrate on one of the sensations when they all competed with the movement of his warm soft tongue in and out twirling sensually with my own. He demanded complete control of what we did with every sensation he created.

"I want you to turn around for me, Kristen." Adam instructed with a soft voice when our lips separated.

I complied facing him, rested on my knees at the edge of the table. I had no idea what to do next unless he spoke. His eyes moved slowly up and down my body with an appreciative expression. His hands opened and trailed behind his eyes as they brushed down my full curves outlining my body for the first time. He licked his lips slowly as his eyes raised to meet mine.

"Lean back on your hands, Kristin. I want you to keep your legs folded under your bottom while your thighs spread wide open for me. I want to see your center." Adam directed as he pulled his hands back from my skin.

I leaned back and kept my feet tucked under my ass while I slowly spread my thighs open. I had never opened myself in such a way for anyone. I remember the feeling of being exposed, vulnerable and yet so sexually aroused by being in that pose solely for him to enjoy viewing my body. Kneeling there for his pleasure. It was so beautiful and haunting all at the same time. I pulled my shoulders back, arched my chest out and tightened my stomach. I felt so powerful and flawless as the heat of his gaze massaged my body. I felt on fire and cold as ice as the air and his eyes traded ownership of my bare skin.

"Pleasure yourself for me." Adam said as he ran the top of his hand against my thigh. "But donot cum."

I felt compelled to do anything to please him. My hand slid down to the warmth between my legs. I had never masturbated in front of another person before. I hadn't done many things until he had me on that table. Suddenly everything was fair game and I was more than ready to play.

My fingers worked slowly. I tried to focus and closed my eyes.

"I want your eyes open and looking at me. Tell me what you are thinking of while you finger yourself." He said as he stepped back and kept his pants on.

I felt if he wanted a show then I was more than ready to give him one. One finger at a time I massaged at the warm opening between my legs. I curled my long fingernails inside the inner lips and swept the hot juices out so that he could see just how wet I was. I coated my outer lips with my sweetness and I used my tongue to stroke my mouth at the same time. Adam smiled softly and bit down on his full bottom lip amused at my immediate response to his command. His eyebrows raised and he grabbed the small round rolling stool and adjusted it to his desired seat height to get a great view of my private show. That was the confirmation of his interest I was looking for. I licked my lips and fixed my eyes on him with the determination of a woman who wanted to get wild and nasty with the man in front of her in sixty seconds or less. And to be honest if I could get him to take over the job of what my hand was busy doing in less than thirty seconds it would be even better.

"I am thinking about you and me on that staircase." I said as I pressed my fingers at my opening and spread my outer lips apart and gyrated my hips forward with all the ease of a high end stripper.

"Well, we know how that ended up." Adam's eyes froze when my hips rolled upward and back down, riding my hand like a pro.

I rolled my thumb over the pink wet love pearl and allowed my eyes the luxury of rolling back for a brief second to delight in the feeling of stroking my own clit in front of his face. "I think of you chasing me up to that room and grabbing a handful of my hair when I turned to unlock the door. Your mouth hot on my ear, whispering for me not to make a sound as you covered my mouth with your hand. You push me up against the door so hard that my face turns to the side. As I look down the hall watching people go in and out of their respective rooms you tell me to smile as they pass."

Adam smiled. "You really would have enjoyed that?" He walked closer so that he could reach for my hair when I blinked my eyes.

"Yes." I gasped.

"You would have liked being against that door while I hiked the dress up while people walked by so that your ass was bare and against my open zipper." He smiled as he pulled at my hair into his tight fist.

"Yes…" I couldn't speak when his hand grabbed my face and pulled my mouth to his.

His tongue was sweet, insistent and spreading like a soft warm flame all over the inside of my mouth. I felt so lost in the sensation that I moved my hand out from between my legs.

Adam's hand wrapped tightly around my wrist and brought my fingers up to his face when his mouth left mine. "Ever taste yourself when you finish, Kristen?"

"No." I tried to lie, answering the only way that I wouldn't feel embarrassment.

He painted my lips with my own fingers as his hand held my jaw open. When my lips were covered and my nose was inhaling my own scent he brushed his open mouth across my cheek as he inhaled and moaned at the smell of me.

"Why would you lie to me, Kristin?" He whispered as his lips moved over mine while his tongue darted out at the juices stuck to my skin. "We both know you would never be able to resist something so sweet."

"I'm sorry." I whimpered as his hand tightened in my hair pulling so that my neck tilted back farther than I expected to look up at the ceiling.

"Of course you are." He laughed. "The part of that little scenario I guarantee you wouldn't have added is anything remotely close to what I plan to do to you now."

"You are hurting me." I whine as his hand pulls harder on my hair.

"Of course I am, Kristin." Adam answered as he licked the length of my throat to my chin. "That doesn't surprise you. Even if you wouldn't have told me, we both know it gets you really hot. I am about to give you what you really want."

Adam pulled my mouth to his. He kissed me roughly biting at my lip. I whined at the pinching of my lip between his teeth.

"I want you to lie on your back with your head at this end." Adam said as he pulled my hair leading me down on the table to lay on my back looking up at him. "Let's see how well you can keep my attention, sweetheart."

"Aren't you full of yourself, bartender." I laughed as he hooked his hands under my neck and pulled me down to have my head dangle off the edge of the table.

"You are about to be full of me." He responded while pulling down on my top jaw and wiggled two of his long fingers slowly down my throat. "Yes, take them nice and deep, Kristin. I want to know I will be happy down there."

I felt that I could gag at how far he was shoving his fingers until his free hand moved down to the warm space between my legs a began a rough inventory of my outer folds.

"Be a good girl and I may reward you." He said as his fingers pinched at my clit.

I moaned and lifted my hips up to ease the ache of being trapped sadistically between his fingers. That is when he found no gag reflex and moved his fingers even farther down my throat.

"Very nice. I am pleased to see you will be able to handle

me." Adam praised me like I was hoping for a gold star or the desk in the front row of the classroom.

The next thing my eyes were watching was his zipper move towards the floor leaving me to discover his silk white boxers which were following the similar path of his pants to the same pool of clothing building at his ankles.

I swallowed dryly when I had my first meeting upside down with what I could only describe as a something you would believe should be registered as a weapon.

I began to feel my heart race and I lifted my head up to turn around in horror like he just produced a tarantula out of his pants but soon his hand had a large amount of my hair in his tight grasp.

"Oh, hell no!" I couldn't help commenting before he tugged me back around and down on my back where I had just came from.

"Kristin, is there a problem?" He asked rubbing the back of my neck to soothe my nerves.

"Okay, the bartender to the doctor thing was a little to get used to." I laughed and looked up at what part of his face I could see past the enormous cock dangling in my face. "But please…you can't be serious!"

"You think this doesn't look serious?" Adam asked as he stepped even closer so that the tip brushed over my forehead and nose. He pulled back and bent over so that his mouth was against my cheek as he grabbed my head to hold it still. "Because it is."

Adam's breath against my skin was enough to melt me right there…weapon or not. His open hands pressed down firmly on my skin and moved down the length on my chest and stomach reaching my hips. A slow sensual massage of his hands worked its magic across my body and soon I was hotter than ever to get my hands on him.

"Open wide. I have a treat for you." Adam purred as he

brushed the tip of his semi erect flesh across my open lips.

I opened my mouth and tilted my head back off the table so that there was more space in the length of my throat to accommodate his size. I had obviously given a few blow jobs and had no complaints but they were your average size and not the size of carwash vacuum hose.

I licked my way from the underside of the tip of his cock to the base of his large sack. It was shaved to perfection so that he was soft and perfectly clean. He smelled heavenly, like a man should. I couldn't help but reach back for his ass and pull him into my face so I could inhale all of his scent. I was now in love for the first time with a body part…every single scrumptious inch of his cock.

I licked his length to get it primed and ready to slide inside. I sucked his balls into my mouth one at a time because taking both was insane and virtually impossible. Adam's jaw clenched and his hands gripped my face as I took him in slowly to the back of my throat.

"Yes, baby." He pushed himself deeper until his length was burrowed to its base. He stroked my throat to appreciate where he was. "That is so hot."

I sucked him inside as he moved back and forth. I held his ass and squeezed it tight between my fingers. Digging my nails into his flesh, I moaned sending sinful vibrations down his swollen cock. I wanted to swallow him whole. The way he would move back as I tried told me he believed I could if he gave me a chance.

"I'm hungry. I think I will have you for a snack." Adam growled as he snaked his hands between my thighs and spread them while gripping my soft flesh in his large hands.

I felt my thighs quiver as his face rubbed back and forth in my wetness while he purred at how sweet I smelled. He parted my bare lips and used the tip of his hot tongue to sweep inside to gather honey from the pot that was filling quickly to satisfy him.

I could have died and gone to heaven right under his skilled mouth. His tongue was so talented that it was like a hot velvety little cock all in itself the way it poked in and out and twisted up and down against my pink love pearl before diving back inside for another mouthful of sweetness. I lifted my hips into his face only to feel the pinch of his strong hands biting into my shameless flesh. He countered my move by giving me an unexpected eight inches down my throat like lightening. I felt my body go limp as I refused to gag on his cock like the good girl he expected me to be.

That is when Adam's oral skill kicked in and went for the prize by sucking in my priceless pearl into his mouth and flicking it like a bead back and forth with the tip of his awesome tongue. His nose fucked my wetness as my hips thrust at him for release. Harder I swallowed at him, moaning around that sweet swollen piece of flesh that I had lost my heart to. His hips began a lovely dance of their own. In and out, sweeping in from the left then the right he grinded down my throat as his balls slapped against my nose.

The sounds of Adam moaning and breathing harder as he pumped in and out of my mouth sent me over the edge. His teeth pinched my clit and I cried out around his cock. I felt a pop and the flow of my first orgasm begin to roll through my hips against his mouth. He released my clit and spread my ass and shoved his tongue roughly inside my pussy then down to my brown bud below. His mouth chewed nibbled ravenously at all the sensitive flesh between and I had no control as my hips jerked harder and faster against his face. His cock throbbed deeper down my throat as my pussy gushed wide open releasing my silky juices across his face.

"Fuck yes!" He hissed as he stood up with his face wet.

Adam held my throat with his left hand so he cold force himself faster in a controlled position down my throat so hard that the skin of his sack slapped loudly at my face.

"Take your reward." He howled as he slapped at my pussy with loud smacks. "Are you ready?"

I moaned and that was all it took for him to drill in a fast thrust up my throat one last time. I swallowed hard and fast which just literally had him buckle over me on the table. I felt the warmth of his cream slide sweetly down my throat.

"Ahhh…" He shook as I continued to milk him for what it was worth. "Damn, wait." He was powerless at getting free from my hold on him.

Adam gripped my throat until I released him to catch a breath.

"You really have a lot to learn, Kristin." He pulled my hair and I followed quickly to sit up and had a proud grin spread across my face as I licked my lips.

Adam pulled my face towards his. "That is not exactly the reward I had in mind." He said before kissing me deep and blending our tastes together in one yummy delectable kiss.

An unexpected swat across my tender ass had me yelping into his mouth.

"Time for me to take you to a place with lots of toys. Call it my own personal playroom." Adam said pulling me off the table to fall into his arms.

"Hey, I have plans for lunch with Abby…remember her?" I asked with a wink.

"Yes, well…." Adam turns away pauses in mid sentence and reaches for his cell sitting on his desk and turns tossing it to me. "Tell Abby that you are going to be tied up the rest of the day and you won't be able to make it."

"Fine, but tied up doing what?" I asked with half a laugh as I began dialing the phone while Adam slipped on his clothes.

He turned and looked at me with a raised eyebrow before picking up his shirt. Slipping it back on his body before walking back to me where I was sitting on the exam table he approached and came within a breath's distance from my face. His eyes danced back and forth between mine as if they were searching for something. A chilling smile slowly moved at the corners of his handsome mouth. The call connected and Abby answered.

"Hello?" Abby answered on the second ring.

Adam's eyebrows raise in question. I cover the phone after telling Abby to hold for a second.

"Kristin is that you? Are we still on for lunch?" Abby asks as I move the phone away to my lap.

"Tied up doing what?" I asked again with a grin.

"What do you think, Kristin?" Adam asks with the smile disappearing from his face. His lips slide softly across my cheek to my ear to deliver the most sinful whisper. "Hmmm? What do you do when you are tied up all day and night?"

I swallowed hard as my face blushed out of nervousness at the idea he was actually serious about me being tied up.

"Uh, Abby. I think I have to cancel. It sounds like I am about to be tied up for the next day or so." I say nervously. "If you need anything reach me at this number."

"Adam Martinez, huh?" Abby laughs. "Here I thought I was being stood up for your gynecologist."

Adam takes the phone from my hand before I can answer. "You are, Abby. It is nice to hear your voice again."

"Have we met?" Abby laughs.

"Your cousin's wedding. I was the bartender Kristin made out with on the stairs." Adam explained.

"Okay, but she was at a doctor appointment." Abby stumbled through to understand what the hell I was up to.

"What can I say…?" Adam laughed. "I was one hell of a bartender." He then passed the phone back to me with a wink and rested his hands around my back to my ass.

"Abby?" I spoke as I inhaled the sweet mix of his skin and the cologne that drove me wild with wanting so much more than I had five minutes earlier.

"Doctor with a wicked shot, huh?" Abby laughed. "He reappeared after all. Seems that kiss was pretty hot to him too, Kris."

"Long story. I will explain later. Call you tomorrow?" I ask as Adam's hands started squeezing and pulling me into his arms. His mouth sucking on my bare shoulder.

"Absolutely. I got his number." Abby said as a reminder.

"Thanks, Abby." I laugh and hang up.

"Ready for a few surprises?" Adam asked with a coy grin.

"No." I answer nervously.

"Good." Adam stopped smiling and guided me to my clothes. "Get dressed. I think you are in for a real treat."

# Hot as Hell

"This had better be good, Gina. I have had thirty minutes of thinking about sleep and one hour left to enjoy it if I find it before I have to be in the shower." I said half asleep and half awake depending on how you want to look at it. Either way as far as I was concerned, I was screwed and it sure as hell didn't look like satisfaction was to be achieved no matter what I did in the next hour.

I rub my tired eyes as my personal assistant and second in command, Gina, in my jewelry and precious stones centered company went on about the overseas account in Romania. She mentioned something about a virus multiplying its way through the company network crashing the delivery and stock programs. I vaguely caught on about someone being unhappy and was expecting a private meeting upon arrival from somewhere far enough that he needed to take a plane to get from there to here.

I rolled my eyes and yawned while she took a moment to tell her live-in boyfriend where to put the lemon pepper on the chicken obviously still in the oven.

"Seriously, this is stressing me out big time here, Natasha. I have the guys in I.T. pissed off because they want answers I don't have. My dinner party was canceled four hours ago because of this mess and Romania has hit the unfriendly skies to greet you to chew your ass for the missing shipment of jewels we sent out a day late." Gina took a deep breath and mumbled something I couldn't make sense of which was not unusual in a conversation with Gina when she was upset.

I rubbed my eyes a second time and sat upright in the bed hoping it would bring me around to tend to the situation at hand.

"Did you call Gregg in Systems Solutions? He is a guru with our systems and will have that virus isolated and history in less than twenty minutes." I inquire hoping she had neglected to any outside calling and I had just solved her first of apparently several issues.

"No." Gina paused. "Greg, huh?"

"Yes, Greg. I put his number in your contact folder. Tell him I want it fixed yesterday and he will be there in the system in five minutes." I advise reaching for the bedside clock on my nightstand to see that it was already midnight. "It's midnight and you are cooking chicken?"

"Long story. You would have known if you read your mail instead of me, Natasha." Gina chastised me while calling Gregg on her cell phone.

"Guess I didn't miss much then." In sighed trying to sink down into the comfort of my bed when a flash of panic ran down my back jolting me back to sit upright. "What did you say about Romania?" I gasped hoping I was confused and lacking sleep from jet lag and just returning back to the states 3 hours earlier after a two day trip to Italy for business.

"You did hear Romania?" Gina asked while she took a few seconds to give Gregg the order to hunt down the virus and eliminate it from the company systems. "Okay, back. He is on it right now."

"I heard that... back to Romania." I wanted Joan to clarify what had them pissed off.

"The delivery..." Gina began to explain before I interrupted to save time and get to the point of the next issue.

"Yes, it was sent out two days ago...."I don't get a chance to go beyond that since Gina decides I need to be updated.

"Correction...sent out yesterday because the virus set all our accounts and delivery systems haywire! We thankfully caught it within the first two hours of the business day but by then the Romanian delivery had been set back 24 hours. By the time I got anyone on the phone there it was too late. He was already in the air and looking for blood…" Gina pauses then inhales with a chilling hiss. "Okay, that sounds creepy, huh?"

"Damn! Gina this is not good." I moan covering my forehead trying to absorb what a mess the largest account for my company was in.

"I know it isn't, I am so sorry, Nat. Kick my ass to the curb and get it over with." Gina said with a somber and expecting tone.

"Gina! Say that ever again and I just might." who else has my back like you? Hell, you are all I need to keep the company going and you know that." I say with a sigh then laugh at how truthful it was. Gina was a one woman army and she saved my ass too many times to count.

"Thanks, Nat, for understanding. I didn't want to disturb you unless I had to. I know you have had a long week." Gina sounded relieved.

"Besides, it's not like that Vladimir creep is the one on his way over." I laughed as I slipped into the comfy warm spot in my huge four post bed.

"Uh…Nat?" Gina's voice broke up as she cleared her throat nervously. "Did I forget to tell you that is exactly who is coming?"

"Excuse me?" I asked in a gasp of disbelief.

"The creep is Vladimir Tomescu. He is on his way here." Gina said with hesitation as if I had the potential to reach through the phone and break her petite neck.

"You have got to be kidding me, Gina!" I growl hoping to intimidate her enough to admit that is was a cruel joke on her part.

"You understand he is coming, right?" Gina asked cautiously,

"You aren't serious?" I hiss hoping she would finally

break and tell me it wasn't true.

"Nat?" Gina spoke slowly as if she was dealing with a hostage situation. "Do you understand?"

"Oh…" I paused as I bit down on my bottom lip to hurt enough to signal the conversation was taking place. "I understand."

"What do you need from me?" Gina offered shakily through the phone.

"Everything on Mr. Tomescu, his company and his weaknesses. I mean every last one, Gina. I need to be able to keep him amused at the least with my interest and knowledge of who and what he is while you locate and deliver those stones back into my hands so I can personally hand them over when he tires of the pathetic diversion on my part." I had to take a breath and focus on this account completely before it was gone.

This guy bought more stones from us in one week than I would otherwise spend a year trying to sell. Whatever this guy needed to be pacified I intended to give him on a silver platter.

"I have my computer spitting out all the info on him available to your fax. Want me to track down his flight and send him a company car to take him to a hotel suite?" Gina asked as she clicked away on her laptop causing my fax to light up like a Christmas tree and sing in shrilling beeps.

"Yes." I reached and switched on the bedside lamp and looked quickly through the information leaping out of the fax onto the desk. "Can you send a picture of this guy? I want to know what I am dealing with."

"It's already there. Didn't you get it?" She asked while rustling and answering her cell phone. "Hang on, Nat. It's Gregg."

I looked through the numerous faxed pages and found no picture anywhere. I was about to ask Gina to resend when I heard the crinkle of paper under my left foot when I stepped out of bed.

"Damn!" I mumbled as I lifted my foot to retrieve the paper.

"Nat, you okay?" Gina asked while hanging up with Gregg.

"Yes." I said as I reached down and peeled the paper off my foot rolling my eyes. "I think I found Vladimir."

I brought the paper to the lamp and swallowed hard at what my eyes rested upon.

"Gina, where did you get this picture?" I asked feeling my hand shake at the image in my possession.

"It is the one he submitted along with his portfolio, security profile and of course his background checks. It is him or my name isn't Gina." She laughed. "Pretty hot, huh?"

"Are you sure this is him?" I couldn't believe my eyes. It couldn't be. He didn't exist.

"Yes, Natasha, it's him. I have had one net conference with him and a buyer from London and he is the one and the same. He is single if that helps out."

"Oh, my." I whispered in shock that a living and breathing version of the picture was indeed on his way. All hell was about to break loose and that was a major understatement. "He is going to be trouble, Gina."

"I got the information sent. Get some sleep while I help Mark eat this bird. Brush up on it while you are in the car on the way to the office." Gina advised. "If he is that hard to deal with you want to be ready. By the way, Gregg caught the virus and sent it on its way to the asshole who gave it to us."

"See you in a couple hours. Call if there are any early sightings of this guy." I needed to be on my guard if this guy is who I thought he was.

I wasn't about to tell Gina who this Vladimir was and how long I had known him. She would truly think I lost my mind.

"He is that bad, huh?" Gina asked in a sad voice feeling

guilty.

"Honey, if he is who I think he is…" I paused and cleared my throat feeling the fear of the expected creeping up on me. "He was going to be coming this way sooner or later and if it wasn't a late shipment it would have been something else. Trust me on this one."

I ended the call and set down the picture as if I was holding something sacred instead. I felt the wind blow in from the terrace window and across my bare neck. A shiver raced up my spine and I felt my mouth go dry. As hard as I tried I couldn't move my focus from the image of him on paper.

His hair was dark and long falling past his shoulders. His eyes were a cool bright blue like the color of small exotic tropical pools of hidden water. His face was hauntingly handsome. Strong and beautiful in structure with every line and definition permeated in the depths of my every memory since I first came into his presence all those years ago. His shoulders wide, strong and defined like a dark warrior ready for war at any moment. I closed my eyes for a moment and his scent filled me. Rich, rare and of spices and woods long since destroyed. His voice was deep in timbre thick with the accent of his people also gone but still universally feared. My eyes moved back to the picture for a last look and he looked to be mid-thirties at the most. I shook my head knowing he is hundreds of years older than the thirty I was.

I wrapped my arms around my chest and barely noticed the nervous stroke of my thumbs against my skin. I felt the fibers of the carpet beneath my bare feet tickle as individual strands. Goose bumps spread across my body in confirmation as a gust of hot air tossed the sheer curtains upward brushed by an ancient breath across my face and back as they returned down to the floor at my feet. My eyelids grew heavy and familiar warmth trickled through my veins. I felt the lazy peace of tiredness slip into my skin lulling me back to bed. My eyes blinked trying to fight what the rest of my body could not.

Strands of my long red curls moved over my eyes before they closed. Red flames danced against the black sky taunting me as I fell under.

*"Shhhh..."*

A deep ancient voice soothed me.

*"Deeper, Cara. Let yourself go. You know you must come when I call for you to join me. There is no other choice."*

*"Please, tell me that this isn't happening."*

My voice stayed silent as mind spoke to him.

*"So much resistance. A disappointment to find when I call upon you."*

The voice echoed leaving a tickled trail across my chest and down my stomach. I gasped at its overwhelming effect.

"Why? Why are you insistent on doing this to me?" I allowed my mind to beg him for answers. "To us?"

*"Ah, my little one, how I have waited so long. Too long. This you know all too well. So patiently I have been waiting, watching...aching, Cara. Why do you ask such now is the question?"*

A sense of sincerity decorated his words. Starved for that tone in his voice I savored each one like a confection allowing them to settle into that heavenly place I stored such gifts alike from him.

"Why do you not answer when I have asked respectfully?" I asserted, determined to hear his reasoning as to what he is up to after all these years.

*"I am not happy that you have found it so easy to forget, Natashia."*

The endearment rolled like warm fluid through my mind while it set off small explosions of hunger and desire through my body in response.

*"Mmm, yes, my precious Natashia, allow the truth to answer for you."*

"Why does it have to change?" I asked as I felt his fingers brush away the curls from my face. I catch my breath at his presence.

*"It was going to change. This you were told from the beginning before you made the choice. Were you not?"*

His words confirmed what I already had known.

"When I offered to sacrifice in turn for his life to continue I was not aware of what you would ask for in return. I was only a child." I pleaded unaware of the tears that flowed from my heart to my eyes.

*"Shhhh...cara, my sweet one."*

He brushed his finger tips delicately down my cheek capturing each drop and collectively bringing them to his lips to savor.

*"Shhhh..."*

His voice hissed and his jaw clenched at the maddening sweet taste of my pain spreading through him. His eyes closed to restrain his body from reacting. "No tears. Not now."

"I'm sorry. I mean no disrespect." I try to sound sincere but knew it was impossible to be deceitful in his presence.

*"Really, Natashia?"*

He offered a last opportunity for retraction.

*"Is that so?"*

I felt the vibration through my arms hum through my shoulders before they paused in my chest. My back arched and my breasts swelled to attention with an all too familiar ache. A whimper escaped my lips as I felt a tightened pinch increase around the hardened tips of my erect flesh poking through my silk camisole.

*"Natashia, answer me."*

His words hot and sensual in my ear demanding my truth while his lips burned the softest curves of my skin.

I arched into his hands. I ached to feel his strength cupped and molded into desired perfection by his skilled palms.

He smelled my need. The sweetness of my sinful hunger for his touch upon my body. The longing of my skin to be against his flesh moving, boiling until he finally plunges within me so deep inside that he pierces his way through my heart and branding himself into my soul.

*"It will cost you, cara."*

His voice stroked my throbbing lips and a sadistic laugh echoed at what only his mind knew.

*"What you want from me will cost you everything."*

My tongue darted out to taste him. It was forbidden but I couldn't hold back anymore. Just a sample of what I knew was there. My nostrils widened and my mouth opened at the scent of his neck as it moved above my face.

*"Now, please."*

My mind begged without any sense of pride.

*"You are hungry, yes?"*

He was amused at the depth of my need for him.

*"Yes."*

My mind answered while my heart beat frantically in anticipation.

*"A small taste to soothe you, my pet?"*

He asked coming closer while his fingers trailed farther below in methodical movements serving a sinister purpose.

"Yes, please." I breathed heavily as if in a desperate fight to stay alive.

When he was close I felt an insatiable hunger. It was powerful and overwhelming. It was not one that I had the power to ignore. I surely never wanted to. He was the reason I slept alone. Only then he would come and open a world of sensual exploration that I knew was not something I merely dreamed of. He was frighteningly real.

It was on those nights that I felt his body settle gently on top of mine. His sculpted arms lifted my small body tightly into the dark embrace of his. I felt surrounded by him in every direction. Safe, warm and passionate. I felt the pang of ache intertwined with mind-blowing pleasure knowing he would have to leave. The feeling of missing his touch even before it left was the chill in the air. It was always that intense. A torturous craving only partially sated for a moment of his choosing. I was left with the painful reminder of the power he possessed over me.

The first time he appeared I thought I was delirious when he walked into the hospital room. I strained to see him through the bandages and the swollen eyes from the car accident I was in earlier that rainy evening. He was beautiful, dark and his eyes glowed like blue blazing stars lighting the room as he smiled. I could scarcely breathe. I whispered the word angel because he had to be. He nodded as he approached and sat on the side of the bed stroking the strands of my curls back like he had done it all my life. It felt like he had.

"I will serve you with your request." He spoke softly as he smiled. "For what I need in return."

"Anything." I felt the sting of tears as my eyes closed shut in a last silent prayer.

"He will survive." He spoke as his fingertip stroked down to my neck. "Worry not, my pet, I shall not claim you in return…"

"Thank you." I spoke too soon unaware I had not voiced my fear and purpose of my prayer.

"Until your thirtieth year. Until then you will be protected and guarded as if already claimed. No other will know of you as I will at the time of my choosing. From this point on and eternally you shall belong to me, my sweet Cara." He was gone when I opened my eyes to withdraw my request.

A nurse slid in on her heels and announced my father's amazing turn for the better. I fell into a deep peaceful sleep and woke five days later. Not remembering anything until he returned in my deepest sleep several months later and stayed close by visiting every night from there on. This night he seemed to more intense, focused and purposeful with me. There was a message in each of his movements, the sounds of his breathing. Everything was like a premonition warning me.

"Lo tentate per commettere gli atti unspeakable avete dichiarato un sin sulla virtù di una bellezza come voi, il mio Cara." His Italian purred through my senses as his lips lowered to press openly against mine while he spoke his message.

*I had asked for him to commit unspeakable acts and therefore declared sin upon the virtue of one beauty as mine, his Beloved. He was my salvation.*

Tragic and dangerous, but hardly the first time. Yes, I now wanted it over with. I wanted to have it happen with my eyes closed and my inhibitions numbed to receive him. I owed him what he expected in turn for extending a loved one's life. I was only sixteen when I cried out the request offering anything in return to whoever would grant the mercy to my shattered world.

"You shall not be granted such mercy, Natashia. You shall be awake and it shall all be because you asked for it. All of it. Then and only then, I shall claim what has always been and always will be mine." He closed his mouth over mine.

For that brief moment I was appeased and relieved as my body writhed at the dance of his fingers within me. In a shattered cry of my release within his hand he suddenly disappeared.

I woke refreshed as if I had slept for a year. I talked to Gina and she hadn't been able to reach Mr. Tomescu which didn't surprise me. I asked her to set up the conference room and make sure the courier was to arrive with the stones Vladimir was searching for. I brushed up on his background and found he was rich, from a long line of ancient royalty and mysterious in how he lived in a dark castle alone. It made sense. He was no doubt Vlad the Impaler himself in a heavenly molded package of six and half feet of mouth watering masculinity. I shoved the papers into my briefcase and tried to find a breath of doubt that he was not really going to appear. Doubt was not in the air.

"Nat, are you ready?" Gina called out as she caught up to my fast walk into the building.

"As ready as I ever will be, I guess." I sighed opening the door and allowing her to enter ahead of me.

"I just got a message from his office. He will be in other meetings through today so he will not be able to make it to the office until later." Gina said as she pushed the elevator button with a red manicured nail.

"Great. That leaves time for the courier to arrive and for me to clear up the other work needing to be done." I breathe with relief.

"Courier should be here by noon at the latest." Gina said as she grabbed my briefcase and handed me the mail from the front desk.

"Any messages?" I asked the receptionist who just returned to her desk.

"Actually there was that came in about four hours ago from a Mr. Tomescu." She answered handing me a piece of paper.

"What now?" Gina asks with a huff of annoyance.

I decide to wait and read it alone fearful it maybe something I would find hard to explain to Gina.

"I am sure it is nothing. Track down the courier and get an ETA from him. I want to be holding those jewels in a safe whenever the man arrives." I announce taking my briefcase from Gina and tossing it on my desk before closing the door for privacy.

I set the message down on the desk and go through the mail instead. Anything to avoid whatever would be inside his message.

*"Open it, Natashia."*

A hauntingly beautiful voice sounded inside my head.

*"Donot be afraid my sweet pet."*

I swallowed hard at his presence suddenly with me during the day which never happened before.

My hand was shaking slightly when I reached for the paper. I felt a chill across my bare neck and closed my eyes to savor the feeling. The rumble of his amused laughter rolled across my skin.

His voice read the message for me as my eyes scanned the words.

*"In the dark, in the moment that you least expect it I shall appear for the first time while you are awake. I will find you and take you as promised."*

His presence was gone. He left me to feel the fear of the unknown.

I didn't eat lunch when Gina brought it in from my favorite deli. I sipped at the smoothie she thought would do me some good. I thought as the cold liquid moved down the back of my throat. Would he truly hurt me? Would he take me from my life as I knew it like a single flower that caught his eye in a field of many? Would he be cold enough to wrap his fingers tightly around me and pluck me from all that I had existed from and contain me for his selfish purposes?

*"Yes, cara, I will."*

His voice seeped into my consciousness and confirmed my fears. I slowly closed my eyes to try and refuse him entrance to my mind. I could feel he had already entered where he was once invited and forever was now welcome.

I heard the sound of Gina's voice talking in the next room. She was upset and quickly hung up the phone. He was good at having everything fall into his hands. Just like a puppet master with whatever he decides to indulge his hands with. It seems to be me and those I loved most that held his interest.

"Whatever you are doing…spare her please and those that love her just as much as I do. I made the offer…she and everyone else I care about did not." I knew my thoughts would find his mind as I mouthed them under a held breath of a prayer.

*"Still so ready to doubt me, Natashia. Bittersweet will be the acceptance of your fate when I see it in your eyes."*

His voice replied softly while his warm breath floated across the back of my neck.

"Nat…" Gina's panicked voice jerked me out of looking out at the sun setting in the distance. "Omigod! I have to go. Mark is in the emergency room. They think it may be food poisoning but are running tests in case it is something more serious."

"He will be okay." I stood up and hugged her, feeling the ache of her heart as if it was my own. "I promise. Just take the company car for the night. Don't worry about tomorrow. Right now you need to take care of Mark."

"Nat, what about the…" Gina tried to remind me of what I already knew was fast approaching but I cut her off.

"That will be just fine. I have dealt with much worse. He is not gonna know what hit him when I am finished. The stones are here and I am willing to wait all night if I have to." I said with a confident smile to humor her into leaving.

"You sure?" She stalled for a moment as she studied my face as if I was hiding something.

"Positive. Now get going and make sure they know your cooking isn't really that bad." I laughed leading her to the doorway of my office.

*"You are selfless, cara. She will not feel any heartbreak because of it."*

His words stroked my ear with a loving sensuousness that I had never felt.

"Thank you." I said out loud as I walked back to the

window and looked at the last of the sun as it settled below the horizon to sleep.

*"I am not to be feared, by now you should know that. We have talked of what will take place many times."*

"Will I come back here?" I asked out loud as if he was physically present to answer.

*"In time you will be permitted to when it is safe. After you adjust to the change and are not a threat to those that you love."*

"Thank you." I said reaching for the smoothie. "Guess I won't get to enjoy this much longer."

*"Fill yourself with any indulgence, my sweet. Soon all you will ever need will be me."*

"That is what you want?" I asked before taking a sip from the cup. "To be all that I seek, want and need without choice?"

*"It is what we both need, Natashia. Soon we shall be together in flesh."*

"You will have to find me first." I spoke with a defiant tone. "It won't be that easy to pluck this flower."

*"You are witty. Clever, yes. Capable of evading me...Never."*

He laughed at my resistance with mild amusement.

*"Try if you must."*

"I will." I announced.

*"I know. I look forward to it."*

I set the drink on the desk and grabbed a pen and my company notepad. I wasn't sure what to write but I knew I had to leave something. I bit down on my lip and thought of the perfect message that Gina would understand. With a smile I began to write.

Two hours after locking up the office I took the last swallow of wine from my glass while I stood at the table in the nightclub. I was feeling warm and strangely excited. I was about to meet the man I had spent the last fourteen years sleeping with.

I walked away from the table and moved through the congestion of the dance floor. The thumping of the beat and the throbbing of speakers dangling above me sent my hips in a soft sway and my hands dancing above my head. I closed my eyes and let the music move through me awakening to the sensual energy building inside.

I could hear his footsteps in the distance. Slow and purposeful. It was the hunter stalking his prey. I lick my lips and feel as an innocent bystander moves his hands up my arms. I grind slowly back against the stranger and smiled at the effect it must have on him as he watched from the back of the room. The stranger's hands moved down to my hips cautiously pulling me deeper into him as he swayed deeper down.

*"Mmm."*

I laughed at the irony of it all. I felt my inhibitions melt away. There were no longer any barriers in doing whatever I felt like. The stranger's hands slid up and down pulling me with him in a hypnotic dance of sexual tension. Slower and deeper we moved back and forth. I felt alive and like I was on fire all at once. The stranger's lips brushed against the back of my shoulder and I rolled my eyes back savoring the sensation of heat and want against my bare skin. The music slowed and I felt arms wrap tightly around my stomach pulling me so tight I remained motionless.

I felt the stranger inhale the scent of my warm skin. I shivered at the burning of another's eyes watching. His displeased hiss that sounded through my mind as a warm tongue licked upward to the top of my shoulder. Hands pressing me deeper while his mind pulled and twisted at mine. I reached back and pulled the stranger closer. His mouth moved from my shoulder to my neck.

"You choose to challenge my patience. The dance is now

over." The stranger's voice echoes down my spine. It is him. "Walk away. There is no need to make a scene in here in front of innocent people, cara."

"And if I don't?" I asked reaching back for him.

"Move slowly outside." He growls into my ear allowing a sharp tooth to sweep over my skin. "Now."

I walk away not daring to look back. My eyes scan the people ahead of me and they freeze on him. There he is sitting relaxed on a tall stool in the corner by the exit. I feel his hands stroking my hips as I approach. His eyes glow a light blue. His arms tight and sculpted through his distressed t-shirt while his long strong legs lay out crossed in front of him covered in faded jeans. He smiles like a man with pure sexual deviance on his mind as I pass. I look into his eyes and they shift to a cool black as the tip of his beautiful tongue brushes over his sharp top teeth. His jaw clenches when I wink at him and blow a kiss his direction. He stands wearing a smirk and towers over the average six feet reaching a closer point to seven. I nervously move in a faster pace towards the exit and he laughs rubbing a hand around his mouth delighted at his first impression of appearing live and in the flesh to me.

After I exit into the night air a rush of a look stolen out of the corner of a stranger's unsuspecting eye hits me silently like a stun gun. The unrestrained movement of a body turning to take a second look as I walk past warns me dangerous tendencies are closer than is safe. Then it is the alarming smell of body heat rising in the air I take with me as I pass by. A sweet delicious hot body scent that speaks in a deep dark whisper that informs all my nightmares are this huge bad boys temptations. I have committed the forbidden act of taunting him as he warned explicitly not to with his chastising expression. The tickle that builds at the corners of my mouth as I try not to smile in response to his need for me. The unspoken dare I served that challenges him. I did not take him seriously. I can feel it in the tingle at the nape of my neck when he pauses before following me. The knowing within he will follow excites me. Fate will soon speak whether I choose to acknowledge it or not.

He walks into the night and inhales feeling the swell of my breasts moving, knowing that the hardening at their pointed peaks is response to his body only feet in distance from mine. The reaction haunts him a thousand lifetime's worth in that brief second that passes. The warmth of his exhale initiates the chase to begin as his heart picks up pace to signal mine. The sound of his nose searching the scents that flow above my passing trail as I walk past fill my senses and my skin crawls. The pool of sweetness that builds deep within prepares me for the inevitable.

The sound of his footsteps as I navigate a corner calls to me to run and hide. The coolness of the unexpected fills the night air as I move fearlessly on ahead. It tells me it is pointless. He can find me anywhere. The tempo of my breathing as the seconds weave tortuously by confirms that he is hunting. Trying to escape will only entertain him. Prickling heat pulses into my cheeks. The feeling of movement and his smell permeating every cell within as it begins to fold around me like a glorious cape wrapping me slowly, tightly. A hiss of his acknowledgment that he has me finally where he has longed to have me speaks of the unbelievable pain to come. The shine of his eyes wild with hunger blaze through to my trembling soul. The flow of blood tapping and pulsing through my veins cries to be untouched. The sinful sweep of the tip of his tongue up my chin to my bottom lip as he searches my eyes denies the pathetic request for mercy. With the shiver of his sharp teeth scraping the tissue of my lips delicately, I feel the promise that his unfathomable need will finally be satisfied.

"Ready to be taken, cara?" His voice heavy with sexual need.

"Seems I have little choice." I breathe nervously.

"You made the choice long ago." His accent purred against my skin as his hands pulled my hair free from the clip that held it up.

So it begins with the taste of him pushing through my lips and charging to claim with anything in its path with brute force. A forced exchange of hot breaths trying to stay conscious when the arousal hits it's all time peak fills the space around us. His arms are like vice grips banding themselves around my wanton flesh. So naive I was to bring myself this close to him and expect nothing to happen.

The first sting of his bite at the crook of my neck confirms my deepest fears. He is not ready to feast quite yet, just a sample of what will come. The pain of his grip pulling and kneading my swollen breast tells me he will never be denied as his mouth gnaws on its vulnerable and frightened tip. The scratch of the cement wall against my back as it peels away the barrier of thin material between us announces I will hide no longer. The burn of the sharp surface as it punctures my skin demands my surrender. His hot tongue sweeping where he intends to feed reveals his only weakness... his insatiable hunger for having me that will no longer wait.

His hands clasp into my bottom and pull me apart while lifting me up to be positioned for attack leave me crying out for help. The separation of my flesh as his fingers clamp down holding me still warns of what he could do if I struggle. The faded whispers of my pleading and the painful silence of being ignored amuse him to release a ragged sadistic laugh in my ear. His long hair brushes my shoulders dancing across my cheek like a glorious mane of a hunter confident it has secured its prey helpless. I scratch and claw at his arms as tears swell in my eyes. The growl of response when I move trying to break free says it was only mildly uncomfortable to him but to me it will be hell before he is through.

Then comes lighting shooting through every nerve burning a blazing trail as his sinks in his teeth to sample my flesh.

*"Mine."*

The claim, his claim, ringing in my ears with the conviction of a worthy Lord and Master when he draws his face back and sweeps his long tongue across his crimson tainted lips.

He gathers the it's wealth of sweetness in a shallow pool on his tongue proudly displaying what he wants from me he can easily take. His hands squeeze tightly pinching the soft flesh of my inner thighs causing me to whimper and arch back against the wall. The spiraling of erotic tickling building between my legs conflicts with the smell of my blood upon his lips. My desire is unfamiliar, uncontrollable and altogether heightened.

The satin heat of his hard length sliding back and forth between the soft halves of the fruit of my bottom intertwine with what my mind dares not to think of happening. The panic of being taken without consent, without choice, without reservation. The defeat in knowing he will do as he pleases and there is nothing that could stop him. The begging in my tears as his need to feed intensifies. The parting of my sweetness flowing into his mouth causes my skin to ache. He thrusts forward to taunt me with his strength and power.

I catch a small breath and moan a plea much to his entertainment. His tongue hooks its tip under my top lip painting my blood inside before lancing his mouth over mine to trap its taste within our primal kiss. The scorching of his exhales from his nostrils as he growls in demand for more stimulates me beyond reason.

*"Submit!"*

His mind speaks as his strong hands demand, splitting my thighs and command pressing me to a breath shattering force against the concrete alley wall.

The sounds of others passing and catching their breaths

as they witness the attack begin to hum. The coos of interest as they slowly step around watching his powerful handsome body dine on my neck collect in a loud choir. The eroticism of something so large taking something so petite slowly and bending it's very will to serve its merciless own draws all types. It flows through the spectators and fills them with hunger of their own. They stop and lick their lips, rearranging their suddenly tight pants scanning the mass of people for a meal of their own. Entranced to watch and terrified to miss anything else that is bound to happen, they stand still slowly gathering to serve as a human wall to conceal the beauty of the aggressive and sadistic assault.

I whip my head back and forth, swearing the most obscene hoping to offend him to drop me. His jaw tightens as he releases my neck and wraps a strong right hand around my throat slowly grinding me to the wall with little effort. I am trapped, bruised, and about to be consumed and devoured.

His face pauses and his eyes turn from tropical blue to sinister black gems that pierce through me. His lips swollen and full offer a pillowy cover to what I neglected to notice before. I feel my heart race and my breathing increase. Long blinding white fangs peek out from the beauty of his handsome mouth. His eyes close half way as if he is feeling a release already. My body shifts against the wall with his movements of his hand below and I feel like I am pinned against sand paper. I wince and attempt to blink away the tears searching the numerous faces for help only to find arousal and more need in their starving expressions.

It is then his bare skin presses back against mine. He is naked and more than ready to fulfill his conquest at having me, owning me. I beg, plea and try to bargain. I only increase his delight and build the anticipation for those around us watching.

His length was not meant for someone of my size. He squeezed my neck slowly as he enters its wide thick tip barely inside my warm wet opening. I gasp and lose more air than I can afford. He studies the fear in my eyes and satisfied he covers my mouth roughly with his not loosening his grip on my neck. The crowd cheers him on, gives suggestions and marvels out the sensual brutality of what is taking place in a dark moonlit alley. He desires his claiming to be witnessed.

I pull at his hair and push at his face to catch any amount of air. He only thrusts his tongue deeper down my throat to the point I feel my soft pink love pearl hum in response. Harder I am pressed against the wall and faster my head spins from lack of air. I feel his huge length advance upward inside. I cry out in a blood chilling scream and he hisses in excitement. My breasts bounce with my movement as my hands grasp at his hand across my throat. Men and women bite their lips waiting for the moment his chooses to impale me on his searing hot flesh. I feel fuzzy and faint as his grip tightens draining my hope for mercy.

"Now, do you accept your fate?" He whispers allowing his wet lips to brush like a feather against my ear.

"Yes." I gasp struggling to stay conscious.

"Do you?" He asks pushing his length a little farther within me leaving me to feel like I will certainly split in half if he moves any farther.

"It hurts!" I protest straining to release his grip on my throat.

"You want me to relieve your pain?" His lips moved across my cheek to my own.

"Oh...damn, it hurts." I moan wincing at his fingers clamping harder on my raw bottom against the wall.

"Answer me..." He growls and moves a small amount up inside me.

"Yes..." I am defeated and weakening in his hands.

He releases his hand from my throat and I gasp loudly for air clawing to get away from his body like a diver that ventured deeper than was intended. I swing blindly swatting his face violently sending the sound a skin slapping through the crowd.

For a moment there is nothing but dead silence as his face corrects back and faces mine. His eyes deepen to a black slate with a glow that takes my precious last breath away. I feel my insides sink and terror fill their place. His nostrils flare and his muscles tighten into mind blowing mounds of power. His tongue darts like a snake's at my lips like a warning before striking. I see his eyes set ablaze and I feel his grip tighten as he centers me firmly against the wall. I only have time to open my mouth to scream as his flesh impales its entire length tearing up into my narrow passage brutally only stopping when its impressive length is completed buried within.

I move my lips to scream and no sound comes forth. I wince and roll my eyes back as the throbbing of his hardness stretches as it swells in its restricted space. I take in a deep breath and he pulls out and thrusts even farther up inside me. I release an ear shattering cry and he repeats the assault again. My fingertips claw at the concrete biting at my back. The sounds of my long nails attempting to dig in for some measure slice through the air and is followed by the sound of his body driving into mine.

Harder he thrusts in and out and tighter my pink bud is pinched by the impact. I feel violated, and on fire all at the same time. His mouth bites catching my bottom lip between his sharp fangs. He swirls his tongue preparing the satin flesh of my lip for the pain of puncture. I feel fire seep through throbbing its way to the surface. His sucking intensifies as does his thrusting. The raw sweet taste of blood fills my nose as he sucks to feed.

His right hand slides around to my bottom and first appreciates the slick wetness glazing his length as it disappears inside my tightness and then reappears even more lathered in juices. Over and over I feel the delicious strokes increase in rhythm and tempo. He pounds and drives himself inside with a force of need and anger. Once he has started he cannot stop or grant mercy until he has finished.

His finger taps expertly at my back opening. I fight to say no but he surrenders my lip in favor of one last deep throat stimulating kiss. I feel the rubbing and the grinding taking over and my body begins grinding back against his. Just as he frees my mouth from his, a long slick finger drives deep inside of my tightest opening. I rear back against the wall and cry out. He pounds upward into me slamming me against the wall.

"Your fate is mine to consume." He hisses as he leans forward and fixes his mouth to my neck.

A sharp prick followed by a burning pain flash through me. His lips fasten like a clamp on my neck causing me lean to the opposite side to afford him more room to enjoy his meal. I feel like a growing pool of liquid weightless and governed by the sinuous movements of his thrusts inside. Over I rock and crash and harder I feel the wave's crash inside. I feel my eyes roll back in my head and the hum that once was now a ragged and intense vibration sending all of my muscles into a wild fit of shaking. Harder his sucking became and the stronger the tickling vibrations hummed through me. I dig my nails into his back and grind my bare skin against the wall for extra sensation. Everything painful was setting me on a pleasurable fire ready to explode. His tongue swirled across the bite marks he made and I felt there was something so powerful about to happen tears filled my eyes.

"Please..." I begged in a struggled gasp.

"Surrender to me, Natashia" He commanded riding my body against the wall with such force that if I wasn't ready to come I would swear he was intending to tear me apart.

Over and over he pounded upward leaving me to gasp and whimper at the intensity of his desire. The crowd called out to him challenging him to move faster and harder. He met their challenge and then some.

I felt there was more that I could stand. I felt the convulsions begin as my legs wrapped around his hips. My mouth locked open as I cried out to the black sky above. The sounds of his grunting and cursing filled my ears as his flesh throbbed and swelled inside pounding and stretching me in a painful dance. I could hear his teeth grind and his breathing quicken as he found his release arriving to him unexpected.

Like a wild animal he bit down on my neck with primal force sucking and growling against my throat as he fed in the haze of shooting deep within me. I felt a throbbing and a pulse build quickly vibrating to the small passages within me he was attacking. I could not hold back and I let the explosion tighten around his jerking length still dancing within me as a shot of his liquid fire fills me.

I gasped for the convulsions to stop. His hips shaking in irregular thrusts hammering me to spill the last of his seed. He grinded against me as he sucked for more at my neck.

"Please, don't take anymore." I begged feeling my eyes grow tired and my body weak.

*"I want it all."*

His mind growled as he fed. My eyes roll back and I melt slowly into unconsciousness in his embrace.

I feel dizzy when I open my eyes and feel his tongue sweep at the tenderized flesh of my neck slowly warming it with the healing gift only it could offer me. The taste of his lips found mine and I felt the chill of the cool air remind me where we were as his hands combed through my red curls.

"Time to take you home with me, cara." He announced wrapping me in a cloak of darkness swirling me into the heavens above to the darkest places I only dare to dream of.

Meanwhile back at the office the following morning a cheerful voice calls out.

"Nat!" Gina bounces into the front door of the office.

"He made it. It wasn't my chicken, after all. I hope it's okay to come back there and that you and Mr. Tomescu are covered up. You forgot my cousin is a bartender at "Jimmy's" where you were spotted grinding with a very hot man fitting Vladimir's description. You are so naughty!"

Gina allows a few seconds to pass before she walks into my office with a grin.

"Nat?" She calls out looking around the desk and under. "Anyone here?"

Gina rests her hands on her hips and finally smiles when she looks at the top of my desk and finds the note I left with her name on it.

**Sweetness,**
**It was love at first bite.**
**Heaven with the second.**
**An epiphany with the third.**
**Don't laugh because it is true.**
**He has literally swept me off my feet and has me heart,**
**body and soul.**
**I am off for a two week vacation in Romania until I settle**
**into the feeling of pure bliss in my new skin.**
**Handle any decisions and matters in my absence.**
**Anything major comes up…call Vlad.**
**Until then…behave.**
*Nat*

Gina waved the note in front of her face and smiled as she closed her eyes. Pulling the cell phone out of her pocket she spoke… in Italian.

"Linea privata di Tomescu della manopola." She directed the international operator. Making herself amazingly comfortable in my chair she waited patiently for the operator to connect.

"Stavo prevedendo la vostra chiamata, Gina." Vladimir spoke softly in Italian. "This must be brief. I am about to introduce her to the others downstairs."

"She is well I hope, Sir." Gina spoke leaning forward to the desk.

"You must ask?" He answered sternly as if insulted.

"I am sure the flight back shook her up a bit." Gina laughed softly at the thought of my trip back to Romania minus the airplane.

"Actually she enjoyed it and even had me stop in Paris. We were delayed, you might say, on top of the Eiffel Tower for an hour." Vladimir said, pausing only a few seconds to appreciate the fresh memory of having tied me to the observation iron wall and taking me in the pouring rain. "Otherwise it was uneventful."

"I am pleased that it all worked out as planned." Gina sighed and set the note from me down on my desk. "I will look forward to both of you returning."

"Arrivederci." He ended the call and she closed her phone.

With a reflective expression Gina turned around and looked out the window. A knowing smile crept across her full lips and her tongue flicked the sharp point of her top teeth.

"It's always love at first bite." Gina says with a laugh allowing her fangs to shine brightly in full view.

# The Office

The setting is a large office if you have one...if you don't then you do now. *If only it was always that easy!* You have left for a few moments and this woman finds her way in. The scent of her perfume lingers in the air and draws you in a curious pace to the door. Your high backed chair faces the wall and you stand in the doorway. The woman asks for privacy so you close the door. Who the hell is in your office asking for you to close your own door? The chair turns and you know now it has to be her. The one from the net. There she is and you can't believe your eyes. She is amazing. Flawless. If anyone has seen her...who could miss her? You are going to have so much explaining to do.

She rises and stands with her back against the wall and asks if you are surprised with a smirk that tells you are in so much trouble.

Surprised? You are having a hard time blinking. Now you could go for that water cooler you rejected last week due to the budget. You make a mental note that if you make it through this alive and with your job you will buy one.

She is wickedly beautiful. The kind of beauty that creates people to walk in doors, whistle out the car windows and call for a double take. It is not her slender figure and legs that seem to go on to eternity that get your attention first but it is her smile. It is amazing. It is mesmerizing.

You almost deleted her email out of guilt. The wife had been in rare form that week and you thought why start down the dark path of cyber sex or worse yet phone sex. It may not be the earth shattering experience it once was with your wife but you could live with it. You know she would pack you up and take your last penny if you cross the line. The few erotic emails you exchanged were hot and left you hard and sore. You even would go as far as to wait till the wife and kids were at the library and grocery shopping to open them. You could swear that this woman could read your mind. She knew exactly what you wanted even before you did.

As tempting as it was that night your finger hit the delete key and her email had disappeared. So you thought. Just as your laptop goes to shut down the mail icon flashes. Maybe it was another email from the office so you cancel out the shut down command and proceed to check it out. It has anonymous as the sender. You open it and there is only an attachment. Your finger hits it and there she is. You are breathless. Your eyes rest upon the keeper of your erotic mind. The line at that moment became enviable. With the awe of that smile. Her lips. Her face framed perfection. How many times you thought of her looking up at you while down on her knees blowing you to heaven. Now she was there in your office and your hand wasn't around your cock in front of the computer to see her.

You know there is no turning back. She loosens the belt around her jacket slowly playing with the ends. You watch cautiously as you step back and fumble the lock on the door. Your eyes never leave her fingers. With her right hand she caresses her left breast under the jacket and settles back against the wall. She squeezes and twists the nipple till it pokes through the fabric of the jacket to greet you. She sighs softly and seems to enjoy watching your reaction more than the stimulation of her own hands.

With her left hand she slips into her jacket and in between her legs. She slides her fingers one by one into her wet opening while she rubs her palm against her clit. She starts to breathe heavy and move her hips back and forth. You can't see where those lovely hands are but you know she is on fire. Your cock rises painfully in your pants and is still in shock she is right in front of you.

You watch her chest rise and fall as she moves her hands faster. You begin to breathe with her. You want to be her fingers...every last sweet one. You want to kiss her deep and fill every last part of her to quench that fire that is taking place in the corner of your office.

You suddenly approach her without thinking. You grab her jacket and pull it slightly down her shoulders. They are warm and bare. She is wearing nothing and you are not surprised. All those emails about what she was going to do to you when she got her hands on you all began just like this. Now you know you are in trouble.

Her hands separate as you pull down harder on the jacket. Her tits stand straight out at you. Your hand instinctively slides gently over one with such appreciation as feeling velvet for the very first time. She looks into your eyes with need and you are feeling too hot for the clothes you are wearing. She lets the jacket fall slowly to the ground and then walks around you staring at you with such directness that it almost makes you shiver. You find yourself confused. It is your office and she is taking complete control.

She is everything you could ever want in a lover. Breathtaking and no inhibitions. She knows what you want before you do. As she stands behind you she starts taking off your tie and your shirt. She does it with such ease you wonder how many times she has done this before. Her husband must be a very lucky man.

She kisses your neck and breathes delicately in your ear. Her hands snake their way down your stomach and to your waist. You feel her breasts warm against your back with her nipples erect tapping at you with each subtle movement. She loosens your pants and they fall to the floor. Your cock is hard in her hands and she purrs how wonderful it feels. She whispers she wants it in her deep. Her tongue trails its way along your neck nibbling every now and then to test your trust. Each nibble is a little harder. Your submission is her goal.

Now she faces she faces you and uses the tip of her tongue to trace your bottom lip then proceeds to outline your mouth. You swear this cat has to have nine lives and you may very well need to borrow one before she is through. You want her so much it hurts. Literally.

Her tongue makes its way into your mouth. As you taste her for the first time her hands bring your hands to her tight ass. She holds them there until you get the message. You can't resist anymore. There is only so much a man can take and it definitely was too much when she walked into your office.

You kiss her neck and taste her perfume. Your hands come up to her breast and you cup them firmly squeezing them for the first time. You pull her into you so they press between you. She silently directs you to the chair and guides you to sit down. She then straddles you and looks into your eyes as she slides your cock into her and sitting firmly in your lap. You could explode right there and still rate it the best you ever had.

She pulls you in close presses her tits into your face. Her back arches for you to enjoy them. Her head leans back and she starts moaning as she grinds into you. She is doing a dance right in your lap. First she rocks back and forth and then you would never have thought it possible but she is doing figure 8's with her hips. She is so warm and wet and tight. You want to fill her up. If only this could last forever.

You feel her move faster and you know she is close to cumming. Now it is your turn to take control. This is your part in every email fantasy she has sent you. You lift her off your lap and stand. Now you want to see just how much she paid attention to what you want.

Like a cat she slides up onto your desk bent over with her legs open for you to see her pink wet pussy. She says she wants you to fuck her from behind. That was your cue and you enter keeping her legs wide apart with yours spread in a stance. You watch your cock slowly slide in. You grab her hips hard and then in one hard pull you slam her down against you and she gasps. She really likes this part. She told you she would. Harder the better. You pump into her deeper and faster and even pull her head back with her hair. She giggles and coos how good you are.

She is squirming and begging for more. Suddenly, she starts becoming erratic and you know this is going to be it. You have broken her and she is now at your mercy. She squeals softly and rises up to stand as you grind up into her deeper. You pull her back against you and squeeze her tits, twist her nipples giving them a little pinch. She puts her mouth onto yours and starts to fuck you with her tongue. She bites your lip and starts crying out to the heavens above. That is all it took and with one last shot you drive yourself home into her shaking at the impact.

You stand holding her with your face buried in her soft hair and neck. You want to keep her around you forever. Without any last words she gives you that heartbreaking smile and dresses. You can't move. This is the part you never talked about. She reaches the door and blows you a kiss. She is gone.

You recover through the day and spend stolen moments looking for her on the net. Surely she will email you when she arrives home. No mail ever comes. You get up late into the night and check on the computer at home. Still nothing. Weeks pass and you realize that it was once in a lifetime and nothing more. One smile and a kiss goodbye. That was the ending she forgot to tell you about.

# The Wager

Jim and Susan had been working in the same office for the past year. Jim had two years under his belt when Susan joined the sales team. He had been the top in their division since joining the company, until Susan showed up. She came in with an arrogant attitude and rubbed Jim the wrong way from day one.

It was the last year of the week and their sales figures for the quarter were just about dead even. They had become so competitive that they had even started wagering on their sales. It was small things like lunches, game ticket, just enough to irritate Jim even more when she would come to collect the prize. Susan strolled in that morning and went straight to Jim's office door. It was open and she walked in.

"So, what's it going to be this time? Playoff tickets?" She asked, taunting him.

"Well, if our team were going to the playoffs that might work." Jim said, leaning back in his chair.

"How about New Years Eve? The loser treats the winner to a night out on the town. Anything the winner wants." She suggested. Jim looked at the luscious woman in front of him and didn't think he could stand taking her out just so she could taunt him all night, then send him home without so much as a kiss.

"No, I don't think so." He replied.

"Your office then." Susan said. She had always been jealous of his large office with the great view.

"And what do I get if I win?" Jim asked, smiling.

"What do I have that you want?" She asked. Jim did not have to think long. He stood up and leaned over the desk.

"You." he said. He figured that would shut her up and he

70

could go back to work.

"Me?" Susan responded, stepping back. "You want me? What, I date you for a week or something?"

"No, I get you for a night. Anything I want." Jim said, sitting back down. Susan was cocky and confident. She had her week planned out well and thought there was no way she could lose.

"Tell you what," she said, crossing her arms. "If you win, I will show up at your door on New Years Eve and you can have your way with me. Anything you want." She extended her hand for the ceremonial handshake. Jim could not believe what she just agreed to. He stood up and took her hand. They shook on their wager and Susan looked around the office.

"I'll be back later to measure for new drapes." Susan said as she walked out the door. "I might want to repaint too."

Jim returned to his work and did not give the wager another thought. He had a meeting at lunchtime with a big client that would seal top salesperson of the quarter, year, even century if he were lucky. He doubted if she would actually consent to her end of the bargain, but at least she would never question his skills as top man in the office again. It would be fun watching her trying to back out of this one. He picked up his phone to confirm his meeting then picked up some files on the desk and put them in his briefcase. He smiled at the thought of Susan actually paying off the bet. He shook his head and headed out the door. Susan saw him from her small cubicle and waved at him.

"Giving up and going home?" She asked, taunting him again. Jim just smiled back and waved as he headed toward the elevator.

It was now 1 o'clock and Jim sat by himself at the table at the restaurant. He kept looking at the signatures on the papers in the folder in front of him. He had called his boss and told him he sealed the deal with no effort at all. He knew it would be easy, but he was still stunned that it took only 15 minutes and it was over. The deal doubled his sales for the year. His boss had told him there would be changes when he finished this deal. Now he was getting a promotion, huge raise and a new office.

Suddenly he remembered the office. He laughed to himself wondering if Susan would get his office after all, even though he beat her sales by a long shot. He never gave their wager another thought as he gathered things up and headed back to the office. He dropped the papers off with his boss then went down to get some things from his office.

He saw that Susan's cubicle was empty and assumed she was out trying to beat him, although she did not know anything about his big deal. Jim's boss had told him to take off the rest of the week. It was a couple days before New Years Eve, so he decided to take him up on the offer and locked his office and headed home.

Susan was talking to a client when her cell phone rang. She ignored it and tied up the loose ends with her current sale. On the way back to her car she checked the number on her phone and saw it was the office. She called back to get her message.

"Hello, its Susan. Did someone call me?" She said to the receptionist that answered the phone. She waited as her call went through to her boss.

"Susan! Good news!" He said to her.

"What is it?" She asked excitedly, hoping that Jim had resigned.

"Jim just signed Boston Vision Software to the biggest deal this company has ever seen. He is moving to a new office so you are getting his job and office. You have done great and deserve the job."

"I, uh…he did what?" Susan stuttered.

"Stop in my office when you get back, we'll go over the

details of your pay increase and benefits." He continued.

"Ok, thanks." Susan said, still stunned and hung up. Jim had beaten her. Her head was spinning, wondering what she had gotten into. She climbed into her car and drove back to the office.

The sun had long since set and Jim was relaxing in his living room, watching an old movie. The last thing he was thinking about was his job, Susan or the wager they had made. He was starting to nod off when he heard his doorbell. He got up and went to answer. He was surprised to see Susan standing there.

"I wanted to congratulate you on your promotion." She said. Jim noticed that she was wearing a long overcoat and high heels. Her hair and makeup looked like she was going out for the night.

"Do you want to come in?" Jim offered.

"I have to. You won." Susan said stepping in to his large apartment. She took off her long coat and revealed that she was naked, except for the heels. "I expect you to take your prize. It would be an insult to refuse. I know I would have taken your office in an instant had I won."

"You don't have to." Jim said, stunned.

"Furthermore, you had better fuck me in every nasty kinky way your mind can imagine so you won't wish later you had done something to me. You won't get another chance." She told him firmly, setting her coat down and walking to the middle of the room. She got down on her knees and put her hands behind her back. Jim's cock was rock hard seeing this woman offer herself to him like that.

"Do you want something to drink?" Jim asked, walking towards her.

"Are you kidding? Just fuck me." Susan told him. "While you're at it, take off your tie and tie my wrists. I might just try to kick and hit if you don't"

Jim walked over behind her. She was offering up her wrists to him behind her back. He obliged and took off his tie. He tied her wrists tightly. He stepped back and looked at her.

"What a prize. Why didn't we have this wager earlier?" Jim said. He walked up to her and undid his pants. He pulled out his hard cock and pushed it into her mouth. She sucked him hard and Jim moaned loudly. He pulled out, not wanting to cum yet. He took her over to the couch and bent her over the cushions. He rubbed the head of his cock on her wet pussy and slid it in. She made a low soft moan when he filled her up with his cock. He started slowly, and then started shoving harder. His hands were on her ass and he could see her juices flowing around his cock. He knew he would cum soon, but wanted to enjoy her as much as he could. He slowly withdrew and rubbed the head of his cock on her tight ass. His cock was wet and slick from her pussy and he started pushing in her tight hole.

"Noooo….." she started to say, but he took one hand and covered her mouth.

"I am going to fuck you any way I want." He told her firmly. "You are my prize and for the evening I am going to use you to get off any way I want."

"God yes!" She hissed when he removed his hand.

She pushed back against him as he fucked her ass. He held her tied wrists with one hand as he rode her like a wild bronco. Jim could feel the pressure building in his cock. Susan could feel it too and pushed back as hard as she could, tightening her ass on his cock. He exploded in her and she screamed when he did. He fell on top of her hot sweating body. He could not believe what had just happened. The woman that irritated him more than anyone had just come into his house and demand that he fuck her. Jim slowly pulled out of her ass. He stood up and she turned her head to look at him.

"Is that it?" She asked. "Is that all you've got?" Jim

could not believe that she was so competitive that she wanted to not only pay off the wager, but also be the most incredible sex in his life.

"Who said I was done?" Jim said firmly, swatting her ass hard with his hand.

Susan yelped when his hand struck her little ass. Jim walked out of the room to get a drink and get ready for round two. He returned to find her squirming against the cushions. He could tell she was extremely hot and ready to be fucked some more.

He sat down on the couch next to her head. He reached into his glass of ice water and took out an ice cube. He ran it down her back and she shivered. He ran it down the crack of her ass and before she could protest, he shoved it into her pussy.

"Fuck! That's cold you bastard!" she protested.

"Just wait till you see where the next one goes." He said, reaching into his glass again.

"Oh no....not...." she started to say as he shoved a cube into her ass.

She was squirming and moaning as the cube melted in her tight ass. He put his hand in her hair and pulled her head onto his lap. She sucked his cock into her mouth and he leaned back on the couch.

"Suck it good and you may get to cum next." He said. She swirled her tongue around it and he started moaning. This only made her increase her efforts on his once again large cock. Soon he was pushing into her mouth as she sucked. He opened his eyes to see the bound woman sucking and it pushed him over the edge. His cock filled her mouth and she expertly sucked it all in and swallowed. She took her mouth off and licked her lips, smiling at him.

"Mmmm, that was delicious." She said. "Now, you were saying about me cumming?"

"A man of my word." Jim said, pulling her up onto the

couch.

He leaned her back and spread her legs apart. Her wrists tied so that she was at his mercy. He knelt down between her legs and slowly pulled them apart. He licked up the inside of her thigh, heading towards her pussy. She closed her eyes and rolled her head back when he drove his tongue into her wet, moist hole. He licked her clit and fucked her with his tongue. His face was getting soaked from her, and she was grinding hard against him. He would get her close, and then back off. Jim knew it was driving her crazy and it would not take much more to get her cumming hard. He dove into her pussy and licked hard. Suddenly she was coming and she screamed, pushing into him.

"Fuck me…oh fuck, that's so…" She said, squealing. Her legs wrapped tightly around his head, making sure he could not pull away. Finally, she relaxed and Jim stood up. He helped her sit up and untied her wrists. She stood up and grabbed her coat.

"Paid in full." She said. She leaned over to him and kissed him. He could taste the result of their fucking on her lips.

"I'll see you after the first of the year." Susan said, walking towards the door. "Come down and see me some time. We can make another wager."

"Anytime." Jim said, smiling.

"I don't lose twice." She replied, winking, then disappeared out the door. Jim was not sure what she meant by that, but knew he was going to have fun finding out.

# Company Policy

The company you work for has just announced an invitation to participate in a study on office stress by a prominent Psychologist. The deal is you visit the office of this doctor and answer a few simple questions. If you volunteer to do so, you get three days off with pay to use when you decide to. You are need of some vacation time. Work is getting mundane. You waste no time getting the directions to this doctor's office. On your lunch break, you call and make an appointment for the next day. Your boss approves the vacation time in advance. You just set yourself up for three free days to do what you please.

You enter the office and there is dim lighting and candles burning. Incenses floats in the air. You feel all apprehension leave your body and feel surprisingly relaxed. You approach the desk thinking you will find some guy who is a deadhead or a doctor who enjoyed the 60's a tad too much. Instead, a secretary greets you by your first name and invites you to have a seat.

After filing some papers the secretary returns to where you are sitting and asks if you would care for something to drink...the usual coffee, water, tea then she tells you they have a beautiful zinfandel that seems to be a favorite. You blink a couple of times and then half laugh asking her to repeat the choices. Yes, sure enough, she did in fact say exactly what you heard.

You think for a moment...*Is this a joke?* You are not a big drinker and everyone knows that. It is after work hours...*why not?* The secretary returns with a chilled wine glass and the zinfandel sweeping back and forth inside almost jumping over the rim as she hands it to you. She explains that it may be about 10 or 15 minutes before the doctor will be with you. That may explain the goblet size glass you are holding. You take a sip of the wine and find it very aromatic, full, sweet and lastly strong. You can feel the vapors escape your nose.

*Wow*, you think. What are you doing here? You search the room for magazines and your eyes locate them in the corner to your left. You pull one off the rack and it is Playboy. You are surprised and then after peeking inside you toss it back in when you hear the secretary return to the desk. Who wants to be holding a girlie magazine should the doctor walk out?

The secretary tells the doctor who is not visible to you that she will finish the findings on the reports for fellatio and multiple orgasms at home... that is if Derek leaves her alone long enough and then giggles. You cannot believe what you have heard. The secretary glances over at you and you drink from the glass looking down to avoid eye contact. Either you are very nervous or thirsty but the glass is empty before you know it.

The next sound you hear is the pouring of more wine into your empty glass. It is not long after that the secretary loudly announces her departure for home.

"The doctor will be with you very shortly. You are going to be so glad you came." She says.

"I just wanted three days off, I really am okay." You say assuring her your need for help was not there.

"You may find you come often after your visit today." The secretary says with a tender smile. "Help yourself to some of our reading material next to you. It will make the time pass and relax you." She says as she opens the door to leave.

You watch as she fumbles the locks closed from the outside of the door. You tap your fingers on the stem of the wine glass and notice it is slowly becoming empty and you wonder how. You feel fine. Toasty fine in fact. As strong as it is, maybe it is actually evaporating.

You grab another magazine from the dark corner and find

it is Penthouse. What are the chances of that? You skim quickly through since it is a new issue and think some person left their reading material behind. You are feeling warm and your face is flushing. Yes, Sir, the toasty part of fine is kicking in. Your cheeks feel on fire. You look at the table in front of you and find a large red hardcover book face down so you decide to flip it over.

The title takes you by surprise *Karma Sutra: Images of lovemaking* are in calligraphy across the front in gold. You hear the phone ring in the back and a woman's voice answer faintly before a door shuts. You think that it will be okay to peek at the contents of the book. What have you got to lose after a couple glasses of wine and the nudie magazines? Anything seems to go in this office.

You open to a random page a third of the way through the book and find the images are of women and men photographed in the middle of intercourse in these various positions. Large color photographs! You are looking at the wheel barrow position and the woman's leg closest to the photographer is bent while she is laying with her upper body across a high velvet open chair and the opposite leg is supported by another velvet chair of equal height. The woman is obviously enjoying this position as you can see one photo shows the tip of his cock at the opening of her pussy and everything is dry.

The next photo was taken after he slid in and out of her several times. His cock was half out of her pussy and her lips were shining along with his cock. Her eyes tightly closed, her cheeks were red and her mouth crying out something that you wish you could hear. Her tits were large, full and hanging down at such an angle you could see her nipples sharp at the tips. The lucky man had his hand around her hip and was playing with her clit and the other hand had his thumb barely inserted into her ass. He had an expression of chaos across his face as if in intense pain.

You can still vaguely hear someone talking in the back office so you cannot help but turn to another page and this time it is one familiar to you. It is one that you have been in although not half as much as you would like. The same couple and it is a perfect side view of the "69" position. His cock is buried down her throat and his one hand spreads her pussy wide open as his tongue has disappeared into her cunt to the point it looks as if he is about to bite her. Again, his lucky thumb has now plunged into her ass up to the knuckle.

You are hot now. You place the book on your lap and slip a hand underneath it to rearrange your own cock that has now doubled in size. The page flips as you situate your hard on and your eyes rest on a position you did not even think of. The man is lying on his back while the woman is on top of him facing his feet. He is sucking on one of his toes as he is doing the same to her. This position gives multiple angle shots and you see that they must have been at it for quite a while. His cock once again buried deep into her juicy cunt while her sweet ass spreads for the reader to see her slobbering over his dick and sucking him in even farther.

You feel your pants are going to rip in the crotch if you do not find a bathroom soon to rub yourself to relief. You look at the last shot, it is a close up of her pussy spitting out its juice all over the base of his cock, and his shock of hair is soaked as if he just stepped out of the shower. Damn! Now you close the book and are about ready to flip it over when the doctor walks into the room. You keep the book over your lap and look up. You have to be seeing things.

"Hi, I am Dr. Jansen. Everyone calls me Jenna. Do you like the book?" She asks pointing to the one thing that protects you from showing her what you have in your pants.

*It has to be a mistake! Too much wine. It has to be.*

"Yes, it is me. I co-authored the book in graduate school with a colleague. We thought the only way to be objective about its content was to photograph actual people performing those positions. I am quite pleased with the success in the lives of my patients because of it." She finishes explaining watching you with an assessing eye.

It is the same woman in front of you. You see that maybe 5-10 years has passed. Her legs are lean and long, her skin has seen a few more summers since the book's publishing but her tits stood out to attention even seeming to be larger than in the pictures. Her hair was longer and highlighted. You look at her hand reach for the book and you pull it into your lap.

"You can bring it with you if you want to. Maybe we can discuss your reaction to the content. I really like the feedback of the readers." She says turning to walk into the office. "Follow me please." She finishes as she opens the office door.

You follow her leaving the book behind on the table. You think of her with every piece of clothing on earth on her body so you will not have to remember her with a cock sliding into her or her beautiful face as she is about to come. She points out the chair she wants you to sit in and it is upholstered in red velvet...are these the same chairs you ask yourself.

"Do the chairs look familiar?" She asks with interest.

You look at her standing behind the desk as she is about to sit in her chair. Immediately you think of being in that chair first and she is about ready to sit on your lap. You console yourself inside thinking any other healthy man would in your circumstance. You sit down in the velvet chair and you wonder to yourself which one her sharp nipples brushed against and which one supported her legs? If you put them together, would you be able to stand between her legs? You size up the height as you sit down and figure you could have a straight shot into her pussy too. Jenna picks up a pen and writes something down as you watch. You raise an eyebrow and she notices.

"Just the patient number and the questions I intend to ask. For research purposes only, of course. Is that okay?" She explains.

"Sure, I am fine and have nothing to hide or worry about." you answer.

She gives you a quizzical look and smirks. She asks the basic get to know you questions and finds out everything up to your last physical. Nothing devastating and she comments what great health you appear to be in. Whatever you thought before has all but disappeared from your mind until of course she asks what she really wanted to know to begin with.

"How did you feel when you picked up that Playboy magazine?" She asks in a serious tone.

"Uh, surprised?" You stammer trying to get a grip on what the hell is going on.

"What about when you picked up the Penthouse?" She follows not missing a beat.

"Lucky. What the hell is this about anyways?" you counter. Is this woman hanging a PHD from the Cracker Jack Box on her wall or what?

"I am studying the effects of stress in the office at home in the sex lives of employees." she finally explains. "I am a sex therapist. That was not explained up front because of the nature of my work. Believe me, your company has been benefited with a grant and I get the last of the information I need to finish this study." She finishes getting her agenda out in the open.

"Wait a minute..." you say, "Am I the only one who responded to this offer?"

"No, the others just were never seen again after the book on the table." she adds, "Which brings me to my next question. Were you aroused by the photos in the book?" She asks curiously with pen in hand.

"Well, you have to admit that a book on the table that no offense, has people fucking, might be enough to shock a few people but when the woman that is photographed with a guy in between her legs comes out introducing herself as the

82

doctor you come to see it may send a few people out the door. Granted, some may be looking for a bathroom others may very well be going to find their woman to help them with the effects following such an experience. Know what I mean?" You say looking directly across the desk into her deep brown eyes.

"The question still stands that I asked before. However, I would first like to discuss why you are sitting in the chair speaking with me right now instead of taking off as the others had." She inquires while her pen runs across the paper. It has to be shorthand she is using because she is finished writing as soon as she finishes speaking.

"Seriously? You really want to know?" You ask while she raises her head and looks at you with complete focus.

It hits you finally. The doctor really wants to know. You give her credit thinking she must be one secure woman to do the work she does. There must be a few happy people right now in bed together bouncing up and down celebrating her intervention in their lives. The thought of two people fucking sticks in your mind for a moment longer than comfortable and you shift in your chair. You decide to give her what she asks for and chances are she has heard it before.

"The reading material was a surprise. When I opened the book and saw these large color photos of a couple fucking, I guess I had the normal response any man would. I had no time to get up and leave by the time you came in. I had to cover myself or offend you. It was one of the two. Call me a gentleman I guess." You finish with a half-hearted smile.

"Did you experience an erection from viewing the photos?" She asks pen flying across the paper.

"Yes." You answer shifting again as you look at her biting down on her bottom lip.

It would be heaven to have her on her knees in front of you right now. Thankfully, she cannot see over the desk because you are starting to pitch a tent in your pants. Her lips must be soft.

"Now, we finally reach my first question. Which position did you like the most?" She asks staring into your eyes in a way that most would find unwise given the topic of the current conversation.

"Uh, well, I didn't get to look at the whole book that is for sure. I doubt anyone could handle looking through the whole book without taking some sort of break." You answer as you once again shift in the velvet chair.

Your hands brush against the fabric and you imagine that must be how her shaven pussy must feel like. You wonder if she still is bare or if that was outdated for her. Maybe you will ask if she gets any more personal about the stiffness the images of her bent over gave you. Fair is fair you think to yourself and smile.

"What is your favorite position during intercourse?" She asks putting the pen to her mouth. "Anything these days. I am lucky if I get into a position with anyone. That one of you lying on top facing his feet was unique." You answer wondering what position she would like you to put her in. *Pretzel maybe?*

She excuses herself for a moment then comes back with the book in her hand flipping through the pages with lightening speed and puts it down in your lap before retuning to her chair behind the desk.

"Is that the one?" She asks and points for you to look down at the photos.

You look down and there is her tight little ass spread just enough as her pussy swallows his cock. You try to bring humor to this situation to avoid another hard on and almost ask if the lucky person ever got his cock back after she was done. No, that would not be a good idea to ask.

"That is the one, yes." You answer with a dry throat.

"Does seeing others during intercourse arouse you to the

point of experiencing an erection?" She asks tapping her pen against the pad of paper while looking at you.

Okay, she has made you have at least two erections that you can think of, put magazines in the waiting room yet neglected to have a damn restroom to finish off in and the icing on the cake has to be the book with her fucking in every position except hanging from a tree. Hell, she probably has that in there too.

The hot doctor must have spent many happy days as an intern touring India spreading her love and her legs to all the country. You would not be surprised if she has a shrine over there somewhere.

What she needs is a dose of her own medicine and you decide you have had enough zinfandel to administer it to her. Screw the three days off. She is causing you more stress in a single hour thinking about diving into her cunt than your work does in a single week.

"Yes, as a matter of fact it does get me hard seeing a cock sliding into a juicy cunt like this." You say holding up the book and pointing at the close up of her dripping pussy.

The doctor clears her throat and shifts slightly in her chair now. You proceed to flip to the page with the "69" position and take a little time to admire it even turning the book a little to be dramatic at viewing it. She shifts back again in her again interested in your burst of assertion.

"Can I ask you a question?" You ask looking at her with a fixed stare.

"Sure, feel free to ask me anything." She answers with a smile that says she is ready to hear anything.

"Does it get you wet while I sit and look at you cumming all over the place? Do you feel like slipping at least one finger under that desk between you and me and touching yourself right there." You say holding up the book pointing to a photo that shows her swollen clit.

Naturally, you tap your finger right on the pink bud you speak of in the photo for added emphasis. She squirms a little, which you completely expected, then leans forward resting her elbows on the desk and puts down the pen and paper.

"Yes, it is natural to respond with such feelings during visually stimulating images." She says in a professional tone. Her answer says you have her right where she didn't expect to be.

"Does it give you an erection right now?" She asks trying to turn the tables.

Okay, this chick is one tough cookie. Your first instinct is to take her hand and help her figure out the answer through tactile discovery. Most women would have told you to fuck off or go to hell and called you a pig. Instead, she wants to know how big your dick is at that moment. She has to break at some moment and be offended. You know how to end this session real quick.

"Would you like to see it?" You ask not moving from the chair but sliding the book onto the desk. Her eyebrow raises and she wets her lips discreetly. "Is that what this is all about?"

"Why, do you want to show me your penis?" She asks again in her professional tone.

"Do I want to show you my package? Sure. I would like nothing more than to pull it out and tell you where it would nicely fit." You say sarcastically thinking she asked for it.

"Then why don't you?" She asks not even blinking with a smirk on her face.

"Why? Well, let me see...maybe 1-5 years in a 10 by 10 cell. Lady, you really need to watch yourself. Here I am answering questions, looking at a book with you where you are exploding all over the place and I could be any psycho and you could end up in some serious trouble." You say sharply as you get ready to stand.

Enough of the talk of sex and arousal. You have had it.

This woman, doctor or not, has pushed you to the limits you had no idea you had. The game was up. Win or lose you were better off going home and taking a cold shower.

"First of all, psychotic you are not. Second, I usually do not take this direction with my sessions at all. I have a camera in the waiting room and I saw you from the moment you walked in." She says standing up from the chair.

"So, why the change in your approach with me? Did I look like I was sexually deviant looking at the magazines and books? Because any man would have done the same thing. I am sure you know that by now with your little camera out there." You respond with a defensive tone.

"Actually, I found it quite exciting watching you look at me the way you did. Our session is over, you are fine and I have the information I need to conclude the study. I am interested in what you thought while looking at the book. Be honest, I would like to know." She asks as she walks closer to you around the edge of the desk.

You can smell her perfume and almost feel the heat from her body. You look into her eyes and you hear her asking a million questions that she does not dare ask aloud. You cannot be reading the signs wrong. This amazing, hot woman wants you or at least to be fucked. Probably both with the way she keeps asking you questions. Just to save you the 1-5 in the cell you decide to answer the question and see what she does with the information.

"What I thought? Well let me see..."You say as you walk around her looking down at her gorgeous legs.

You feel her breathe in deep and hold it as she leans on one hand to the desk while you pass her. You stand behind her. Ready or not you were going to find out what was the doctor's real agenda.

"I thought about how the apex between your thighs must feel. I imagine it is exactly as the velvet chairs your tits brushed against as you felt that cock sliding in and out of you. I thought about what it would feel like to put my fingers in it and wiggle it around to get your hips moving. I thought about the taste of your sweetness on my tongue as I snaked it in and out of you while I shoved my face in between your legs. I thought about sucking on your chest. Massaging until you arched your back up to me and then biting firmly as I slid into you." You stand closer behind her and can smell her heat and her perfume.

Her hair is against your cheek as you lean over to whisper in her ear. She closes her eyes and takes a deep breath. Either you are right about her or you are just about to feel a lot of pain followed by sirens.

"What I thought about more than anything else that no photo of you could tell me in your book was..."You lean into her and whisper, "What noise do you make when you come? I know you make one...So, what is it Jenna? Hmmm?" You finish not moving.

You think this has probably either bought your way out of her office or at the least proved your point. The ball was now in her court. She turns around to face you not letting any space between you. Her chocolate eyes are on fire and you can feel her heart beating between you. She softly leans over to the side of your neck and breathes in your cologne without touching you.

"Would you like me to tell you or would you like to find out for yourself?" She whispers in your ear leaning closer than safe to you with as excited as you are.

That was all the restraint you had left. You are thinking you are about to call a cell home and not even care. Your cheeks are hot and your package has just reached an all-time tightness in your jeans. The woman was asking for it now.

"Do you want to fuck me?" She asks after a thoughtful pause with a serious balls-to-the-wall look in her eyes.

"I want to make you scream." You announce and bring

her mouth to yours with your hand behind her neck.

You pull her into you as her tongue searches for a place to hide in your mouth. Your hands slide down her waist and you finally hold her in your embrace. Your mouth leaves hers and slides down her neck sucking hard as it makes it way down to her shoulder while your hands pull back the shirt.

The doctor sighs deeply and you feel her hands slip into your hair. She is just as ready as you are. You want to fuck her in every way possible and make the book seem ancient.

She leans back against the desk and rests on her hands while you brush the blouse off her shoulders revealing her white lace bra that serves no purpose other than to glow against her brown sun kissed skin. She obviously had some work done to defy gravity. You slide your tongue down between those luscious tits and she tosses her hair and head back moaning how good you feel.

"You smell so good." She sighs with her eyes heavy and hungry for you alone.

You slide your hands behind her back and unfasten the hooks to her bra. Before you release the garment you run your tongue into her cleavage then slowly up her chest, throat and finally nibble on her chin before biting her lip. As her tits bounce free from their lacy prison, you suck on her bottom lip and then her tongue as she offers it soft and full to you. You explore each other's mouths for an eternity grinding into each other almost to the point of biting.

You pull back on her hair wrapping it around your fist and pull downward so her neck pulls back. You trail breath soft kisses down her cheek and finally land on her throat where you first suck lightly then increase to where she tries to push you away fear of leaving a mark.

She cannot push hard enough to keep you away. You cup your hand under her tight ass and pull her hips right into yours letting her feel what you cannot hide anymore. She loses strength and her hands grab your head and hold you to her neck to suck even longer.

"It feels so good!" She calls out with enthusiasm.

You waste no time in sliding down to her breasts and she leans back on both hands as you take each one into your mouth as if feeding out of ravenous hunger. Biting and twisting her nipples between your teeth hoping to make her squeal in pain.

Nothing could be better than this you think. That is until your start licking your way down to the sweetest taste in the world. You lower to your knees and slide your hands up her skirt into the inside of her thighs while eating her navel then blowing lightly on her stomach. She spreads her legs slightly open so that you have access to do what she needs you to do.

Her skirt is a wrap and buttons in the front. You have it off in no time and come to face the most appetizing delight you are about to consume. Her sheer panties scarcely hide her pink shaven pussy. Her preference remained and you are grateful. You shove your face into her and blow a long hot breath against her clit.

"Yessss!" she says giving you permission.

Your hands slide up to the back of her left hip holding the elastic as your tongue slips between her legs and firmly goes to her cunt all the way up over the outside of her panties to her clit and biting through the material holding the little bud delicately between your teeth. She sucks in a deep breath as if she just stepped into uncomfortably hot water. You hope as you proceed to rip off her panties in one quick tug of your hands for the reaction.

"Ohhhhhhh!" she exclaims.

Now you let the fabric fall to the floor. You lean her to a half sitting position on her desk bringing one of her beautiful legs up to rest on the side of her on the desk. Her pussy was clean, pink, shaven with perfection and the lips swollen with a few little pearls of juice at the base. You lick them first, come up, and kiss her deep. She moans and pleads for you not to stop as you slip your fingers into her wetness. You swirl them in and out painting the outside of her cunt and inner thighs with her juice.

She slides her fingers into your hair as your hand squeezes her tit. You feel pressure on your head to go down and you know what she wants. Making her ask for it is necessary given the last hours of torture you endured looking at her bent over in the book. You tease her and nibble the insides of her thighs always coming close but not close enough to what she needs to ask for. She pushes your head back to her cunt but you continue to move somewhere else. Finally, she almost whimpers.

"I want you." She begs.

"Want what?" you look up at her. Then proceed to lick her thigh.

She grabs your face and shoves it between her legs and demands "Eat me. I want to cum all over your face!" she states firmly.

That was all the invite you needed. You take your hands and pull her lips apart so she is wide open to feast. You suck, you bite and you almost chew her to climax. She rakes her cunt back and forth across your face, moaning deep in her throat like a lioness. She shows control as she keeps both hands back on the desk until you hear her reach her peak.

"Oh, fuck, Yesssssssss!!!!!" she cries out and grasps both of her hands on your face and shoves your mouth over her cunt and you suck down hard over her clit.

Her juices trickle down your cheeks and over your face. She shakes, squirms, pulls your hair and almost falls off the table. You are almost afraid to fuck her now when you see the intensity she has with an orgasm. You fumble your pants down half in confusion and half in wild need to put your rock hard cock into this woman somewhere...anywhere.

Not missing a move in her own abandon her hand is gripped tight pumping up and down your cock. She sucks on your shoulder, biting you and making you jump. Before you know it, her mouth finds your chest and your nipple biting and pinching it between her teeth. You never thought of such a thing and now she could make you explode right there if you do not pull away. She spins around and has you flat on your back with you watching her dance her way down over your cock. You would bet she knows how to belly dance the way she is riding you.

She leans back on her hands as they rest on your thighs and her tits are bouncing up and down and side to side as she uses your cock to anchor her. You grab her boobs as they swing together and squeeze them and she moans even louder telling you once again how good you are making her feel. She starts to bounce harder and faster and you know it will not be long now. You grab her hips and slam her down on you a couple times and she cries out.

"Fuckkkkkk Yesssssssss!" She calls to you. That is not good enough. You sit forward, she falls back still attached and wiggling on your cock, and you pull her legs up over your shoulders and tell her to look at you. Her brown eyes burn through you and you slide yourself back and forth into her first slowly then you drive your cock in deep and fast. She grabs your ass clawing at you.

"Want me to fuck you hard, Hmmmm?" You say between breaths pounding as hard as you can into her silky depths.

"Yes!" She moans and arches her back, looking into your eyes as you take the final dive in her fast and hard.

The floor quakes beneath both of you and you collapse on top of her. You wake later next to her and she kisses you softly like an angel.

"Would an early appointment next week work for you?" She says as she smiles sliding into your arms.

# Moonlit Dream

It is late and the air is softly flowing through the trees. The breeze rippled the surface of the open water. The stars glitter and the moon casts a soft light to my shoulders and the path before me. An internal longing, a hunger far out of control, drives me. I feel my soul aching for something...anything to sustain itself for another moment without you.

I walk in a different direction than usual. I smell the flowers no longer seen. I feel the texture of the grass though I walk on a plain path. I feel the warmth of the moonlight wrap around my body. I feel the freedom of the weightlessness in water though I am on land. I see past the water and the other lands in between and now I see you.

You are taking the same steps, the same path to me. My senses are aware of everything. Everything they are not supposed to be. I hear you breathe. Feeling each exhale against my cheek as the sound dances softly in my ear. I feel you coming closer. I close my eyes and see you clearly. I stand and you circle me. I am peace. The longing lessens. I feel tears fall from my eyes, the joy of you coming to me again.

I feel your fingertips glide from my hands up my arms. I feel the warmth sink into every pore as they touch my shoulders. I feel the heat of passion build as they float across my neck bringing me to you. I draw my lips to yours. The meeting is delicate. Our lips opening to exchange each breath released. We could survive this way. One soul breathing for another

I taste you first with restraint as if you may not be real. I then go deeper searching for more. Your hands pull me against you. I feel like I am melting into you. You have come to be satisfied. Together we shall find our need fulfilled.

The surroundings change to suit our needs. Everything conforms to our desires. You trace my lips with a single fingertip. I softly smile at the vision before me. I whisper your name and tell you I need you. You sit on the edge of the bed. A bed shared by no others and never to be shared again.

With our eyes looking into each other, searching for the love hidden for this moment, you unbutton each barrier holding me from you. I feel freedom as more of me is revealed to your touch. I do the same to all that keeps you from me. I move my fingers down your chest to your pants and ask you to stand. I free you and cradle you in my hands. I kiss your cheek. I nibble at your earlobe. I taste my way down your neck, your chest and going down on my knees I kneel before you. I look up at you with a silent request for permission. Your hands slip into my hair and draw me to the gift granted.

I can smell you as I dreamed it would be. Skin soft as a rose petal. I have savored nothing as much as this. I lick my way around your shape as it grows. I suck each jewel as if polishing to reveal their beauty. You are aching for my mouth. You guide yourself into me. Slowly you move in. My tongue is the magic that will draw you in. My lips keep you captive. I suck you in for security. Holding you as you grow deeper into me. You are mine. I want to swallow you. You feel you could lose yourself this way and not regret one moment. You pull me back and you out. You lift me up and kiss me deep. This time it is a spark to ignite a flame. It burns in both of us. The sweet pain is calling. We must answer.

You sit on the bed and I stand before you bare except for the wanting. I bring your mouth to my breast. I caress your neck...run my fingers through your hair. Drink me into you I ask. I feel the sucking intensify. Your mouth is my heaven. I want inside of you. I moan. I need you so. I ask you to give me more. Your fingers follow my command. I feel them step down my body as you suck me in. You draw heavily from one breast and then to the other. Hungrily, you bite at me, licking me. Your hands sliding down to my secret door and your fingers touch the sweetest spot of all.

They slide delicately one by one inside. I become weak as they tap against my clit. You support me. I beg for you to wait but it is not heard. You suck and plunge deeper as your hand grabs my universe. I cry out, shaking, collapsing into the palm of your hand. I tremble and you are ravenous in my weakness. Now you shall feed.

You lay back and then kiss me to share what there is to come again. I know where my place is to be. I settle myself over you. I straddle your face and venture to your South. I worship this pole. I again suck you in and feel you enter me to taste me again.    Your tongue probing and my lips inhaling you down deep. I moan and you feel the vibration. Like waves you ride with them down my throat gasping against the release. You fill me and I drink you. I shall never be thirsty again. I am not complete. Not yet. I find my way heading to your North. I straddle you and lay on you to taste us blended together. Sweetest taste in the world.

I touch every inch of you. We will be one as I rise up over you. You watch me slide you home. You grasp my hips to set the movement. I bring your hands to my breasts to do as you will. I move faster grinding into your body. You guide my hips where you need me to be. I cry out and call your name. I beg you to take me and claim me now. You tell me not just yet. You ease me onto my back and tell me to ask for it again. I ask you once more to open me and release me above all else. I shudder as you enter me looking into my eyes. The sweet satisfaction of your penetration. You travel deeper. With your eyes you break through the barriers never broken before. As you do I call your name and ask for to join me there but you go further still never leaving my eyes. You refuse to turn back. You want nothing less than all I have to give and demand for me to give it to you....to let it go. I arch my back and squirm but you drive yourself into me anchoring me still. You ask who I belong to and I moan. You demand to know who...pulling me deep into you with your eyes.

You. I belong to you. I look into your eyes and the fire calls me in. I answer the sacrifice for this moment. I no longer belong anywhere else. I look within you and I find my home. I vow I belong to you. You whisper that you shall never have to ask again and release yourself deep within me. My legs wrap around you to hold you prisoner. You touch every last place inside of me and claim all or it as your own. We dissolve into each other becoming one. Deep in this night there is nothing left to long for.

# The Switch

Phillip hung up his phone in disgust and stood up from his desk in the small insurance office. He looked to make sure there were no clients there before he spoke.

"The nerve of some people!" He said, shaking his head. "They should be a little more discreet if they are going to try to defraud an insurance company."

"What happened?" Lucy asked. Lucy had been working in his office for nearly a year, and was fast becoming one of his top agents. Philip smiled.

"Nothing to worry about. I handled it. It just irritates me to no end how some people think they can get away with anything."

Lucy smiled. She admired how firm he was, and knew it was the reason his agency was so successful. She didn't have to try hard to get clients because he had such a good reputation. She often wondered if this was part of the reason he was still single. He was a driven man that was full of strength and passion, but whenever a female came into the office, he always withdrew. It had taken a couple months for him to even get comfortable talking with Lucy casually. Philip walked towards her desk.

"Big plans for the weekend?" he asked.

"No, we are just going to stay home." Lucy replied. "It's nice to just do nothing sometimes. How about you?"

"I don't know where to start. I will be here tomorrow getting some things ready for the convention, then on Sunday I have to go take some pictures of the Franklin property for the file."

"Don't you ever take a day off?" Lucy asked, knowing

the answer.

"Someday I might, if I find a good reason to." Philip said, heading back towards his office.

Lucy and her husband had invited Philip over to their place a couple times, but he never seemed to have any free time. Lucy looked at the clock and saw that it was after 5:30 already. She finished up her work and got ready to leave. She stuck her head into Philips office to say goodbye as she left, but he didn't even notice.

It was about an hour later that Philip realized that he was alone at the agency and decided to go get some dinner. He looked around his office to make sure he wasn't forgetting anything. He picked up his keys and his cell phone and started to leave. He walked towards the front door of his small insurance office when he notices a purse lying on the floor near the door. He had seen it before and realized it belonged to Lucy, his top agent. It was lying on its side and looked as if it had been dropped. He grabbed the phone on the desk by the front door and punched the button next to her name. A man's voice answered that he recognized as her husband.

"Hello?"

"Yes, this is Philip from Blacks Insurance. Lucy seems to have left her purse here."

"Yes, she mentioned that she had forgotten it."

"I am leaving now and can drop it off it you want." Philip said.

"That would be great. She was worried about it."

Philip hung up the phone and left the office. He started driving towards Lucy's house. It was down a long drive and hidden from the road. He had never been there, but knew it was quite nice. Modest, but very well kept he thought as he pulled up and admired the well groomed lawn. He got out of his car and went towards the door. He rang the doorbell and looked around the small but well landscaped lawn. He was admiring an old willow tree when he heard the door open.

"Oh no…" he heard a voice say as he turned. "Sorry sir. Welcome to my home."

He looked down and saw Lucy there; wearing nothing more than what appeared to be a tight black corset and panties, as well as a leather collar around her neck. She was kneeling and had her head down. Philip didn't know quite what to think.

"Invite your guest in." He heard her husband, Frank say. She stood and with her head still bowed, motioned for him to enter.

"Tell him what you have done." Frank said.

"I was careless and lost my purse. Thank you sir for finding it and bringing it to me. I am in your debt."

Philip was a bit in shock. He knew that Lucy was a very diligent agent, and was frequently tops in sales in the district. He slowly started to take it all in.

"Tell him why you invited him in." Frank said.

"Yes Master," she said in barely a whisper. "I was careless and for my punishment you are to watch me get whipped. Is this acceptable to you sir?"

Philip stammered, "Uh, I… well…"

Something stirred in him that gave him a shiver. "Yes, "he heard himself saying. "That would be good." Frank laughed.

"Come on in, Phil. Relax. Lucy, get him a beer." Frank said walking back into the room.

Lucy ran off towards the kitchen. Philip walked into the large living room, not really knowing what was going on. Lucy returned with the drinks and kneeled in front of them, head down. Frank got up and put a leash on Lucy's collar. He took her to the middle of the room and Phil watched as her wrists were pulled up over her head and chained to a metal ring in the ceiling. Frank then chained her ankles to a long rod that kept her legs spread wide. Finally he put a large ball gag in her mouth and pulled it tight.

Lucy was facing Phil and had a look of fear on her face. Frank stood behind her and smiled. He reached over to the table and picked up a leather flogger. Phil was squirming uncomfortably as the bulge in his pants got bigger. He hoped Lucy wouldn't notice, and then thought she probably had other things to think about at the moment.

Frank suddenly swung the flogger and it hit her ass hard. A muffled sound came from Lucy. He continued and she seemed to push into each stroke.       After a minute Frank stopped. Lucy tried to catch her breath. He walked around in front of her and her eyes got wide when she saw the riding crop in his hand. Her eyes darted to Phil and back to the crop. Frank stood behind her and she closed her eyes tight, waiting. The crop hit her hard and she screamed a muffled scream. She kept her eyes closed and this time tried futilely to avoid the crop. Frank lectured her while using the crop, but the words went unheard to Phil, who was engrossed in the scene unfolding before him.

"Phil…Phil…"Philip looked to Frank and realized he had asked him something.

"Sorry, what?" Philip said, still in a daze.

"Go out to the big willow tree out front and get and nice green switch." Frank said.

Lucy tried to look at Frank and was shaking her head frantically. Philip stood, and felt his cock pushing against his pants. He ran outside and quickly broke off a long thin branch hanging from the willow. He pulled the few leaves off and ran inside, not quite knowing what to expect yet, but knowing that this was the most exciting thing he had ever witnessed.

Inside he started to hand the willow switch to Frank, but Frank shook his head and said, "Your turn."

Lucy suddenly started struggling against the chains and tried to say something in protest. She knew how badly the switch hurt in Franks hands, but she had no idea what to expect from Phil. Her body tensed as Phil, still in a daze, stepped behind her.

"Slave, this is what happens when you are careless. Understand now?" Frank barked at her, now standing in front of her and moving in towards her face as he reprimanded her. He nodded at Philip and stepped back.

There were tears in Lucy's eyes and she knew now was not the time for any more protests. She had been here many times before, but never at the hands of another. The thought of what would be happening to her tender ass scared her. She wrapped her hands around the chains that were attached to her wrists, and at the same time felt her pussy becoming very wet.

Philip felt his hand going back. It came forward and hit her ass hard. He heard her scream into the gag louder than she had with the riding crop and her whole body jumped. Philip saw the large red welt start to appear on her little ass. It was much larger and brighter than anything Frank had done with the crop or flogger. Frank walked around behind Lucy. He smiled when he saw the large welt. He ran his fingers over it lightly and Lucy jumped. The pain shot through her body again and she started shaking from the anticipation of more.

"Nine more please Phil." Frank said stepping back.

Philip continued and felt a smile creep across his face. He heard a harsh voice counting in his head, almost yelling, as he struck her ass again and again. About half way through he realized the voice wasn't in his head, but coming from his mouth.

"You little bitch, making me come over here to bring you your purse! Don't you think I had anything better to do?"

Lucy was sobbing around the gag now. Frank had a huge smile on his face as he watched Phil beat his wife's ass. Phil reached ten and stopped. He stepped back and took a deep breath. Lucy was limp and quiet now, her ass marked with red stripes. Philip set the switch down on the table, his hand trembling. Frank walked over to him and put his hand on his shoulder.

"Thanks for coming over. I think it did you some good."

"Yeah," Philip said, "I…it…yeah"

Frank walked him to the door and shook his hand. Philip looked over at Lucy, who was hanging limp in the chains and he could hear an occasional moan coming from her. He smiled and walked out to his car. He realized that his cock must have been nearly bursting through his pants the whole time. He thought about why this made him so excited. He didn't quite understand why, but he knows he wanted more.

The next day he showed up to work early. He waited and wondered what Lucy would say when she got there. He wondered what he would say. He didn't have to wait long. She came in the door carrying a pillow and a willow switch. She smiled at him as she went to her desk.

"Good morning Phil!" She said cheerfully, as if nothing had happened the night before.

She positioned the pillow in her chair then walked over to his desk. She placed the switch on his desk and smiled. She walked over to her chair and carefully sat on the pillow. Philip looked at the switch. He took it in his hand and decided he didn't ever want to let go.

# Jennifer

We have a silent code at work and that is to never answer the phone during report. That is the time when staffing is most likely to call with the "I know you think you are going home but you can't speech" when no one else is available. The phone rings and my lapse in judgment are due to an expected Dr.'s call back on a patient.

"Fourth floor R.N." I answer.

"Good, Jen, it's you." I hear Mitzi's chirpy little voice on the other end. She runs our staffing office for the hospital. Her specialty is dealing with us nurses who feel 8 hours is enough time served.

"No, Mitzi, I will let you talk to someone else." I try to say quickly but fail. Mitzi is faster than any telemarketer around.

"Honey, you know who's up to bat for 5th floor?" She giggles into the phone. Of course she can taunt us because she knows there is a security door on the staffing office. I think I know why.

"Do you know it takes a really sick person to do your job?" I say sarcastically. Mitzi knows I am kidding...partly anyways.

"Actually, Jen, that is your job...taking care of sick people and there are two for you all night on 5th floor. I have to go the phones are ringing. Goodnight" she says as the phone is clicked over. Bitch!

The thought of paging security and suckering them into letting me into the staffing office to retrieve an invisible purse comes to mind but not for long. The girls come in to relieve me for report.

I head up the stairs to 5th floor with the idea that this could be worse. Much worse. The whole floor could be full and I would be alone. I get report and settle into the desk. I get some charting out of the way and by then it is time for rounds. I get the vitals on the guy in 4A and note he is due for discharge to the nursing home for comfort measures only.

I continue on down the hall to the lady, Anne, in 2B. She is sleeping with Valium on board and will leave tomorrow via family who has a guest house ready to take care of her in. I check her vitals adjust her sheets and clip the call light to her side rail. I get ready to leave when a framed photo catches my eye.

I pick up the photo and see the family smiling after a long day of fun in the sun. There are uncles, aunts, grandmas, grandpas, cousins scattered and grandchildren sitting on the grass in front. I study each face left to right and it is then that I see him.

He is ruggedly beautiful. His smile could light up at least half of L.A. His dark hair and his dark eyes almost distract you from the fact his arm is around an equally amazing creature. She is exotic in her features. Great! Ken met Barbie. I know there must be some law against two beautiful people being together. Talk about cheating the less fortunate gene pools.

Their skin glows and must have just been kissed by Fiji or Bermuda before the photo was taken. Irregardless, I feel my mouth go dry. He must be a treat to look at everyday. I put the photo down and close her curtains. I turn off the television and think about him as I fill her water pitcher.

He is the guy in my fantasy opening the door to the cabin. I have just hiked three miles into the deep woods after splitting my canoe during a portage. I can't believe my eyes thinking he must be a mirage to my dehydrated soul. He takes the lead and gives me a smile that has me drying off in a towel absent of clothing by the fire in no time. My mountain man replenishes me with a warm drink from the antique wood stove.

He is quiet because everything about him talks to me in the silence. His accent soothes me, his eyes warm me and the touch of his hand seduces me into complete submission. He has asked for nothing and I will give him everything for that moment, his presence within me to never end.

The water splashes over the water pitcher and sprays out at my uniform. Great! Now that I am cooled off with reality I grab a towel and curse the faucet. My shirt is soaked and the fact is white isn't going to help matters any. Thank goodness it is 12 midnight and has 7 hours to dry.

I return the pitcher to the bedside and get ready to leave the room when I walk into a human wall. I would guess 6'2"-6'4". Incredible smell... a cross between Armani and roses. Roses? I look up and see a huge bouquet of multi-colored roses. Above them I see my mountain man. What? I must need my contacts rinsed. I blink and find a hand extending towards mine. I wrap mine as much as possible around the large fingers. The warmth spreads through my arm and up into my cheeks.

"Hi, I am Elijah, Anne's nephew. I just got back from London on business. How is she?" He says in a rugged voice that cuts the silence in the room like a jagged knife.

"No problem. She is doing great. Anne will be ready to be discharged tomorrow. Are going to be the one taking her home?" I ask letting go of his hand. I am still only able to see his eyes because there is a bouquet of roses in between us. I quickly count and there has to be at least 20 in there.

"Oh, sorry" He says as he backs into the hall bringing down the bouquet at the same time.

In the light I now see him. He is breathtaking. It is him. The man in her photo. First thought is naturally that Barbie must be parking her pink corvette. Or did they bring his beachcomber jeep? I smile lightly at the idea of a pink corvette in underground parking. Now that you don't see everyday.

"Can I set these in her room if I am quiet?" He asks holding the bouquet out from him to get my attention.

"I am in your way. Go ahead. I will be out at the desk if you need something." I say attempting to pass around him.

"Actually, I do need your help if you don't mind." He steps back into the room blocking me.

"Do you have a phone I can use with a calling card? I read the signs about using the cell phone in the hospital." He in informs me.

"Sure, put the roses down and I will show you to our visitor's room. I bet you are tired after your flight. Your family is probably just waking up in London." I comment figuring that is who he is calling since I haven't seen Barbie claiming Ken by now.

"My family is probably still sleeping actually...at least Anne is." He says with a laugh.

"Oh, I am sorry. I saw the reunion photo on Anne's table and figured you and your wife was responsible for those adorable kids in the front." I reply.

"My wife? Oh, you mean the lady next to me? That is my twin sister, Elise." He says. "Beautiful isn't she?" He laughs and then clears his throat.

"Well, that reminds me not assume anything doesn't it?" I laugh.

We reach the room and I turn on the table lamp. There is a couch and a small table to the side. I hand him the phone book. Making eye contact with him gives me goose bumps.

"Just in case." I say as he grabs it.

"Do you mind staying a minute? I really would like to talk with you." He asks putting his hand out and touching my shoulder.

106

"Sure." I answer and sit on the couch while he picks up the phone and dials. After a few seconds he realizes there will be no answer.

"So, what can I help you with?" I ask looking at him out of the corner of my eye.

"Will my Aunt need anything to be more comfortable when she leaves the hospital?" He asks settling into the couch.

"Everything is taken care of and hospice will be there every step of the way with you after discharge." I inform him and pat his knee as I slide up to the edge of the couch to stand.

"Another thing I would like to know is since you were so polite to ask about my family ...how about yours?" He smiles and puts his left hand over my right on his knee.

"Uh..."I stumble with my words looking at my hand covered by his.

He notices what I am looking at and pulls his hand back and apologizes blaming it on the European influences he has been accustomed to over the years doing business in other countries. I assure him no harm was done and I watch him start to wiggle out of his jacket.

His dress shirt glows against his face. Then it happens. Our eyes lock completely on one another's. Why did he have to look into my eyes? My ears are turning red I know it. I can feel my face blushing. The energy his eyes project is intense. My chest feels cool drafts of air from the fan that blows back and forth in the corner. Just then I remember my wet shirt! I look down and my skin is dark and the outline of my bra is completely obvious along with my nipples that are standing straight out. I look up in panic and he is looking at my chest then darts his eyes back to mine.

I realize this one of those defining moments. I can use my creativity and slide out to check an invisible call light or I can bet on never seeing him again and make light of it. Which do I pick?

"This is the new look for night nursing uniforms. The wet t-shirt look. Do you like it?" I finish and I can't believe I said it! His eyes blink and he starts laughing. Thankfully this gorgeous man has a sense of humor.

"As for family...I have a cat that waits for me at home and that is it." I answer his question. "I will let you rest...you have a long day ahead of you getting Anne back home." I say as I stand up and walk to the cabinet to get him a pillow and blanket. "It was nice to meet you, Elijah. Good luck tomorrow and tell London hello for me." I finish as I hand him the pillow and blanket.

I brush past his knee and think of the fantasy I am leaving behind in the room as I walk towards the door. I get ready to turn the knob when the door doesn't open. I look up and see his hand is about a foot above my head keeping it shut. He is quick and silent I think to myself. He also must have something on his mind that we haven't talked about.

"Don't turn around. I am going to ask you something only once. I feel you. I look into your eyes and see more than I do anywhere else. If you feel the same ways don't leave." I stand frozen at the door. I can't believe what I am hearing. Great! I meet the man of my dreams and I am in a hospital and I am working. Figures.

"Just my luck." I say and slide my hand slowly up the door and lean my head against it.

I stand there pondering what I am going to do when I feel the clip in my hair open and my curls spill out over my shoulders. I hear it tossed onto the table in a corner. Elijah slides his right hand up my back very slowly while leaning his right hand on the wall and door. His hand makes its way to the nape of my neck and his fingers tilt my face to the side to face him. He is so hot I close my eyes afraid I am going to melt right there.

He kisses my forehead softly then my cheek and neck. I

am feeling dizzy. The effect of his lips brushing against my neck is over whelming. He nibbles my earlobe then softly dances his tongue inside my ear. I am getting wet and it is almost too late to turn back now. Elijah whispers something in French with warm exhales and I softly moan.

"Elijah…" I say with a dry mouth.

"I want you more than I have wanted anyone in a very long time." he whispers in my ear.

"I am working. I can't. Really. I want to so bad." I say feebly.

With that his mouth is over mine as his hand holds my neck. He tastes just as I had imagined. Delicious. I can't refuse. My body won't let me. I feel weak standing there and that's when I feel him slip his hand from my neck and down my ass as he bends down. He picks me up and locks the door with his left hand. All I can smell is his cologne in his hair and I wrap my arms around him. He brings me to the counter of the kitchenette and sits me down on it. I am face to face with him and I am speechless.

"Please…"I stumble on the words as his mouth covers mine and invades its depths.

His hands move from my hips up the inside of my shirt and make their way to my breasts. I think of his lips and teeth around them as he pinches and squeezes them.

"Oh, God." I say softly.

With that he pulls my shirt over my head and tosses it to the floor. He wraps his hands around my back and puts his face between my tits sucking and nibbling as he unfastens the back of my bra. I run my fingers through his hair and pull his mouth to suck one then the other. He rolls my nipples between his teeth and tongue like little beads. His hands slide down my back into the elastic of my scrub pants. His left hand slides under my bare ass and he lifts me up while the right pulls off my panties and scrubs with no effort at all.

Again I am sitting on the counter looking at him as he slips off my shoes. Then my socks. My pants are then yanked from my legs with one quick sweep of his hand. He lifts my right leg and kisses the sole of my foot and trails his tongue up my shin and inside my knee. His shirt is unbuttoned with his left hand as he makes his way up to my thighs.

I move my hands through his hair, down his neck and pull the shirt down over his shoulders. That is tossed into the growing pile of clothing. He pulls my hips forward and cradles my neck back having me lay across the cold hard counter. He slides his shoulders under my knees and with one hand on my stomach and the other under my ass he pulls my cunt to his mouth quickly.

Wasting no time his tongue dives into my pussy sucking at me with his lips. The tip of his tongue is working my clit in deliberate strokes like my well used fingertips. I crunch forward trying to shove him away but he pulls me onto his face harder with each attempt I make. My hands and hips betray me and grind and squeeze him into me.

I can't hold out much more and begin moaning deep and soft. My hands reach out for something to hold onto for leverage and I grab the support beam for the cabinets above me. I feel the vibrating in his moaning massage my clit. His tongue dives deep into my soaked pussy and I imagine it is a small cock fucking me with perfection. His left hand pulls up at the hood over my clit and he starts sucking the little bud furiously.

With that I arch my back and his right hand plunges three fingers into my cunt fast and hard. In and out. I let go of the support beam and grab his head as my hips bang against his mouth and fingers.

"Ahhh, I am going to cum!  God, YES!" I cry out.

My body writhes and jerks while I shudder in defeat against his face. My thighs hold his face prisoner in my finish. I am completely defenseless as he sucks the extra juice that could possibly be left.

"Mmmm Baby, you are the sweetest thing these lips have ever tasted." He moans as he pulls me up to sit. Our mouths lock and the taste of my release mingle between us.

"You know what?" I say breaking the silence.

"What?" He returns the question in a verbal volley while kissing my neck and sliding his fingertips between my thighs.

"You may just be right but there would only be one thing sweeter yet..."I say with a playful smirk. Elijah looks up at me and smiles like a kid at Christmas looking under the tree.

I slide my hands down to his pants and take off his belt tossing it into the pile of our clothing. His cock pushes against the zipper as I free him. He slides his hands under my ass stepping out of his pants then slips off his shoes. This man is not only hot but he is coordinated. I wrap my legs around him and he carries me over to the couch.

I am in his lap and can feel the length of his hardness along my bottom pointing to the ceiling. I think to myself this is going to be one rough hard ride. I hold his face in my hands and search his eyes. So much energy...deep and dark. I want to harness it all. I kiss his cheek and chin. I suck my way playfully down his chest. Sliding off his lap and onto the floor I take him into my mouth. I stimulate his underside with sharp flicks of my tongue.

His hands find their way into my hair wrapping strands in between his fingers. He leans his head back, slides his hips forward and closes his eyes.

"Oh yes, baby, that's it!" He moans as I take him in deep. He looks down and he watches me work him and his breathing quickens. I make slow deliberate strokes.

"God, you look so good sucking my cock." he purrs.

I feel his hands pull my head down deeper on him. I suck hard and move faster. His legs are starting to tighten up. His cock starts to throb and his balls get hard and tight. I don't want him to cum yet so I slide my mouth off him and start to suck his balls. He holds my hair back wrapped in his left hand and his right brings my mouth back over him once again. This time I slide my middle finger down into my pussy for a little extra lubrication before bringing it up to his ass. I slide just the tip of my middle finger in slowly and he gasps.

"Oh, God, yes!" he cries out.

His hands work my mouth faster on him. Now it is time. I start moaning deep so the vibrations are strong and take him down to the back of my throat. I shove my middle finger all the way in his ass and wiggle it as he lets out another cry while his body jerks sending shots of cum down my throat.

"Ahhh, Yes!" He calls out and I slide off for a moment to swallow only to have his hands shove me back on him for more.

Holding him like a candy cane I lick him clean and dry. I slide back into his lap and kiss his lips individually with delicate sucking then both searching deep within him with my tongue. The taste of us combined is heaven.

"Now that is the sweetest thing I ever tasted." I say with a satisfied sigh.

"Yes, I agree...now how about after work you come home with me to give me a little more TLC?" He says with a grin.

# Forgiven

I call you to apologize again. No answer. I decide to take a long bath and drown my sorrows in a small chilled glass of wine. The room is lit with candles and the air has the scent of jasmine dancing.      I turn on the small radio to listen to something besides the sounds of my longing for you inside my head. I close my eyes and fall into a gentle sleep.

A noise wakes me. I grab my robe and put it on quickly. I feel beads of water skate down my back and between my legs. The cool air that kisses them on my skin sends chills up my spine. I take the candles into my room. I call you once more and you don't answer.

It's raining outside and I wonder where you are. We always made love when it rained. I feel my heart ache and I surrender to the punishment of a night without you. My words cut through my mind like a jagged knife. The searing burn of needing your touch only reminds me of what I have done. I blow out all but one candle and sit on the side of the bed. Something catches my eye in the corner of my room sitting in the chair beneath the window. You stand up and walk towards me. I am numb with shock. I stand up and start to step towards you. You stop me by bringing up your hand. Your eyes flash a glare.

"Take it off!" You say soft but directly.

"What?" I ask pondering if I have some jewelry on that you want back. I have nothing to offer you.

"Take off the robe now!" You say as your eyes shock me with their piercing stare.

I feel the energy surge within me. You have the right to be angry but I hate being told what to do. You know it. It makes me more than difficult. I start to give you a look of defiance but you will have none of it. You have your own idea of making yourself heard loud and clear.

"Do it now!" You raise your voice, "Or I will!" stepping closer to me.

My eyes glow green and I feel the heat rise and know something is going to explode. It is the energy we share that can freeze the sun or melt the North Pole. I can't accept less than all of what you have...I take it without asking. That is what started all of this and you know it. You also know that you have just started something that I will end up finishing.

"Dare you!" I say with a tone of sarcasm and smirk. You move forward and pinch out the candle's flame. I back up against the wall. Now there is darkness that is only interrupted by the flashes of light from the storm outside. You block me from moving by placing a hand on each side of me against the wall.

"I am not the one in trouble," you hiss at me. "Now am I?" You breathe deep through your clenched jaw.

I feed on your anger and only become more obstinate. I will make you pay for telling me to disrobe as if your wish is my command. I untie the belt to my robe slowly playing with the ends of the tie. I look at you and your face softens in satisfaction. I only want to make you suffer more. Your eyes drift down to my fingers.

With my right hand I slip in and caress my left breast under the robe and settle back against the wall. I squeeze and twist my nipple till it is stiff. I sigh softly as you watch me. With my left hand I slip into my robe and in between my legs sliding my fingers one by one inside. I rub my palm against my clit and moan out loud. You can't see my hands only the fabric moving in the areas beneath that they disappeared to. I am on fire and you know it. I see your cock is hard and pushing to get out of your pants. Your breathing grows heavy and you finally have had enough.

"Show is over you selfish little bitch!" You are looking me dead in the eye.

You pull my robe open and in turn my hands also come apart. My tits stand straight out at you round and firm. My hard nipples are taunting you. If your eyes were your hands my nipples would have been twisted right off for the way I have behaved. You see my left hand and it shines with my juices. Again, I smirk knowing that makes you very angry to be left out. I bring my fingers to my lips and suck each one clean like a candy cane.

"Yummmmm!" I say in gratification smacking my lips.

I slide off my robe and let it fall to the floor. I unbutton your shirt. Walking behind you, I wrap my arms around you and slide it off while kissing your shoulders. I undo your pants and let my hands dance across your chest and stomach. I move them delicately as the travel lower. You feel my tits pressed against your back and my skin is so hot it almost burns.

Finally I slide my hands in to grasp what no fingers can substitute. I don't even have to pull it out because it eagerly jumps into my hand. I pull your pants down kissing my way down your back and I playfully bite your ass. You whisper how good it feels even though I have been so bad. I run my hands sharply up the sides of your thighs. I push you towards the chair in front of the window. The lightning flashes and you see my face. I am determined and my mind is set. You can't stop me if I tried.

"Have a seat!" I say as standing and facing you.

I brush my hand up the side of your neck and pull your face into my tits with deliberate force almost suffocating you. You bite each nipple quickly and hard in defiance.

"Pay backs are a bitch!" You say when I yell in pain.

"And so am I!" I snap.

Without further warning I impale my pussy down your

cock stabbing my insides deep within when reaching the base of your lovely tool. You place your hands on my hips and I raise my hands into my hair pulling it up and then holding it to the back of my head. I can grind you into oblivion and you know it.

I have different movements when I am top. Sometimes in a hurry it's up and down like a jackhammer. When we are being gentle saying "I love you" while fucking I rock tenderly back and forth sucking on your neck moaning in soft, hot gasps in your ear. When I am angry or feel like revenge for being scolded, which can be often, I move my hips in perfect rhythm making an invisible 8 on the top of your thighs.

I watch your face wince and turn red from the stimulation. It will take a 10 good figure "8's" to make you explode. I have it down to a science. I always make you explode. Overconfident at 72 I expect to see your face show your finish and you calling out my name.

Instead your eyes flash open and are glaring into mine. Standing up with me still attached to your cock you leave me no choice but to wrap my legs around your waist. You push my thighs down as you stand at the edge of the bed. Without effort you flip me around onto all fours landing on the mattress.

"You are still in trouble you little bitch!" You confirm shoving your cock up into my pussy so hard that you knock the wind out of me.

You whack my ass with your hand and I scream in pain filled excitement.

"What do you say you nasty little cunt?" You demand an answer.

"Please..." I say in a whisper as tears run down my face. Another smack sounds before I can feel the burn of skin racing across my ass. "Please!" I gasp in alarm.

"What do you say when you want it?" You yell pulling my hair and head back.

"I am sorry. Please fuck me...hard!" I beg.

"That's a good girl." You say and pump into me with wild abandon.

I slam my ass against you and rise up to grab your ass from behind hoping to hold you in me. Your hands grab my tits and my mouth finds yours. I suck your tongue with force. You shove up into me two more times before I scream calling out your name. Squeezing my tits hard you explode cumming into me in complete exhaustion.

"God, I love it when you fuck me like that!" I say in between breaths.

"Yes, Baby, you are forgiven..."You respond pulling me down into the bed with you. "After you suck my cock clean." Then shoving my head in between your legs.

Little do you know that this part I see as a reward for being so difficult.

# The Pool Table

*Part One*

The two girls were having fun in Kate's big new house. Kate's husband was gone, so the girls were enjoying the big room downstairs with the fully stocked bar and new pool table. They giggled as they tried to shoot the balls, and after a few drinks, their already meager billiard skills were declining. Julia was winning this game, and was getting ready to shoot. Kate walked over and put her hand on the table, blocking Julia's shot. She smiled as she looked down at her friends open blouse, admiring her firm breasts.

"Let's say we make this interesting." Kate said.

"What did you have in mind?" Julia asked, grinning up at her cute friend.

"If I win, you can lick me." Kate said.

Julia had only a couple balls left on the table, while Kate had yet to make a shot. She winked at Kate and proceeded to shoot. She missed and Kate got ready. After making 5 balls in a row, Julia was wondering if she had been had. Julia got up to shoot, and nervously missed again. She sat on a stool and took a drink. Kate stepped up and shot two balls in. Only the 8 ball remained.

"I am going to enjoy this." She said, and then pocketed the winning ball.

Julia's eyes got wide. Kate walked over to her and took her hand. She led her to the table. Her hand was up under Julia's shirt, pinching her nipple as she laid her back on the large pool table. Before Julia could react, she was nearly undressed. Kate pushed her back against the end of the long pool table onto the green felt. Her firm little ass rested on the edge of the table.

Kate crawled up onto the table where Julia lay. She slipped off her tight jeans and revealed no underwear and a shaved pussy. She crawled over Julia's face and pushed her wet pussy onto her. Kate grabbed Julia's nipples and pinched and pulled as Julia licked and moaned. Julia's hand went down to her own wet pussy. She heard Kate talking softly as she moved around on her face.

"Ooh yesssssss....lick it. You are a good little pussy slut. Ohhh that's the spot.....lick me good." Kate purred.

Julia jumped when she felt hands on her legs. She tried to get up, but Kate held her down. Kate's husband had been there the whole time, waiting. Julia's legs where hanging over the edge of the table, leaving her pussy vulnerable.....

Kate took Julia's wrists and pinned them under her knees while she was grinding her pussy on Julia's soaked face. Julia felt a large cock pressing against her pussy. She moaned as it slid in. She hadn't felt a cock in such a long time and it hurt as it pushed into her. Kate was getting louder now.

"Roll her over now." Kate's husband barked. He pulled out long enough for the two of them to flip Julia onto her stomach, bent over the edge of the pool table. Julia felt Kate pull her face towards her outspread legs in front of her. She also felt her hands being pulled behind her back. Her head was spinning too much to object to anything. Leather cuffs were slipped onto her wrists. She continued to lick Kate, harder and faster. She felt his large cock rubbing on her pussy, in and out slowly. Suddenly she felt a finger slip into her ass. She jumped and tried to pull her outspread legs together, but realized they had been taken captive too, tied to the legs of the table. She felt his wet cock pushing against her tight virgin ass.

"Oh please, fuck that little ass" Kate screamed. He pushed in slowly into Julia's ass. Julia tried to get away, but he held her hips tightly as he pushed in. Julia screamed into Kate's pussy.

"Fuck her hard. Yessss....oh god......that looks so good. Fuck this little slut." Kate said in a moaning voice. "Lick harder! Oh you are such a good little pussy slut."

Kate started to jerk into her friends face as her husband pushed into Julia's ass. Julia could tell Kate was coming, and she wanted to come too.

"Noooo......don't make me come! Stop it....slow down." Kate screamed at Julia.

"Oh fuck....I'm coming." Kate was sobbing as she came hard on Julia's face.

Julia could feel her face getting soaked. His thrusts pushed her over the edge and she started to come too. Julia shook violently as she came. The cock in her ass kept pounding, and she thought he would never come. He slammed into her hard and stopped. She was screaming as she felt her ass fill up.

She opened her eyes to see Kate gone. She heard a voice.

"Kate, I did not give you permission to come, did I!" her husband barked.

"No Master. I am sorry." Kate said, her voice shaking.

Julia looked to her side and saw Kate kneeling on the floor, her head down.

"Get over here now" he ordered. Kate crawled over to him and went to work. He didn't have to tell her what to do. Julia felt her tongue on her ass, licking up the cum dripping from her. Julia moaned and tried to move. She had no idea what to expect next, but figured whatever it was, it would probably be even more mind blowing than what she had just experienced.

When Kate had finished, Julia could only hear what was happening.

"Please Master...." Kate said, her voice shaking.

Julia was dying to see what was going on. She thought she heard the rattle of small chains. She was straining to turn her head to where the sounds were coming from. Next thing she heard was muffled moans from Kate, who was obviously gagged now. Suddenly, she felt a hand in her hair, pulling her head up. Kate's husband whispered in her ear.

"This is what happens to a naughty slave who comes without permission. I believe you came too. Did you ask before you did?"

The next thing she heard was the sound of leather striking Kate's ass, and a loud moan. She jumped, wondering if she was next. The smell of Kate still on the soft green felt, and the sound of the whipping almost made Julia come again.

Julia thought back to the first time she met Kate. They worked together and were both getting into trouble with practical jokes all the time. They got along well and became friends quickly. Julia knew that Kate and her husband had a "special" relationship, but she never imagined this would happen." Kate had shown her welts on her ass before and although she didn't know why, it always made her wet.

It occurred to her that she didn't know her husbands name. She only knew him as "Master."

Julia was brought back to reality when she realized the whipping had stopped. She still heard Kate sobbing softly around the gag. She wondered what was next as she squirmed, still tied securely to the pool table with her legs spread apart. She listened as the chains rattled again. She saw Kate being led to the table, her hands secured behind her back.

Kate was pushed onto the table and her face was close to Julia's. Julia watched as the gag was removed from Kate's mouth. Julia understood why this man was called Master. She feared what was going to happen to her, and at the same time, her pussy was so wet it was dripping down her leg.

"No, I don't want to…." Julia started to say as the same ball gag that had silenced Kate was now being pulled tightly into her mouth. She tried to shake her head in a futile protest, but a strong hand held her head against the felt of the pool table.

"Since you were the reason Kate came, I thought I would let her take care of your punishment." He whispered into her ear.

Julia froze as she watched Kate pick up the same whip that had just made welts on her ass. She saw that same grin on her face that had appeared during the game and she realized just how set up she had been. Kate disappeared from her view and she felt her warm hands caressing her ass.

"You little pussy slut, you made me come and got me in big trouble." Kate said softly. "I won't be able to sit for a day now, and I think you should join me in my discomfort."

Julia jumped as Kate's hand came down on her ass. She moaned around her gag. As Kate continued her lecture, her voice grew louder.

"I will tell you when you can make me come. Do you understand?"

Julia lay there silent. She jumped when the whip hit her ass. She screamed into her gag.

"I said, do you understand?" Kate repeated. Julia was breathing hard and tried to moan acknowledgement so the whip would spare her. Her ass burned. She could not understand how Kate could possibly enjoy this. She was trying to beg to be let go. The whip came down on her ass again. She arched her back and bit into the ball in her mouth. She was breathing hard and drool was running down her chin. She felt totally helpless. There was nothing she could do to stop this. They owned her now and she was at their mercy. When this thought entered her mind she felt her pussy burn. Julia realized she was hotter than she had ever been in her life. Kate was relentless with the whip on her ass. Julia was worn out and her head was lying on the table. She was still breathing hard but was unable to fight anymore. She felt Kate's breath on her neck.

"You are my little slut now. Master said I could have a

toy, and now I have one." Kate said as she looked Julia squarely in the eye. "I think I want to fuck my slut now" She whispered.

Julia watched as Master helped Kate put a large strap on dildo around her little waist. Kate took some lube and stroked her rubber cock. Julia knew her pussy was dripping and the dildo would slide right in. Why would she need to lube it unless…..

Julia lifted her head and tried to say "No Please!" but it came out "NmPmmgh!"

Kate disappeared from her sight again. She felt her small hands again on her ass. Kate slowly rubbed the welts on Julia as she spread her ass checks apart. She rubbed her large rubber cock along the crack of Julia's ass and pushed against her tight hole that Master had taken for the first time earlier that evening. While she teased it Master had gotten on the table and was taking off Julia's gag. He replaced it with his large cock. As he slid it into her mouth Julia felt her ass being filled again. Kate started fucking hard as Julia sucked furiously. Kate was screaming at her, but she didn't hear. Her head was spinning again as she realized she was totally owned and used now. She was simply their toy, to use and fuck for their pleasure alone. She now put all her effort into pleasing this couple, and hoped that it would never end.

# The Pool Table

*Part Two*

Julia walked around the large pool table. She looked at her prizes. Kate was bound to one end of the table, legs spread and tied and her wrists behind her back. There was a ball gag secured in her mouth. Julia walked up behind her. She stood there and caressed Kate's ass. Julia was wearing a leather corset and stiletto heels. Kate had worn the same outfit many times while using Julia. Now the tables were turned. Across the table from Kate was Master. Not much of a master right now, Julia thought. He was in the same predicament. Legs spread, wrists tied and ball gag in his mouth. Julia walked around the table slowly. She picked up a vibrating dildo that was lying on the pool table. She lubed it up and stepped behind Master.

"This is to warm you up for later" she said as she rubbed the tip of it against his ass. He jumped as she slid it in. She turned it on and he started to moan. Julia slowly walked back to the middle of the table. She picked up a large strap on in a leather harness and put it on. She walked around behind Kate as she stroked her large rubber cock. Kate had been in this position behind Julia many times, and it was time for some payback. She slowly rubbed the big cock against Kate's pussy. Kate moaned around her gag as Julia slipped it into her.

"You like this?" Julia asked mischievously. "Oh yes, I can tell you do. You want to cum, don't you." Julia started fucking her faster. Kate always had to ask Master for permission to cum. Master was watching from the other end of the table now, helpless to what was happening.

"You had better not cum. Master will not like it." Julia said, laughing. "Not that he can do much about it though."

Julia fucked harder and Kate was screaming around her

gag. Julia slid a finger into Kate's ass. Kate started jerking on the table and Julia smiled wickedly, knowing she had just pushed her over the edge. Julia pulled out slowly and left Kate breathing heavy on the pool table. She walked around to the other end of the table where Master waited, tied and vulnerable.

"Your turn" Julia said, pulling the vibrator out of his ass. The large rubber cock strapped to her was wet with Kate's juices. She held his hips tightly and pushed her cock into him. He moaned in protest. She shoved it in fast and hard.

"Let's see how you like taking a big dick in the ass. See how it feels? Do you enjoy it?" Julia screamed. She kept slamming into him. She looked at Kate, who was lying exhausted on the table, drooling around that gag in her mouth. Julia smiled at her and continued her assault on her master. He was moaning loudly and pushing back into her. She reached down and grabbed his swollen cock.

"Oh look at this. I think you are enjoying this!" Julia said, stroking his cock as she fucked him. "Don't you dare cum. Same rules apply to you as they did to me. You get punished for cumming without permission." She said, taunting her now captive owner. She fucked him harder as she stroked his hard cock. He started cumming and groaned loudly. She pushed into him hard and felt his cock shooting on her hand and onto the floor.

"Uh oh," Julia said giggling. "You came without permission."

Julia undid the strap on cock and left it in his ass. She released his ankles from the legs of the table. She took hold of the collar he was wearing and pulled him to the carpet. "Look at the mess you made." She said, undoing the ball gag in his mouth. "Clean it up."

Julia kneeled down next to him and pushed his face into the cum. She pulled him up and licked it from his face. She stood up and put her stiletto on his head and pushed his face into the cum he had spilled there. She watched as he tried to lick it up. Julia was so hot at this point she needed to cum now. She wanted to reach down to her wet pussy and rub it. For some reason she could not move her hand. She closed her eyes and felt herself struggling .The bite of leather on her ass brought her back to reality.

"Ready for some more?" She heard Kate say as the whip struck her again. Julia left her fantasy behind and got ready for the next blow. Julia was bound to the table in just the way she had imagined Master and Kate.

"Yes please, Ma'am." She heard her self say. The whip came down hard on her ass and she jumped. Julia knew she was their property and her place was here, pleasing others.

# A Day of Indulgence

I am not answering my cell or the phone at home. I am taking the day to myself out of pure selfishness. You call several times and are getting very annoyed. Work is hectic for you and you think this is the biggest display of disrespect yet that I have shown. What a cunt I am for not picking up the phone. I knew better and you were getting increasingly angry. What a way to treat you.

It is getting close to your lunch hour and you happen to get a call from Jill asking where I am at. You tell her, *"In a hell of a lot of trouble for the way I was acting."* Jill acts surprised then said she remembers where I said I was going on one of my stops. Victoria's Secret. She said there was a guy there that hit on me the last time we went together and she was sure I was going back to pick up some more clothing with a hopeful discount.

This interests you. My defiance today and the stud at a lingerie shop hitting on me. Together these are the reasons that I will not answer the phone. I needed to learn my lesson and you decide to once again show me who is in charge. I was about to find out it was not me. You are so furious you can't think anymore. I never behaved this way before and you were not going to stand for it. I knew better and you taught me well.

Jill asks how much trouble I am going to be in and you inform her this was not going to be good. She steps in as a best friend and asks if she can make things a little better and get her fun too. You are game for anything but want to be able to watch when it happens. Jill tells you to take off from work and get over to the shop.

Soon Jill is on her way and will make arrangements with

the manager to let you two in the back entrance so you will not be seen as soon as you arrive at the mall. She calls up the guy from her cell and asks him if he would like $500 cash for an hour worth of time while he is working. He said he was ready for anything especially when he heard I was going to be the toy.

You meet Jill in the back of the store and she tells you to follow her lead. The idea is that you won't be seen by me and I am to be oblivious to you being there. That is until the last moments. You decide this is the best way to find out how loyal I am to my Master.

I am in the store and the only customer. Jill calls the guy to the back and you get introduced. You ask him if he knows me and he says unfortunately not but would like nothing more than a taste of me. You don't tell him that I belong to you. You tell him this is his chance to do whatever he can to fuck me right in the store. If he does fuck me he makes an extra $1,000. Jill shows the guy the cash in her hand that she was on the way to deposit into her account. He says it is a deal.

He is hot and his mind is spinning with the idea of fucking me on the counter in a corset he wants me to try on. You tell him you want the doors locked and for him to give me some believable excuse so that I trust his intentions and think nothing of it.

He walks away with confidence and approaches me. With a handsome smile that most hot and bothered young women would purr to see, he informs me that the security system wants the doors locked for an hour so that they can upgrade the systems.

At first I offer to leave but then see that he must be honest...sexy too. I didn't want to stop to come back later. I knew I was going to be in trouble anyways. If the scenery was going to be stimulating for the next hour why not stay put?

I start by putting on several different out fits having each making me wet. I think of all the ways you would enjoy my body covered in lace and silk.

The guy comes back to you and you tell him he is going to lose money if he doesn't start getting my attention. He is leery about you two watching and Jill offers another $500 but emphasizes he needs to get going now.

The guy walks up to me and says over the door...there is a teddy he thinks would look really hot on me. He says for me to try it on and tosses it over.

You and Jill can see everything on the monitors in the back. You can see me touching my body and every so often even my pussy. You want to slap me for not asking. I was already in trouble for that from before.

My defiance excites you even though you will never admit it. Jill watching and being a part of it added to it.

Jill reminds you that at this moment you are about to find out whether or not I am loyal to you. You ask what she is going to get out of it. She said to fuck the guy and have me and you watch. Jill had her own motives after all. He was not the bait...I was.

She asks for permission to touch me to make the temptation even harder on me. You agree. Jill tells you after this you will know if I truly am going to be worthy of you as my Master.

The guy tells me the ties in the back of the corset can be hard so maybe he can help me out. I am fumbling the ties and almost give up and then decide that since no one is around I might as well try it on right.

I walk out and the guy is standing with his mouth open. His mouth is amazing, full and sensual. You can see me staring at his lips...you know how I love to bite at yours. You see the expression on my face. It is not as if you have not seen me with others before at your wishes. Certainly not without your permission.

You wonder if this was a bad idea as I turn around, his

hands slide down my back, and he begins to knot up the strings to the corset on purpose. He is setting me up to be stuck in the garment! What a devious little bastard the young stud is.

I ask what the problem is that is taking him so long to tie the strings up. He mumbles and then slides his easily at the back of the corset that just rests at the top of my ass. I take in a breath and am paralyzed.

I feel his hands slide over my ass. He presses into me causing me to brace my hands against the mirror. You watch his mouth come against my shoulder and you see my eyes close.

Your heart races...I am going to let him fuck me you think to yourself. You want to walk out and slap me for such humiliation.

Jill puts her hand on your arm and stops you from walking out. She tells you to watch because her money is on me.

He slides his hands up my waist to my tits. Your pulse is flying. What a nasty little cunt I am. My eyes open in a flash and I spin around. I tell him I can't and grab his wrists. I need to go. He tells me that I can't and just to relax.

It is at that point that Jill starts peeling off her clothes in front of you. Her lack of inhibition turns you on. Soon she is naked and nipples sticking straight out. She hands you the money and says to enjoy the show.

Jill comes out to the dressing room and I am shocked. I ask her what the hell she is doing there and ask where her clothes are. She winks and tells me that the salesman has a wicked way of helping out the customers. He tells Jill that I am being a little difficult about having some fun. I look at them and the shock on my face leaves you smirking. Maybe I am not such a slut after all.

Jill walks up and tells the guy that he is going about it all wrong. I blink my eyes in surprise and Jill backs me up against the wall. She tells me to put my hands up over my head and he needs to hold them there and stare in my eyes.

I back up thinking it is a joke but she tells me she will make one phone call and I know who it will be to if I don't do as I am told. I swallow nervously while my heart races in anticipation. Whenever Jill rats me out to you I get it all night long.

Jill slides her fingers down between my legs and then comments on how my pussy doesn't lie. I try to speak but she takes her hand without my juices and covers my mouth while the wet fingers she gingerly inserts into his mouth then pulls them out and kisses him deep as his eyes stay locked on mine. She asks how sweet I am and he confirms my mind blowing sweetness.

Wasting no time, Jill starts rubbing my tits and asks if he likes them. He says he has since he watched me changing on the monitor in the back several weeks ago. She asked him if he was hard when he watched. He said he was. She asked if he pumped himself off with his hand while he watched me and he said he did that too. Jill asked what he enjoyed most of all. *"Hmmm…"* He thought out loud for a moment then said it was when I touched my pussy then licked my own fingers. He said he exploded right there in the back room against the wall. I am getting hot thinking about his hand over his cock and getting off watching me.

You start thinking about how I love to watch you stroke your cock. You know between that and Jill's hands rubbing my tits and them sharing my taste that I have to be really wanting it now.

Despite you and Jill and your devious plans for me, you still have yet to hear of me doing anything wrong. Except, of course, for touching my pussy without asking. You already know how to discipline me for that. That was simple.

Jill slips her fingers back into my pussy and starts to wiggle them. She tells him to keep watching me and tell her when he thinks I am really hot. At the same time she starts working his cock. I love the feel of Jill's fingers in my pussy and watching her stroke his hard cock is really starting to get me going.

The guy tries to kiss me. I turn my face to the side and his mouth lands on my neck. He tells me to kiss him and Jill's fingers stop abruptly inside me.

I tell him, "Not without permission."

The guy asks, "Permission from whom?" Jill's fingers restart and then she gets down on her knees and starts to suck his cock.

I tell him, "My Master."

He lets go of my hands and gets ready to put his fingers near my pussy and Jill stops him and says it is off limits. He again is confused. He says he wants to fuck me hard. Jill tells him he needs permission. He says forget the Master and the money and let's start to really fuck. Jill says he needs to have permission to touch me.

At this point I am dripping wet and want to get off so bad...Jill's fingers or the guys cock or my own hand. Who cares...I need to cum.

Jill works her magic with her mouth. The guy starts moaning as he glides in and out of her lips. He keeps looking at me and then tells me how he really wants to fuck my pussy. He describes what a sweet tasting piece of ass I would be to ride.

I am missing out on everything. I am wet and insane as he pulls Jill back up and pushes her down on the display counter. He keeps his eyes locked on mine as he begins to lick the outside of her pussy like a cat working on a small dish of sweet cream. Jill squirms back and forth and starts fucking his face pulling his hair with her hands.

His hand is still pumping his cock and it takes all that I have not to get down on my knees and suck him hard. I think of you and remember who I belong to. I wish you were here.

You watch Jill screaming as the guy eats her alive. I stand there pouting like a child in a nasty little corset. You decide I have proved my loyalty by denying myself any pleasure with out your permission.

You walk out of the back room and Jill gets wild. She tells the guy to fuck her and he bends her over the table and starts sliding into her ass.

The guy watches as you enter the room and I drop right to my knees on the ground. I apologize for being disobedient and you tell me to shut my selfish little mouth. You yell at me and tell me how bad I was and needed punishment. I agree, "Yes Master."

You instruct me to lie back on the counter as well and watch the guy fuck Jill. The guy watches me lay back on the table and spread my legs. My pink shaved pussy ripe for eating.

You tell me I won't get any cock but I can use Jill's tongue if she wants to eat me. First I have to beg her to eat me.

Insulted and feeling left out I start to feebly beg and you tell me what a whiny little bitch I am.

"Yes, Master," I agree.

I plead with Jill to eat my swollen pussy and she finally brings her mouth over the top of it. I grab her hair and her mouth devours my cunt as her teeth bang against my clit as the guy fucks her harder.

He starts telling you what a hot little pussy I have. You tell him it is *owned* by you.

I love the way Jill's tongue massages the inside of my pussy and start to feel myself cum. You twist my right nipple ring hard and I am gasping.

The guy says he is going to explode and you tell him to pull out and spray my face...but don't let my tongue touch his cock. I am being punished.

With two tight strokes of his hand he sprays his load all over my face and hair. You spank Jill's ass really hard in one swat then shove your fingers in her pussy grinding her to cum. Jill screams into my pussy and I explode all over her face.

The guy dresses and goes to clean up. I ask for permission to get up and you grant it. You tell me to get my things and you were going to take me home and let me suck your cock after I give you a bath. Naturally, I thank you.

Jill dresses and tells you she knew I would never disappoint you. You tell Jill that you taught me well.

The guy wants to know if he gets the money and you two remind him of the deal...he never fucked me.

He asks you what my problem is with the Master thing. Jill says that I am your pussy, your bitch and I can't even pee without your permission which is why my not answering your call got me into trouble to begin with.

He is surprised and says he can't believe the control you have...I won't even fuck unless you say so. You tell him that is because I am a good little cunt. I smile next to you in pride. My reward, after all, is having just earned the privilege of sucking your cock when we get home.

# The Wedding Party

We learned of each other through friends. You and I had to be the wildest people they ever knew. We often socialized with the same groups of friends, yet we never ended up meeting face to face. Either you were away on business or I was tied up with other interests.

We had something in common. My best friend from college was engaged to marry your best friend and partner from you advertising agency. I have heard of your antics for the past two years from Janet on lunch breaks and various girls' night parties.

My favorite and eventually yours was the nasty little bachelorette party you whipped up with Jack for Janet. We were told it was going to be all her fantasies come true including a private male strip troupe that would entertain us. Thinking this was the most romantic gesture a woman has ever known we cheered Janet into accepting it. Janet and the rest of us took it hook, line and sinker.

We arrived at a studio in the warehouse district. The main door was blocked by a twenty something buff blonde beauty in a bow tie and nothing else. As his wide uncut cock swept back and for the table top with his movements while he welcomed us to the wildest event of the year. For an extra tease he assured us that noble Jack and his groomsmen went to great lengths to ensure that whatever goes on will not make it to any of the society pages of Vanity Fair. The sun bronzed god announced the paperwork that sat on the table had to be signed by each and every person invited and entering the door.

We all stood there baffled as he passed around a copy to each of us giving each partygoer a kiss on the cheek and a quick tap on the ass. After whispering and the giggling stopped he explained the documents were in fact legal and binding. We were informed that by signing the agreement we are aware the participants would get a copy of the tape to enjoy for later viewing pleasure. However, none of the tapes would be allowed to be distributed or reproduced outside the ones that were given out at the end of the night.

Rebecca, one of the two lawyers present was satisfied with the wording and assured I had no reason to question the contract because it was explicit in detail that copying or distributing for profit or personal agenda of the participants was a violation and would be prosecuted. All of the invitees were close friends that were either carrying medical licenses or had large enough companies that the repercussions were heavy shall that happen.

I was famous for trying anything twice. Not a surprise that I am the first seen on the video signing. I even slipped the tasty blonde one of my business cards and winked to the camera. The rest followed my lead and kissed the naked host leaving him covered with lipstick. When the video camera panned in for a close up of him waving the signed and notarized documents for proof he was proudly covered in lips.

When we entered the room we all gasped collectively. There were cameras everywhere with men and women dressed up in corsets, chaps and collars. If it was leather and kinky it was there. I felt a rush of fear and anticipation goes up my spine.

While the others started to huddle closer together for comfort. I knew that the happy hour we invaded earlier would kick in so I decided it was time to get the party started. I didn't do this every night and I knew the rest had chaotic schedules too. This was our chance to celebrate Janet's upcoming marriage and a chance to show Jack what he will have to deal with should he fuck up with Janet. The night would prove to defy the expectations of Jack of any of his groomsmen. The tape was proof.

Jack gets the tape and calls you to come over with the rest of the guys in the wedding party. After beers and pizza he pops it in the player. It is priceless. You see me signing the document and smirk. The lens pans in for a close up when I am asked if I am ready to play. I answer in a voice you expect out of a high priced phone sex operator. While Jack chokes on his beer I purr for him to give me whatever he has got. You comment under your breath that you are watching the woman of your dreams.

The party went on for hours. You watched me be a whipping post and beg for more. I turned the tables and flogged a corseted red head girl who whimpered to taste me. There was nothing that I wouldn't do you thought to yourself. I liked the idea of being watched. I let a large heavy set man cover my shoulders and stomach with hot wax and I took a spanking over a desk from another man. Other women were entertaining to watch as well, but you could see this was exciting me. It wasn't a joke. That was what you had been looking for. The uninhibited woman of your dreams was before your eyes telling a submissive she was very bad and to kiss her feet.

When the tape ends you ask Jack to work some more of his magic. I was just what you wanted and Jack was going to make it happen. He comes up with the idea of arranging a pre-wedding weekend trip to Miami to have the wedding party make sure all is going as planned for the big day. It was a wedding that would be catered by the finest chef and entertaining guests with everything to live swans floating in a pond to champagne falling from ice sculptures at each table. With all the money going into the details it surely would make sense that we all go down and make sure that everything was going as planned. Besides the girls all needed to get fitted for their dresses at the boutiques Janet's mom hired to make them.

Jack calls Janet's mom and makes the plans. Janet's mom will simply call her and summon the whole wedding party down there for a long weekend of fun in the sun and getting the last fitting on the tuxedos and dresses. Jack tells you the rest is up to you. He can't wait to tell Janet that her wild girlfriend is about to finally meet her match. You make him promise that I will not know of your intentions other than meeting the maid of honor.

Taking Jacks' advice you call all the wedding party to inform them of the weekend and that their tickets will be sent by courier for the flight. You save my number for the last call. I answer in a breathless voice on the fourth ring. I sound so hot even in a rush. You give me the details and ask me to dinner the night we arrive to discuss the details of our job as best man and maid of honor. You have me write down you cell number and tell me to call you when I get to the hotel and settled in. I tell you I look forward to seeing what makes you such a big deal. You laugh and wish me a good trip.

The week passes fast and soon I am standing at the front desk of the hotel checking in. I get to the room and decide it is a good a time as any to call you. I leave you a voice mail to tell you I have just arrived. We meet that evening for dinner.

A trail of my clothes leads to the shower. It's clear and surrounded in glass. I stand under the hot water letting it massage my back. I wash my hair and let the lather cling to my breasts. I begin thinking of you and massage my arms with the sponge. I wonder what you cologne smells like, and the size of your hands. Did you really like the video as much as Janet said you did? You had seen me.

Now I wonder about what you look like. I start the scenario in my nasty little mind. Your hands are rough and strong as they squeeze my ass. I imagine the length of your fingers as they enter me and the taste of your mouth as it hungrily invades mine.

My heart beats faster at the thought of you. My mouth turns dry and I open my lips to the hundreds of drops of arm water falling down upon me like a child in a summer rain. I put the condition on my hair. Standing with my eyes closed I pinch my nipples and then stare down at them in pride. Will you bite them? Will you suck them hard asking for more? I imagine the sensation of your lips on them, surrounding them and biting them.

I dream of your oral talents and where I want your tongue first. I slide my hand down over my pussy and find my clit rock hard and begging for attention. I close my eyes to think of you and slide three fingers into my cunt. I pull out the middle one to rub the one thing that is always sure to get me off.

My left hand finds my mouth. I take each finger one by one slowly and slide them in and out with the rhythm of my fingers below. With a spare finger I tease the other hole that I fear to enter. The burn of virgin flesh stretching causes me to gasp. Soon my ass is gobbling its way to my palm. It feels so good. Inside I wiggle a finger and waves of pleasure vibrate within. Slowly they build and I begin to lose strength standing. I let my knees weaken and slide down the shower wall and coming to lie on the shower floor. I am moaning out loud and out of control. My fingers ramming into both voids that need to be filled by you. I cry out for mercy.

Suddenly, I feel I am not alone. I open my eyes and am so startled I can't scream. I see a large built man about six feet tall standing just outside the shower. He has nothing on and the only thing besides his huge thick cock that catches my attention is the tattoo on his left pectoral of a panther and the word "Challenge" above it.

Holy shit! It is you. Janet told me about how the sight of you at the marina in swim trunks showing off your new tattoo got her begging Jack to get one. I swallow hard as the water sprays my eyes and reminds me of the position I am in and you are obviously intending on more than shaking my hand. You are more handsome than I had imagined.

"Faster...finger yourself!" You scream at me. I blink stunned that you are actually there naked and stroking your cock in front of me. Damn! You are watching me fingering myself on the shower floor!

"I said to finger yourself! What are you waiting for? Show me how you get off." You demand, pumping your hand roughly up and down your cock to show me you are serious.

I spread my legs wide, arch my back and close my eyes shoving my fingers as deep as they will go sending mind blowing pleasurable pain into my cunt and asshole. I look at you and see the intensity of your face. My pussy is packed with my fingers and I am squirming around leaving you to want nothing more than to pin me down and nail me into the floor.

"I am going to cum!" I wail in a shattered scream.

"Do it! Fuck yourself" You yell. I moan and shake in waves of surrender at your feet. You open the shower door and pull me out onto the bathroom floor and position yourself between my legs. You support yourself above me with your left hand while using the right to rub the tip of you cock against the opening of my slippery cunt.

"Is this what you need? Look at me!" You say in a deep demanding voice.

I am ready to move to put space between us and you counter my move with putting both my wrists into your left hand, pinning my legs open with the weight of you between them.

"Please..." I say unconvincingly.

"Now that is more like it!" You interrupt and slowly bring your face closer to mine. I look into your eyes and the reality of what is taking place sends messages of panic through me.

"I will scream." I whisper shaking at the thought that

anything could happen.

Your face lowers so close we share the same breath, eyes locked on one another. I feel the tip of your throbbing cock against my cunt. My juices are running down my ass sending cold chills below.

"Yes, you certainly will." You confirm as you slowly slide your cock into my tight pussy.

I never thought size could be an issue. Never had a problem accommodating any lover before. Not too tight and definitely never loose. Those legal exercises not only benefited my lower abdomen but they gave the sweetest cunt you would ever know a great workout.

As you shove yourself as deep as you can go I lose my breath. I close my eyes and arch my back. You slide back out almost to the tip of your cock and then back down in again. You put your mouth on my chin and bite softly then down to my throat and you bite harder then suck at my neck leaving marks behind.

"Ohhh noo." I cry out loud.

Your mouth slides down to my shoulder and continues to send shocks of pain and pleasure through biting and sucking. Your cock spearing my insides faster. I am pushing my hips up to meet yours trying to get all of you that I don't even have room for. Wanting all the pleasure, all the pain.

Your mouth finds my breast and you suck furiously on I. I can't take much more. You let go of my hands and I grab your face, bringing it to mine. My mouth fucks yours as you fuck my cunt.

Deep, hard and fast. We are biting each other's lips. We are viciously slamming into each other. It is an unbridled and sadistic twist of power exchange taking place right on the floor of the bathroom. Neither of us will succumb to the other. I claw your back and grab your ass pounding you into my cunt.

"Please now!" I beg, calling out your name.

"Ahhhh" you moan as you answer my hips question.

You grab my ass with both hands squeezing hard and grinding yourself so deep you knock the wind out of me. I can't take much more of this and you know it. You look into my eyes and pull my hair causing me to let my head bend back to expose my neck. You pump yourself into me like a jackhammer on steel. You bite my chin then nip your way to the middle of my neck.

I quiver at the sensation as you find that special spot that makes me powerless. You suck hard and bite every time I move. I feel you consume my resistance. The fat tip of your violating cock hits my cervix with such force I know that you have won.

"Fuck yes!" I scream, startling you.

Concern for the other hotel guests getting alarmed enough to call the desk has you change your approach. You shove your mouth over mine to quiet me. I rip my nails across your back and ass causing you to slam down into me even harder in pain…purposefully to demand my submission.

"Give yourself to me now!  Offer yourself to me!" You growl through clenched teeth.

"Oh my fucking…"I am interrupted by the puncture of your cock slamming into my cervix again.

"You will cum now bitch!" You command, pulling my hair hard and savagely attacking my neck as it is exposed.

I feel the fire travel through my body. The searing pain of your assault on my skin, my cervix and the release is my only hope. I surrender, bucking and flailing my body beneath you. Your body shakes and your cock jerks without your hips moving. I felt your body tighten above then spasm, twisting into places inside I was not aware of till that point.

I cry out from the sensation of another orgasm erupting. I feel a sudden pressure and then a pop ricochet through my walls. I look into your eyes and the grimaced expression as you give in shooting warm cum into the very deepest part of me. Breathless we lay there and stare into each other's eyes. I am still in shock that this is happening. You run your hand through my long hair.

"Nice to finally meet you." You say, leaning down to kiss the tip of my nose.

# Martin & Iris

It had been a long day that would make anyone regret not calling in. Iris was no exception. Everything that could go wrong...did! It all started with the early commute. The moron in the BMW in front of her slammed on his brakes almost costing her a trip to the garage not to mention the coffee stained linen suit and the interior of her new car. After escaping the near collision Iris locked her keys in the damn car. By the time I retrieved them I was 10 minutes late for my first meeting of the day.

"Yes, and be a doll and send a nice bottle of tequila to...Pedro is it?" James says with a giggle looking at me. Iris smiles sourly and nods her head yes.

"See, Riz that is why sometime I can see your ass warming this chair instead of mine." James says and rises to leave the meeting.

Iris gives James a look that lets him know he will never be more right in his life. He knows she feels like cringing when he calls her Riz. Everyone looks at her in disbelief in the office when he calls her that. It will be the whisper of the office that James was calling Iris "Riz" again.

Most would not dare call Iris that without fearing physical harm. Iris fought hard to get through school and win a position at the company with aspirations of nothing less than to run the company. She has goals beyond walking some rookie on a leash until he gets a clue. Yes, Iris was about to spend her weekend in a suitcase. Alas, Mexico was not going to be the destination. Iris glares at James and while telling Jessi, her secretary, to cancel her flight and reservations for Mexico.

Iris drives into the garage thinking she could just scream.

Walking into the kitchen she throws her keys across the counter. Iris presses the answering machine to play in the background as she pours a much needed glass of wine and strips for the shower. She has an hour to make the plane and the company limo should be picking her up shortly.

Iris listens to the sounds of three calls from work...Jessi giving her trip information, her neurotic Aunt complaining about her brother's wife and two hang ups. Iris gets out and dries off while having Jessi call Seattle for her.

While Iris waits for Jessi to retrieve Seattle she looks into the mirror. She thoughtfully applies mascara and a soft red liner to her plump lips. After dabbing off a lost particle of mascara Iris decides mom was right. Her eyes are such a deep bright green that she was rich in natural beauty and had two emeralds to prove it. Iris' red hair sets off the beautiful green color all the more.

Iris sprays a sweep of perfume across her bare neck and chest. She watches her nipples pucker tightly at the cool lilac scent that blossoms from her skin. Iris strokes her tits softly, cupping each one appreciatively. Admiring her lush shape, Iris moves offer a side view to look at the profile of her tight athletic body. She admires her large breasts. They bounce and move freely with encouragement but quickly go back to defying gravity appearing amazingly perky with their nipples pointing upright to the heavens above. Iris feels a tickle of excitement and brings up her left leg to rest on the vanity.

What a beautiful smooth shaved pussy lingered below. It definitely needed some attention after being neglected by her business tracked mine. Iris slides her right hand down and parts its sweet pink lips. The wetness excites her and she indulges in playing with her nipples with the other hand. As Iris watches her hand work her cunt she thinks of what it would be like to be down there eating such a delicious meal. Soon Iris' hips pick up rhythm watching her fingers work like a rotor going at mind blowing speed. She knows the minutes are flying by quickly.

Now another woman is with Iris in her mind. The beauty's long hair tickles Iris' thighs as she shoves her tongue deep inside. The dark beauty's nails dig into Iris' flesh. What a rough little bitch she is. Iris' mouth gets dry as she moans involuntarily. Iris taunts the goddess to suck harder. Iris pinches her clit and gasps.

Iris leans back, imaging her wicked lover settling her sweet box over her face. That first salty sweet taste of her is heaven. Iris sucks savagely on her little bud, sending her to ride Iris' mouth trying to tame her quick learning tongue. Iris grabs the wench's ass, squeezing her voluptuous curves. Iris spreads out her fingers generously to pinch all that tender sensitive meat on her back end. Iris thinks of her tits bouncing and her hard nipples poking and brushing against Iris' stomach as she grinds into Iris' mouth. Iris pushes her hips down farther so that the crack of her ass is in view. With an instant skill acquired from desire alone Iris licks and prepares the vixen's ass to be eaten as Iris' fingers attack the beauty's cunt.

Iris wants to cum so bad. She can see it on her frustrated face in the mirror. Iris rubs her clit faster, jamming her fingers deeper than comfortable. She watches her body jerk frantically. *Yes, I am almost there,* Iris thinks in a heated state of mind. Iris commands the wench to eat her pussy. *Such a good little wench you are,* Iris coaches the lover out loud while imagining the beauty shoving her finger into Iris' ass while biting Iris' clit with unforgiving teeth. *Yes, that is it,* Iris confirms with a loud purr. *Almost...so close,* Iris encourages her vixen between her legs. Iris opens her eyes to see her cunt swollen, swallowing her fingers in the mirror.

Iris needs more and creatively dips into her mental bank of fantasy and pulls out a lover that fails at finishing her off without disappointment. The third lover, this time a man, enters the room.

This beefcake is dangerously built with an astounding height of six feet with an extra seven inches to spare. Stud is dark and hot with sinfully thick unruly dark hair that teases the middle of his back. He walks in on Iris and the hungry vixen with a scent of Armani and sex waiting to happen like they have never known before. He was a walking hard on waiting for a ménage à trois. He drops his clothing and lifts the wench off Iris like she was light as a feather. Instantly the vixen is lying beneath Iris eating her cunt as Iris rides her face. The thick cocked stranger seems to have grown a few more inches to surpass any expectations two sex starved sluts like Iris and the wench dared to have. Wedging his beautiful member into Iris' slippery pussy causes her to have her eyes roll back in painful pleasure leaving her toes curling into the carpet below her feet and the vixen's head.

*Damn, a fuck that never disappoints is just what you are, Big Boy,* Iris thinks as the bulging vein rippled cock stretches her almost to the point of tearing. Biting her bottom lip sadistically makes it all the more for Iris and tears form in her eyes at the stinging pain spreading across her mouth.

The dark vixen below chews Iris' clit flicking her fiery tongue across Iris' silky lips while the stranger pumps her hard in long deep strokes. The stud begins moaning deeply each time his cock is fully buried in Iris' tight pussy. The talented oral goddess below sucks his balls roughly, causing him to squeeze Iris' swollen tits in reflex. Iris cries out as the vixen's sharp tongue assault her clit further. Iris rises up, straddling the vixen's mouth and the stud pulls out and quickly impales up into Iris' unsuspecting ass. To soothe the burning of stretching virgin skin the vixen sucks slowly on Iris like one would savoring a rare ice cream cone, rich and creamy. Iris leans back and begins claiming the stud's mouth with her own.

Every place within Iris builds to the point of exploding. The stud pounds harder as the vixen's tongue sucks his balls and licks the rim of Iris' ass that he is invading. Iris reaches down and pulls the vixen's hips up to devour her dripping pussy. Rubbing her face in it moaning into her crevices, Iris rams a couple of her left fingers into the vixen ass. Without mercy Iris pulls at the opening of the vixen's dripping cunt causing her to yelp in pain. Iris calls her a bitch and sits harder on the whining vixen's face, demanding her to eat Iris' cunt and to use her teeth gently.

The stud is a wild well hung stallion fucking Iris' ass. As he works Iris over, her lips make crude smacking sounds while the stud and Iris share the job of eating the vixen's spicy-sweet pussy. Iris grabs her left tit and squeezes it so hard that cries out simulating the stud's wicked grip on her chest. *Here it comes*, Iris thinks with a savoring lick to her pillowy lips.

*RINNNNGGGGGGGGGGGGGG!* The phone calls out.

Iris tries to rub faster to finish but the shrill double ring ruins the fantasy. Iris drops down her leg feeling cheated and ridiculous. Walking naked and frustrated to the bedside phone she impatiently clicks on the conference button. The rookie gets on the phone after being hunted down by spirited Jessi. He gets impatient and has the nerve to interrupt Iris' verbal assault telling her she should have known better. Iris tells him to tuck his tail between his legs because she is taking over to do the job right. He is still babbling and apologizing when Iris disconnects. Iris slams half the wine while pulling down her suitcase from her walk-in closet.

Iris was told that the client set up the arrangements for her to stay in the estate house. He would be flying in for the weekend from New York. This property belonged to the company so Iris had no reason to think twice. They would be having dinner at 8 pm in the dining room. Iris looked at her wardrobe and decided on casual and conservative. Her plane is scheduled to leave Minneapolis at 3 pm and arrive in Phoenix just in time to get to the estate for dinner. Iris gets packed and is on the plane in no time. While Iris waits as people board the plane for coach seating her cell phone rings.

"Yes?" Iris answers flipping through her briefcase for a missing document.

"Why did you choose to let someone incapable of doing a job right when you can do it flawlessly with out effort?" An unfamiliar voice asks.

"Seattle is sinking fast...Word has it so is your ass!" Stopping to pick up on the unfamiliar voice. "Wait! Who is this?" Iris asks realizing it may not be Boy Wonder after all considering the tone.

"What did I just ask? I think I was perfectly clear. Your answer disappoints me as does your tone. I will work on that later. For now you will be expected to change quickly into what will be laying on the bed in your room. There are no exceptions. Should you not wear what has been chosen for our meeting I will leave your presence until you are suitable. Do you understand me?" The voice finishes. Iris has to laugh in amazement at the absolute gall of the person on the end of the conversation.

"Also to add to your obvious amusement which is completely unfounded, trust me on this, my car will meet you at the airport. Daniel, my personal driver, will greet you. Save the inquisition...he will not answer you except for what he has been instructed to. Have a good flight." The stranger ends with a click for goodbye.

Iris was stunned. It took at least a good fifteen seconds for her to come back around and close her mouth. Iris tried to pull up his number to tell him to kiss her ass but nothing was available. Iris then takes the next step and calls James who immediately interrupts her as if he was expecting to hear from her.

"Iris, this client is very particular. Very! There is a reason he didn't let the accounts close. This guy knows you far better than you care to understand right now." James growls on the phone. Even that didn't deter Iris from cutting him off.

"James!" Iris snaps back at him. "Listen to me!"

"You are fucking clueless, Riz, to what and who this guy is but soon you will." James explains as the plane backs away from the gate.

"And?" I raise my voice.

"And this client was very insulted when he requested you to handle the account and you handed it over to Boy Wonder in Seattle." He finishes as the plane now is heading towards the runway line up.

"Good God, James! He wants me to wear something he bought...God knows what. May I remind you that I did not get a Master's degree to become a high priced call girl with business skills? There are lawsuits ready to wear my name and ...yours. I will not stand for this!" I yell and startle the newlyweds in the row beside me.

"No, I am sure you won't because I suspect the plane is about ready to take off. Riz, you can do this and we both know it." James says with a giggle.

"Damn you! This guy is not worth it, James." I say in an angry whisper as the plane picks up speed. The static starts to interfere.

"I will be on the return flight tonight papers signed and in my hot little hands. Be ready. Keep the fucking light on so you can see me coming!" Iris lowers her voice to a promising firm tone.

Iris snaps the phone closed and slams it back into her briefcase. She closes her eyes and breathes deep. James' image passes through her mind and she instantly sees red. Son of a bitch! He will pay. Iris feels a rush of competitive venom race through her veins being chased by a bitter-sweet fondness for the very man who put her in this position to begin with.

Iris knows the game all too well. She was born into it.

150

The manipulation and power struggle between her parents gave her glimpses into the weakness that both genders exhibit when under pressure. For her it is sad and rather depressing to think about. Not so much her own parents' demise but the mess that results from what can be ultimately avoided if everyone would be rational and think objectively.

Iris was hired for the partnership by James because Iris was the only one who went in guns blazing telling him that she wanted his job, title and his clients. He played some mind sparing games and he lost rather quickly much to his delight. The rest of the interviews were cancelled and for the first time in the history of the company Iris was hired and signed on as a partner. Not on wit alone but armed with a portfolio that rivaled his and being a woman to match.

Iris never loved or respected a man as much as she does James and the fact that he can get under her skin like he does is not a surprise to her in the least let alone him. He is a mentor, father figure and big brother all in one. Only James knows her better than herself. At the wee hours of a particular strategy meeting he told her that he found theirs a partnership that will meet its end when Iris finally takes his place. He vows to happily sail off to the islands with Kari, his southern belle wife, when it happens.

Iris remembers her Dad's slurred business speech at the dinner celebrating her partnership. Iris squeezes her eyes tight thinking the memory could disappear. After a few Manhattans and rejections from a cocktail waitress who could smell him a mile away, her Dad stepped up and embarrassed her once last time. James and Kari unfortunately had to witness it along with half of Merra's Bistro.

"My baby is grown up. She will make more her first three months than I did last year. So what? Who cares? She deserved it. She did right. She was always smarter than any rich asshole I ever came across including all you pricks in this room looking her up and down right now." He stops to sip the last of his drink then roughly puts it on the table in front of him. Iris sinks down into her chair as Kari stares in disbelief at the way he refers to his only child.

"Here is some advice for you, girl. Makes no difference what that college degree taught ya. I can give you this advice for free. Those bastards will eat you alive out there. They will smell you coming. That's right. Keep your legs locked tight together. That is what they really want. They care less with what your were born with upstairs in the head. It is brutal and they want nothing less than the clothes off your back and you laying face down. If that happens look them in the eyes every time. Don't back down, don't ever lie down and definitely don't bend over. Don't let them know what gets your tits hard and be ready to grab them by the balls and squeeze till your last breath. Kick them…" He stops and coughs then hick ups. Thank God he pauses leaving time for someone to step up and save the particle of dignity that Iris prayed that she would be shown enough mercy to leave the restaurant with.

"That was inspiring there, Sir. I would like to add to that." James steps up and winks to me slapping Iris' father on the back much harder than needed. Iris could have died right at that moment. She was frozen in humiliation and James knew it.

"Let's congratulate Iris on achieving what took many of us half a career to accomplish. It is all to come in good time and may we all be able to enjoy it with her when it arrives." James finishes with clapping and deafening loudness that causes my Dad to stumble off past the bar and out the door.

Seven years later and it still seems like yesterday. Iris wiggles in her seat in search of comfort or a way to evade the further memories. Either at this point would be welcome.

Iris never saw him again. He died in a single car accident two weeks after the dinner party with a bottle in his hand and divorce papers in his pocket. James went to the memorial with her. Kari helped her mother pack and move into a condo the company leased out to executives. The monthly payments were to be out of her check but Iris never got an answer from James on why she never had the payments withheld.

When her mother passed away in a peaceful sleep the following year from a stroke Iris felt so empty. She felt like it closed every part of her past with the lid of her casket. There was virtually no family left for her to lean on. James and Kari stood with Iris while she cried, screamed and cursed her father for sucking the beauty out of the woman's life before she had a chance to realize what she was worthy of. Iris broke the door going out of the memorial service feeling like she was going to snap. James stayed behind taking care of everything while Kari took her away for the weekend.

Iris returned to a new life and an apartment filled with pictures of her mother and her that Iris scarcely remembered. Her mother's tattered quilts lovingly mended and presented on an heirloom quilt rack that her grandfather made long ago left Iris with a sense of faith that she would never be alone again as long as she had James, Kari and Jessi.

Iris learned later that James sent Jessi into her closets armed with a briefcase to fill with old pictures to take to Antiqued Treasures on 5th and Grand. James and Kari told the shop sky was the limit for whatever it took to make Iris' mother a part of every room. Iris cried when she walked in and James was there cooking a dinner and Jessi was casually finishing up her paperwork on her computer. Kari handled the after funeral correspondence and the legal strings that needed to be tied up. James wrote off the last minute bills to a gold card. Iris promised to pay back every cent.

"Try it and I will have you in the smallest office with the rookies hired last year." James smiled and gave Iris his affectionate wink he saved only for Kari or her. He wouldn't hear of being paid back a single penny.

James' actions made sense when Kari revealed in a private that Iris' life was a mere shadow of James' own childhood. His generosity was self serving as well genuine. He felt he healed his own internal scars by making things right for me. Iris loves James with a respect and was committed to making sure she never lost sight of what it was Iris owes him. That was to be the most aggressive and ruthless partner he could have imagined. Even if it meant kicking his ass once in awhile while Iris was at it.

The plane lands before Iris opens her eyes. Iris takes a few moments to gather her carry on suitcase and her briefcase. Her cell rings the second Iris steps in the aisle smashed between the lovebirds and a set of kids that should have been tossed down to the luggage carrier long ago. Iris grabs the cell snarling.

"James, you will pay dearly. I know where you live and you might just want to leave the light on to see me coming." Iris hisses as she makes her way down the aisle.

"We will address this unbecoming tone tonight. Welcome to Phoenix." The voice chastises Iris much to her shock.

*It is him! The bastard has the audacity to criticize my tone!* Iris thinks to herself as her eyes scan the people around her who may hear an upcoming outburst of anger slip through her lips.

"Sorry, the pilot beat you to it. And another thing..." Iris starts her *"let's get something clear"* speech only to be sharply interrupted.

"Quiet! Don't waste our time trying to impress me with an attitude that should have been left at home. It will not be tolerated and will be subject to modification. Understand me?" The voice again departs the one sided conversation with a prompt click to disconnect.

Iris' mouth again is wide open in shock. *Who in the hell is this guy? He acts like I am some piece of high priced meat being flown in from exclusive ranch that caters to business men. Subject to modification? He probably is sitting at the table with a knife and fork in hand with Daniel tucking a linen napkin under his chin as he awaits for me to arrive to his table.* Iris thinks as she pushes her way through the lovebirds and the Brady Bunch with the determination of the marines invading land. Iris dashes through the airport and finds Daniel before she can lose the thought of her last phone conversation. What Iris lays eyes on only makes this situation more bizarre.

A man who is in his mid-thirties with no expression in a black suit approaches her. He stands with his arms folded in front of him with the formality of a military presentation.

Not a hello or greeting. Iris smiles and extends her hand. She is baffled at his resistance to reach out respectfully. Iris used to particular, wealthy clients. She has had some real clowns but this guy thinks he runs the whole circus!

"Daniel?" Iris asks. With that he extends his hands and takes the baggage from Iris' blatantly ignoring her intention of shaking hands to greet each other.

"May I?" The handsome valet asks says after already taking possession of them.

"Sure." Iris answers following behind him as he walks away with her belongings.

"Welcome to Phoenix. When we arrive at Martin's estate I will carry these to your room." He says as he walks towards the black limo waiting at the doors.

Iris sprints to keep up and make attempts to ask what his employer's problem is. He is quite effective in avoiding the conversation as he opens the door and motions for her to get in. Iris keeps her right leg outside the car and looks at him firmly.

"I asked what Martin's attitude is from? Please answer!" Iris looks directly into Daniel's eyes. He knows it will not be worthwhile to ignore her persistence.

"Martin expects formality, respect and he will in turn

give that, Madame. All that you want to know is best to be addressed with Martin. Please allow me to close this door and not delay us anymore than we already are." Daniel finishes properly.

Iris moves her leg in and receives a grateful smile as the door closes. Before Daniel gets into the car, Iris notices he takes a call and is speaking when he steps into the car. Knowing things are becoming more intricate as the minutes pass that she is left in the back of the car leads her to believe it is not his wife he is talking to but the arrogant prick himself.

"Yes, Sir, the contracts are to arrive by courier to the estate as requested." Daniel finishes while turning on music for Iris. Iris catches on to who is on the phone and leans forward so that he can hear her or Iris can interrupt, whichever comes first.

"Daniel, please tell Martin I have the contracts in my hands with duplicates." Iris speaks loud enough for him to hear shaking the contracts for added effect with an insistent smile.

Daniel sets down the phone and turns off the music almost if by command then proceeds to drive ahead through a private lane for express drivers. Iris hears a click then to her surprise Martin's voice.

"Please don't interrupt Daniel when he is at his duties. Open the silver cabinet and enjoy your ride. You should be able to accomplish that without further trouble I presume." Martin's voice then suddenly disappears as he arrived. *Should be able to accomplish that?* This man's arrogance has no limits!

Iris opens the silver cabinet that is elegantly placed in the seat facing the back. Inside is a black velvet envelope with a crimson wax seal keeping it closed. Iris opens it and it is a note in gold embossed letting. The message speaks volumes as Iris reads it carefully the first time. The second time softly as if to whisper the message to her memory as the words echo out loud around her.

*Iris,*
**There came a time when the risk to remain tight in the bud was more painful than the risk it took to blossom.**
*~M~*

Iris goes to close the door and notices a single red ribbon dangling a charm at the end. It is a circle divided by three sections. Iris knows she has seen the symbol before. It has another section instead of the two commonly used for "yin & yang". Iris pulls on the ribbon to see where it is attached and soon finds a single black long stemmed rose appear. Iris grasps it with delicate fingers and in turn is gasping at the prick left in her finger tip. Nice… he neglected to have the thorns removed. What sense does that make? Iris brings the finger to her lips and sucks at the wound.

"Curious, tenacious and self-reliant even in discomfort. How becoming and interesting. I know I have made the right choice." Martin's voice echoes from somewhere into the car.

Iris rolls her eyes at the extent this guy goes to make some warped impression. *Okay, James Bond, get off on your little fantasy while you can.* Iris thinks quietly bringing the note to her lips smelling the cologne so vivid it makes her sigh. This man is very unsettling. Anais Nin, black velvet, gold font, a single black rose and the smell of him in her mind. Martin seems to command Iris as if she is an unclaimed vessel that he is navigating further out into the unknown toward his private lair.

Iris looks ahead and can see Daniel smiling in the rear view mirror as he watches her smelling of the scent on the velvet embossed note card. Iris quickly slips the note into her briefcase and tries to approach the front seat to chat with the chauffeur but is greeted by the window divider rising as she gets there. *Damn!* Iris says as she sulks back into her seat. She decides to figure out what this guy is about before they come face to face.

Iris gets on the phone and sends Jessi a picture of the emblem in the ribbon. She makes sure to tell her about the recent phone calls. Even Jessi agrees that the man's elevator must be jammed somewhere between reality and disturbing. She tells Iris to give her two minutes and she will call back.

In the time that passes Iris finds the city disappears fast and soon they are racing down a beautiful winding private drive. They coast up to gates that block the car from what looks like a mission influenced palace. The old wrought iron gates that stand majestically in front the car have an "M" in the middle. Iris finds it odd since the company was founded by James and is carrying his last name starts with an "S".

The estate is a glittering jewel basking in the last rays of evening sun before it falls to sleep in the distance. The white sand castle rests in the backdrop of the endless desert. The car moves slowly through the gates and approaches the house. The car just arrives to the door when Iris' cell rings. She answers as Daniel opens the trunk retrieving my bags.

"Where the hell did you get that charm thing on a string?" Jessi asks with concern in her voice.

"What are you talking about? I told you! Did you find the meaning of the symbol on the charm?" Iris snaps.

"Riz, the charm comes from a jeweler that designs privately for very an exclusive client. Initially when I spoke to him he seemed to think I was wanting something made and was more than happy to talk. I told him a friend gave me his number when he asked. When I mentioned the charm he asked me to send the picture so I did on my cell. That is when he went cold and became really short with me. I get the feeling he wasn't suppose to talk about it if anyone asked about the charm. He excused himself to call someone then saying our conversation was over. I was instructed to never call again." Jessi finishes.

"Hmmm," Iris breathes out looking at the charm resting

securely on her fingertip. "I know I have seen this somewhere before." Iris says out loud trying to recall.

"Sure you have, Riz. Remember Joy's farewell party?" Asks Jessi. Iris' eyes widen with sudden awareness. *That is it!* Iris realizes why it looks so familiar. How could she ever forget?

Joy was the intern that spent the summer with the company from Britain. Her jet black hair was always pulled up tightly in a bun. She always the same thing everyday. A crisp white blouse under a black tailored suit that fit her to perfection. Her heels had her towering over most of the employees at 6 feet even. A to the point strategist, Joy was the epitome of business discipline. Never late and never absent she would work diligently to do whatever she was assigned. No one ever heard about her private life. They only knew that she was from a wealthy family growing up in Britain and Austria.

At the end of her internship Joy accepted an offer in Australia to handle the international investors in a trading firm. Jessi and Iris decided to plan a party for her and asked her input. To their surprise she mentioned her fiancée' and a get together their friends were having after her last day of work. Joy wanted the two of them to come but felt uncomfortable with anyone else coming from the office. She even had her own car for the evening picking up the guests. Jessi and Iris were to ready to be picked up at 8 p.m.

Iris laughs at the thought it would only amount to a conservative dinner getting wild with a spicy sushi at the end. Joy reminded them to be open minded and bring a sense of adventure beforehand. If only they had known! Jessi offered to bring her camera to record the moment but Joy was adamant that it was not allowed under any circumstances. Iris remembers thinking that maybe Joy is in the mob family and the whole story about Europe was a front including the faint British accent she used. Again, we were absolutely clueless to just what it was we were being invited to.

That evening Jessi and Iris dressed in cocktail dresses, little make up and hair straight. Iris surely didn't want to embarrass Joy at her party. The car dropped them off at a home overlooking Minneapolis's river front district. Nothing could have prepared the two unassuming women for what was to greet them at the door.

The door opened into a very quiet entry way. A woman in a French maids outfit just like the kind you find in a Frederick's catalog greeted them. She had Jessi and Iris follow her through to a back hallway dimly lit with candles. Jessi and I thought for sure they were about to walk into the wrong dinner party when they stood at the French doors. The maid opened them in unison and they stepped slowly into a sea of leather and skin. Iris clears her throat to suppress a giggle when Jessi whispers "Oh shit!"

There they stood like two statues as everyone mingled around them as if they weren't even there. Men and women in suits passed as well as those in scarcely anything but pierced body parts, dog collars, leashes and perfume. Iris mentioned the sound of bells ringing and that maybe an angel finally found her wings causing Jessi to choke. Interestingly that is when a clump of nude women passed by whispering to a voluptuous woman with silver bells dangling from her nipples. A waiter goes by and they swipe the last two flutes of champagne. Iris whispers to Jessi when their glasses are empty they are slipping out quietly…together. There was no way they were at the right place Iris insisted.

With the last sip of their champagne Jessi and Iris made their way back to the door. Jessi at one point was approached by a young lady wanting to offer her services. Jessi bewildered almost handed her a business card till Iris grabbed it and reminded her that James would hardly be amused that their company was advertising at an alternative play party. Just when they are about to leave Joy comes in the door with her fiancée. It just became all the more interesting to Iris and Jessi.

Joy greeted them with a kiss on the cheek which of course was very out of character for her. Missing was her trademark white blouse and waist length black blazer. Instead she was wearing a thigh length black silk jacket plunging open to almost her navel. Iris caught her breath as Jessi grabbed her arm in comfort. Joy was standing at least 6 inches above her average 6 feet via chandelier stilettos that seemed to defy reason. The straps weaved defiantly up her sleek bare legs and tied just below the knee. Her black hair spilled over her shoulders shining a beautiful blue in the lighting. Iris was speechless.

Ben was an equally yummy sight to behold. Blonde and sky-blue eyed with a chiseled body he was invigorating to look at. He was bronzed by the Australian sun and quiet except for saying a "Good Evening" to both of them. His tailored black suit was complimented by a silver shirt that clung to him. Iris was just getting a quick look at his choice of shoes thinking how well Joy dressed him when something catches her eye and Jessi's as well. Iris quickly assumes so when she feels Jessi's nails sink into her arm.

Discreetly rolled up in Sir Benjamin's pocket was a whip of some sort. Very similar to a horse whip. Iris begins to ask about his equestrian interests when two lovely ladies in waiting assist Joy with the removal of her jacket.

Joy stood in front of Jessi and Iris with a smile that rivaled a cat after devouring the mouse. Her nipples were pierced with a gold chain dangling between them Instantly they became erect to the kiss of cool air and warm stare of her stunned audience. A soft chain secured in the middle trailed down her stomach anchoring itself on a large gold hoop Iris was sure was pierced permanently to her clit. It certainly didn't appear to be a new fad in costume jewelry. Iris blinked as she stood looking at Joy's bare pussy waxed to Brazilian perfection. Jessi sets Iris' arm on fire with her nails and Iris gasps. Joy smiles knowingly and asks permission from Ben to thank the hosts for the beautiful party. Joy's firm ass moves across the room and it is then that they realize Ben doesn't tame horses but Joy's beautiful crimson ass instead.

They look nervously at a sun blazing smile coming from Ben. Iris gives a pathetic "how nice" smile and tries to make small talk about their future plans. It fails miserably when Ben pulls out the whip handing it to a passing server who seems to be collecting an array of leather goods. Iris puts her empty glass on the tray much to Ben's amusement as she attempts to adjust a paddle to serve as a coaster for my glass.

Something tells Ben Iris feels a chill flying up her arm as her hand finds it difficult to settle on one place for it. Too many seconds pass before Jessi and Ben witness Iris releasing the paddle from her grasp so the waiter can move on. A nervous smile creeps across Iris' face when Ben winks at Iris causing Jessi's eyes to dart back at her and realize she is blushing like a school girl.

Joy made her way back after what seemed an eternity. Apologizing to Ben for her length of absence, Joy then thanks Jessi and Iris for being respectful in attending without co-workers in tow. They visited with Joy much to the comfort of the endless champagne that passed by. Our departure was signaled by the sound of wood slapping skin resulting in the yelp of a lady bent over someone's lap. The fifth glass of champagne had everything in dizzy perspective for both Jessi and I. We bid Joy and Ben success and stumbled our way to the door. I grabbed a napkin on the way out to dab the tears of laughter that were going to come as soon as Jessi started her verbal reprisal of what she had just been subjected to. The emblem on the napkin was the same as on several ankles, ass cheeks and shoulders.

"Iris! Helllloooooo! Are you even there?" Jessi yells.

"Yes, settle down!" I yell back. "What did you say?" I ask.

"BDSM." Jessi exclaims.

"What the hell is that?" I respond looking at the charm more closely.

"It stands for B&D Bondage & Discipline, D&S Dominance & submission and S&M Sadism & Masochism! It is not limited to just some cuffs and a few hot candles, Riz. There is a lifestyle out there that many people take seriously. " She started sounding worried.

"Well, I am sure it was not for me to find and meant for someone else. However, I found it in the cabinet with a note meant for me in the car. Martin called me and told me where it was." Iris told her trying to figure out whether to get out or make some excuse to leave.

Daniel stands at the door respectfully with his back to her till Iris finishes her call.

"I am sure that it was not meant for you. I checked the company records and the cars we have out there are in use tonight and you aren't in the logs. Martin has not used one of the company vehicles in over a year. You are in his limo, my dear. He just landed in from New York. I would imagine Martin has a private life that as exciting as it may be was definitely not something he was intending you to participate in. He has never even met you for heaven sakes. Besides anyone knows you are as straight as straight can get." Jessi takes a breath while typing loudly on her lap top.

"But…if I am wrong, Iris, then you are in for the thrill of a lifetime. You would be so lucky. I hear the guy is so damn hot he makes you melt with a look. Gillian in accounting saw him in the London office last week for account balances and this Martin guy was brutal chewing people for slacking off. He doesn't take any shit. She said she could hardly think of

163

numbers except attempting to give him hers. I guess he blew her off." Jessi finishes with a much needed breath.

"Jessi, you are kidding…aren't you?" Iris asks reaching for the door handle.

"I am not. This guy is not to mess with." Jessi answers quickly.

"Not that …well that too but I mean about everyone thinking I am so straight that I am on the verge of narrow? Really…people think that?" Iris asks with a hint of disappointment that she may have a limitation others knew of and she didn't.

"Riz, safe is fine. If it is what you want then who the hell cares what anyone else thinks? You just would be the last person anyone would approach about tying up and beating for just sheer wicked pleasure. Anyone who knows you that is. Oh, and you can't find anything out about him. It is like he appears all over but doesn't leave anything relevant behind. I can't find any personal info on him. Not even a birth date. Watch your attitude. You know how you can get, Iris. I don't think he will tolerate it. Keep me posted. Hey, if you need anything just call. By the way, first tip…a *"flogger"* is not a cocktail."

Jessi laughs so hard she has to hang up. Iris swallows hard and can feel a million butterflies fill her stomach. The door opens and Daniel extends out his hand to see Iris out of the car.

Iris takes a deep breath and walks up the steps. The door opens with the help of an older gentleman in a tuxedo who flashes a sober smile.

"Welcome, Master has been expecting you. I shall inform him of your arrival. Daniel will escort you to your room. I will show you the way to the dining room after you are changed and refreshed. Dinner will begin at 8 pm." He ends his British flavored speech with a wave of his right hand silently directing both Iris and Daniel towards the winding staircase that seems to disappear into a dimly lit upstairs.

Daniel goes around Iris when she stalls at the door. Iris thinks over the idea of questioning Jeeves but he must also read minds because he raises his eyebrow and gives her a silent "not in this lifetime" message with the mere twitch of his thin lips. Daniel has made it half way up the staircase before looking to see where Iris is at. Jeeves looks up at the ceiling impatiently and Iris decides holding out at the door is going to get her no where.

Iris walks up behind Daniel and notices the walls are adorned with art. Impressionistic pieces delicately dance within the candle light. Tchaikovsky serenades softly in the distance adding to the warmth. If this guy comes out in a white tux and a small Hispanic person at his knee named "Tattoo" Iris wouldn't be surprised. The mystery intrigues her as she moves slowly up the stairs.

The room Iris is escorted to is decorated in french renaissance period. The four post bed is breathtakingly large with ivory organza curtains surrounding it spilling from a hoop hanger above it in the center of the high ceiling. The smell of peonies and roses fill the air.

Iris is speechless. She hears the door close before she can say goodbye to Daniel. Iris absorbs the room and notices the amazing floral arrangements in plump vases in almost every corner of the room. The detail was amazing and Iris had to touch the petals to believe that they were real. The cost of such flowers presently out of season must be astronomical.

The sheer black cocktail dress lying on the bed on display and a box containing black stiletto pumps next to it didn't take long to catch her eye. Not far from the dress a set of lingerie and thigh length black silk stockings lay accompanied by a garter. This guy had the nerve to buy her underwear? Now her blood starts to rush to her ears and cheeks.

Fuck the fragrant high end flowers! Iris picks up her cell phone and tries to call out but "No Service" comes up instead of a dial tone. Iris is about to search for a phone when a small lilac velvet box catches her eye on the pillow.

Iris picks up the box and feels the texture tickle her fingertips. Iris opens it and finds a delicate gold bracelet. Beautiful links softly hug a single letter "M". It has to be for some one else. Her name starts with an "I".

Iris is starting to believe the room was also prepared for someone else. Who the hell would be so damn bold as to set out $700 in fresh bouquets, gold jewelry and lingerie for a contract signing? Iris puts back the bracelet and closes the lid. Jeeves will have to return it to the right room or show her to another suite. One of the two is out of place.

Iris grabs her briefcase and carry on bag and proceeds to the door. She fumbles it open and then starts to wander down the hall finding another room that seems equally decorated to impress. It is in a matter of moments that Iris freshens up and then takes the papers in her hand and opens the door to find Jeeves stale faced waiting for her.

Iris asks him to wait and runs back to retrieve the velvet box. She asks if there possibly is another laying on some other pillow that has the letter "I".

Jeeves doesn't laugh and instead takes the box and looks at the ceiling again in disbelief. The wave of his left hand silently directs her down the dark hallway following the scent of fresh flowers.

Iris enters a door and finds herself in a formal dining room that has to be the size of a medium size house. It is empty except for an elaborate long table. I think that they have yet to be using another room for the dinner. Jeeves slides the papers from her hands before she can even feel them leave her grasp. Iris turns to look for him but he is gone.

Jeeves is replaced by the presence of a beautiful waitress wearing a revealing black and white cocktail server's dress. She has the same stilettos on that Iris does. She has soft blonde hair pulled up with a pearl clip. Her blue eyes are seductive and as she approaches, Iris feels a disturbing but immediate attraction to her.

The woman's lips are full and soft. Her skin is flawless and shimmers with a desert kissed bronze tan. She slows as she comes closer carrying a tray with a single flute of champagne. Her lips part and her tongue mischievously strokes her top lip before her bottom lip is involuntarily pinched between her teeth. Iris shifts in her stance as the gorgeous creature stops in front of her.

Iris feels a sudden impulse to kiss her. Not on the cheek but deeply and passionately. Iris clears her throat and feels the warmth between her legs grow moist.

Iris is captured by the woman's exceptional beauty. First looking at her waist that is perfectly framed with a bodice that beckons Iris' eyes up to her chest. Her cleavage is making her own heartbeat faster.

Iris envisions sucking on her...biting her as she allows her gaze to travel up her neck. Her throat is surrounded by a very simple yet dramatic choker that is silver and obviously made of steel. Right at the middle of her throat is a small heart shaped lock that apparently is the way the choker is joined.

Iris' gaze is distracted as she hands her the flute of champagne. Iris catches the sparkle of the woman's bracelet on her wrist. A single letter "M" dangles from it. The goddess leans forward as if to whisper a loving secret...her scent intoxicating and surprising to Iris. The woman kisses Iris softly on her right cheek. Her breasts rubbing against Iris' own create a static shock that surprises both.

The woman giggles softly and then takes her free hand and holds Iris' chin and draws her lips to her own. Iris feels almost faint as she has never been so close to another woman especially in such an intimate way. Her thumb pulls down on Iris' chin opening her mouth without effort. The woman's tongue slides in and she warmly exhales into Iris. Iris tastes her. The woman's voluptuous chest presses against her own. One woman's skin warming the other. Iris feels like she is melting. Iris' hand slides to the woman's cheek and to the back of her neck pulling her close. The woman sucks Iris' bottom lip then runs the tip of her skilled tongue down Iris' throat to the middle of her chest where her tits swell squeezed together. The exhilaration sets Iris' nipples on fire. Iris closes her eyes and gasps.

The woman's tongue races back up Iris' neck and dives into her open mouth. The two kiss for a few seconds before Iris hears someone clearing their throat signaling their arrival into the room.

Iris scrambles through thoughts of what to say to explain what even her mind can't as she pulls away. Surely making out with the staff is not a good way to start negotiations on a troubled deal. Iris remembers the waitress and looks for her.

In a blink of an eye the goddess is on her knees and the tray is left on the table on her way down. Her hands are flat on her thighs palms up with her thighs spread apart. She looks straight ahead. Iris has little time to look down at her new position before the one who interrupted them is standing behind her. Iris looks up and finds her eyes meet his. His hand strokes her head and she remains still. Iris feels the burning of embarrassment fill her face and as his stare pierces her Iris immediately look down to the waitress.

"Kira, please check her stockings to make sure they are fastened properly." He asks in a soft deep voice.

"Yes, Master." She responds in a whisper loud enough for only the three to hear.

Iris glances up to his face and can see his brown eyes sinking into hers. Iris feels as though he is slipping into her body and she cannot do anything about it. Iris feels powerless and completely vulnerable. Iris begins to step back as she hears a hand extend towards her.

"Do not move. Kira's only going to do as I instructed her to do." The tall gentleman says in a deeper voice than Iris was expecting.

Iris feels Kira's fingers start at the base of her heel, stroke around to the back of her calves and the tips of her fingers find themselves wrapped on the inside of Iris' thighs. Iris feels the chill of anxiety at him watching and her pussy starts to twitch.

Iris is trying to escape the thought of Kira between her legs while her hungry mouth is searching for her nectar. Iris closes her eyes as the waitress reaches under her dress, Iris holds her breath. The woman reaches Iris' pussy slipping her long nails under the material of Iris' thong, sweeping the wet lips of her pussy. Her fingers then tap at the crack of her ass as they move upward finally stopping at her waist. Like lightning the waitress' hands return to her thighs with palms facing up.

"And Kira?" The gentleman asks in a lower tone.

"Master's garter is missing." She responds still staring straight ahead.

Iris is more nervous and confused than ever and looks back into his face.

"Finish Kira. Tell me." He says sounding irritated that Iris is studying his face longer than he finds appropriate.

"Damp, warm and swollen, My Master." Kira answers.

Iris is thinking of her answer when he dismisses Kira. The waitress exits fast leaving her amazing scent behind.

The man steps closer and Iris tries to look anywhere but into his eyes. This is the point Iris needs to both make a move and take control of the situation or she can see things getting far out of hand.

"I guess I will go first. My name is Iris and you are?" Iris extends her hand confidently.

"Martin." He responded and glides his hand over hers.

Martin keeps hold of Iris' hand with a firm grip looking

down at it enclosed in his large dark hand. After an uncomfortable pause he speaks again.

"What is damp, warm and swollen?" Martin asks with a smirk and eyes sparkling at the opportunity for truth to seep from Iris' lips.

"The first two would have to be the champagne and the last of the three would most certainly be your ego." Iris says with a laugh thinking humor has to win him over and show her assertiveness at the same time. Iris naively smiles with pride.

"Your wit has a place and a time at the expense of another. When you are dressed appropriately I will speak further with you. For now you are excused." He says releasing her hand and walks away.

"Listen this is really quite entertaining but I don't have the time to waste on dramatics. Why don't you, Martin, come back over here pull out the plume pen in your satin lined pocket and grace the dotted line with your approval. It is ideal for you and our company. Walk away from it and the loss is yours." Iris says in the same tone she uses in every board meeting when people start to get lazy and the numbers show it.

Iris watches Martin stop quickly and walk purposefully back to her. He stands within inches of her at an uncomfortable whisper close distance. Iris shifts her weight nervously to one foot then the other thinking the movement may cause him to step back for her comfort. He breathes in deeply as if she is a rare flower he wants to savor the scent of.

"I am not intimidated by anything including fingers sliding over me while you watch, quotations that stimulate my sub consciousness, large accounts that can expand my profile or another who thinks he knows me so well that my mere submission to something I don't acknowledge or participate in can be bartered with, counted on and expected just like the garlic butter on his bread at a cheesy deli on Tuesday's late lunch special. This is business not the price is right. My attention or your general amusement is not criteria. We are not trying to merge Burger Stop and Pancake Heaven here. We are here to join millions of dollars and make a mind blowing profit. Let's leave this for Valentine's Day and the cutie that catches your eye selling lingerie at Victoria's Secret or Leather Is Us. Here is where reality sets in. Getting me, Martin?" Iris hears nervousness in her voice that surprises both of them.

With that said Martin steps closer and looks into Iris' eyes. She can feel him softly exhale. His lips parted, appearing inviting in a wild, rugged and unpredictably hot way that taunted her. The heat from his body surprisingly intoxicating. Iris can feel him lean in and down to her ear. Iris closes her eyes to prepare for anything.

"You are excused." He says firmly. Iris looks up into his piercing gaze. His smile is absent. His expression disciplined.

"I…" Iris starts to say but is soon talking to herself as he walks off leaving the door open behind him.

*Congratulations, Iris…you have just met the Prick of the Year!* She can hear her inner voice chiding.

The door fills with a beautiful presence and captures Iris' attention. It is Kira. Iris feels like butterflies and chaos are invading her all at once. Iris notices her finger curling upward and back down in a signal to follow her.

Iris is fully prepared to get her things, that is if Jeeves hasn't tossed them out to the drive by now.

Kira says nothing when they enter the suite Iris changed in and hands Iris the garter, thong and bra with two slender perfectly manicured red finger nails. Iris looks at her with surprise. Kira gives a disapproving look and shakes her head as if scolding a precocious child. She makes no move to offer privacy and refuses to speak which Iris expected. Martin probably has a remote hooked to her that shocks her collar the minute her mouth begins to open, Iris decides looking at the under garments in her hands.

Iris wonders if she knows that she could easily have her on the catwalk in Milan by Tuesday making $500,000 for simply looking luscious like she does now. Iris decides conversation and any attempts there of are useless. Instead she concedes to undress and redress in front of Kira.

*Who the hell cares anyways? I will be out of here in a matter of an hour tops.* Iris decides with a smile looking at Kira. *Humor the kinky bastard and no one will need to know. James will seriously owe me for this one.*

The thought of making demands upon her return fills Iris' mind. *A new office, a secretary for Jessi.* Kira shifts as Iris bends over to slide on a pump. Within two steps she is behind Iris wrapping her long fingers over her mouth.

Iris never had a woman touch her before, men tell her what to wear or dismiss her presence when it was not satisfactory. Iris is used to being in complete control of almost every situation. Now everywhere she turns it seems that she is not. Nothing makes sense and yet everything is so stimulating. A force holds her that she is not yet aware of and keeps her from running back to all she have ever known before this day. What is most unsettling is that Iris craves even more. In some insane way Iris is hungry for Martin.

Kira's hand moves from Iris' lips and down to Iris' left breast while the other has found its way under Iris' dress and between Iris' legs. Without notice Kira's fingers enter Iris' pussy. Iris is in shock and stands frozen afraid to move.

With skill Kira's left hand pinches and rolls Iris' nipple without mercy between her fingers. Iris catches her breath and Kira leans her face forward to lick Iris' cheek. Iris instinctively turns to the side and kisses Kira.

As Kira's fingers run wild in Iris' pussy her palm grinds Iris' clit. Iris is cumming in spasms before she can stop it from happening. Iris moans and gasps in Kira's mouth. Kira supports Iris as she moves her right hand back up to their faces and slips her dripping fingers between their lips.

Iris knows she should move or do something. That would be what she would have usually done but Iris never felt more alive than she did at that moment. Iris thinks of Martin and feels a nasty desire to think he is watching. Sucking Kira's fingertips and her tongue leaves Iris wanting Kira all over again.

A knock at the door and the sounds of someone walking past separates the two quickly. Iris hurries to pull her clothing back into place as Kira dutifully smiles and patiently waits.

In fortunate timing the door opens and it is Jeeves. He stands quietly waving both women out the door with a slow sweep of the hand. Jeeves smiles at Kira like a loving great uncle enamored with his sweet niece but as soon as Iris passes looking for equal approval his eyes roll tiredly up in the air.

Iris thinks about what Jessi said earlier and wonders if this Martin is some kind of high end business man who role plays as a classy pimp to the rich assholes with kinks that even their maids won't touch while their wives are out for the day cleaning out Sak's 5th Avenue.

Iris thinks of how gorgeous and disciplined Kira is and she starts to feel smugness for this twisted prick that has her living under his thumb. *What does she get subjected to? Why? Poor Kira.*

Kira leads the way back down the spiral staircase and through a dark tunnel to yet another staircase. This one seemed to be going to a wine cellar. Great...her knowledge of wine will not impress the man in the least. Iris is better off with cheese.

Iris decides to wing it in hopes of avoiding the topic of her first female sexual encounter with his toy he probably isn't too happy to share. Iris just starts to feel like she is coming back to reality when she gets the surprise of her life.

Martin is standing in a plain room with a row of chairs facing a stone wall. On that stone wall various chains, leather bindings and ropes dangle. Iris has been in one bondage club in her life, not that Jessi needed to know that. Iris decides that she can pretty much assume that she has the picture clear.

Martin is just that. A Master/Dominant and cute Kira is a chosen slave. Iris looks at Kira to give her a smile of support but doesn't find Kira beside her. Iris looks to both sides of her and then realizes she should look down for her.

There Kira was once again at Iris' feet with her palms facing up and thighs spread staring straight ahead. Iris ponders the effects of breaking the trance with a smart comment about Yoga being more beneficial and far less demanding than her current arrangement. Ultimately Iris decides to keep it to herself since she wants to make it back out of the basement playroom.

"Kira, that is all. You have done very well. You are dismissed for the evening. I will call you when I need you next." Martin says petting her head.

"Yes, Kira, I would like to speak with you later regarding a few ads in Paris we have opened for modeling campaigns. It is for Klein and Destiny couture during the spring fashion season. You would be perfect. I will come see you before I leave if you don't mind." Iris says while Kira stands.

"Freely, Kira." Martin says while walking over to align the chairs to the exact millimeter.

"Thank you, Madam but I have only an interest in painting and have a studio opening next year. However, if you would be so generous with your time, Madam, I would like to paint you at your convenience if Master permits." Kira says looking over at Martin for permission.

"Yes, Kira, that is a wonderful idea." Martin says with approval giving her a kiss on the cheek upon his return to her side.

Iris rolls her eyes much to Martin's disapproval as Kira softly departs up the stairs. The look on Martin's face grows more surprised as Iris shakes her in disbelief.

Iris walks over to the wall and reaches out touching one

of the leather straps. Iris imagines Kira or anyone for that matter fastened against the wall. At the mercy of Martin's hand or an audience's twisted whims. Iris strokes the leather and discovers it is soft on the inside. A sense of strength and awe fill her. Before she can think correctly, Iris speaks.

"You know, Martin....Or should I call you Master?" Iris asks, grinning and looking back at him as he walks closer to her.

"Martin." He says with a smile stopping short of standing on her toes. Iris backs up and finds her ass rubbing against the harsh stone wall.

"I truly admire the trust and devotion to turn you over physically, mentally and emotionally to another. It is as sacred as marriage. Which, of course, is why I never married or found myself bound to a stone wall in leather bindings. "Iris says as she strolls down the wall touching the ropes and chains.

"That is so very true." Martin agrees following behind her.

"Kira is your only I hope. She is a beautiful person and must make you very proud. She obviously enjoys serving you. I find it hard to accept that this is all she will have in life." Iris says turning to face him leaning back against the wall.

"You understand completely, Iris, just have yet to accept and ask for it. You have a hard time admitting what you truly want." Martin says passing around Iris to admire either her body or the chairs. Iris decides that it must be the upholstery on his chairs when his hand reaches to appreciate their position.

"Kira is collared by me. She is not a sexual slave. If I wanted that I could have it but that is not what Kira's role is in my life. I have no one. She is here to live peacefully and by choice she can come and go. I have the responsibility of supporting her, educating her and in all respects she is more like a daughter or niece to me. She will never have to worry about her welfare as I will provide her with anything that she ever

175

needs. Kira is studying art and soon will have her Masters. She is highly gifted and this commitment she shares with me keeps her focused and free from the pressures of the world. I am very proud of Kira. She is perfect." He finishes looking up at a clasp on the chain and pulling to test its strength with a tug.

"I guess I am here on business and not here to question a client's lifestyle. I would like to get the paperwork finished and then we can close the deal and I will leave you and Kira in peace." Iris says moving a step back against the wall as he steps closer.

"That is your wish? If so the papers were signed upon my arrival home." Martin asks studying Iris' lips as she bites tenderly down on her lower lip.

"By the way, I am sorry about removing the rose from the cabinet where the note was. I know now it was not intended for me and I will give it to Jeeves as soon as I get up to the room to change." Iris attempts to distract his focus on her mouth and step away from him.

Martin leans down and brushes the seat of one of the chairs. He looks up at her with a soft smile and suddenly looks informal and relaxed.

Martin is incredibly attractive and Iris is sure he knows it. He unbuttons his two bottom buttons on his jacket and motions for her to have a seat and join him. Iris sits relieved to see the real Martin emerge.

"Thank you. I know I was a bit harsh on the phone. I find I have little time for games and I guess I probably should work on being more patient with others. Your changes were inserted and the final contracts and whatever displeased you was corrected." Iris says looking at him searching for acceptance of what otherwise is a pathetic apology.

Somehow when Iris looks into his eyes she feels a surge of fear that he is well aware of whom she really is. He knows she isn't sorry. He knows that she would have rather been in

Mexico than spend her time off time kissing his ass. His slow smile tells her she has hid nothing. Iris can feel her heart race and she shifts nervously in the chair to Martin's delight.

"I didn't change the contracts, Iris, since the disappointment in Seattle. I thought you would have noticed that when you were to review them on your ride here. Contracts need constant review or do they not? So much depends on wording and the legal implications." Martin pauses looking at Iris deeper than she thought humanly possible.

Iris licks her lips nervously and he knows. Again, that smile comes across his face.

"Did you read the contracts, Iris?" Martin asks sliding forward in his chair getting ready to stand.

"Read them?" Iris stumbles on the words.

Iris feels like she is on the stand and sworn to tell the truth. All or nothing. Iris takes neither option and out of sheer opposition chooses to squirm out of it by blaming his demanding calls.

"How could I with your interruptions every fifteen minutes?" Iris raises her voice in a defensive tone.

Martin stands up and steps right in front of Iris' feet preventing her from rising and doing the same.

"I hardly was the one throwing tantrums with James about having to finish a job that was yours to begin with. I would think more time would have been yours to read those contracts had you not misspent a majority of it asking Jessi who, what where, when and why I have charms made." Martin says looking down at Iris.

Iris swallows hard and feels the burn of guilt and shame set in. Iris looks at her hands and wonders what she was thinking behaving that way. Iris thinks of everything she said and feels ridiculous. Her nails shimmer in the lights and a thought brings her back. Her hands are that of a 35 year old woman. Iris is not 3 years old. The fire within her starts. James knows it and steps back as Iris stands up a breath away from touching him.

"Excuse me?" Iris snaps looking up at him. "Whatever you overheard or listened to was not an invitation to critique the conversation. Didn't approve of what was said…too bad. I guess we forgot to ask you to participate." Iris finishes walking past him towards the staircase. Iris has a signature on the papers. There is no reason to put up with his delusions of grandeur any longer. Iris starts thinking about late flights going to her Mexican hide away and making a mental note to get Jessi on the phone and book her a seat.

"You are not excused, Iris." Martin calls out making no effort to see up the stair case.

Martin's voice makes Iris' blood boil. She stomps back down the stairs and almost trips pushing the chairs out of the way to get face to face with him.

"You know, Martin, I didn't ask!" Iris yells at him. Martin looks down. He puts his hands in his pants like a man who just lost the game he was sure to win and surprised at the outcome.

"Yes, that is right! I didn't ask your goddamn opinion you self-absorbed son of a bitch! Another thing if this cheap piece of lace you entertained yourself with me wearing gives me a rash you are so done!" Iris yells loud enough for the next floor to hear.

Iris cares less. She hopes Kira is listening and getting a clue. Iris will give her a chance to get off Fantasy Island.

Martin slips his right hand out of his pocket and slowly a giggle begins to escape him. Laughter follows as witness to him laughing right in my face! I am so disgusted I want to smack him.

"Fuck you!" Iris snaps and moves to slap his face.

With unexpected quickness Martin grabs her right wrist in his before she makes contact and spins her around to face the

178

wall. He pins her hand behind her back and pushes her firmly to the cold stone. Iris is caught off guard and gasping at the whole situation.

"You have so much to learn." Martin hisses in Iris' ear squeezing her wrist.

"I know enough to know that you have two choices. Either let go of my wrist and hope I don't call my lawyer or make the biggest mistake of your fucking life and find out just how much of a bitch I can be!" Iris says trying to free her wrist and attempting to kick him at the same time. The stone wall is unforgiving to the sheer dress and her skin. Soon both start to give pissing her off even more.

"It seems so far what has taken place is you attempted to hit me. That is one of the many issues we are going to deal with." Martin growls into Iris' ear bringing up her wrist higher into her back causing Iris to whimper in pain.

"James is expecting me to call anytime announcing the closing. You asshole! Jessi..."Iris gasps unable to finish her sentence because he leans into her with his weight pressing her harder against the wall.

"The only one James is expecting a call from tonight is from me." Martin whispers so close that Iris can feel his lips brush the nape of her neck.

"James will have your ass for this! You'll be lucky if he doesn't hunt you down himself." Iris screams causing him to cover her mouth with his left hand.

"That's wonderful! I haven't seen my brother in a couple weeks." Martin chides in my ear. "Tell me, Iris, how is Kari doing? You really should take some lessons on how a lady should behave from her. After all, James trained her with a very firm hand."

Martin released his hand from Iris' mouth leaving her to collect her thoughts. *What is Martin talking about? His brother? Kari?* Martin's breathing dances across her skin as

Iris searches for what he is meaning. *What the hell do James and Martin's brother have in common?*

Iris remembers a conversation not long ago that she had with James. James had to cancel meetings for a client and Iris offered to do it. Iris was in his office while he took a call from Kari and started to pull up his schedule on the computer. It had a block time of 8 hours duration and reservations to fly out to Phoenix. Iris remembers it was strange since they knew every client and every deal active in each other's day. Iris offered to take the day's schedule for him and bring in Trent from Kansas City to run the office for the day. James refused and told Iris it was a private matter telling Kari that "Big Brother" needed attention at the same time as refusing her help. The name in the files on his computer screen said "M.S. - confidential" and James clicked the screen off as soon as he realized Iris was looking at it. Iris started to relax. *Son of a bitch James!*

"Interesting James doesn't tell you everything isn't it, Iris?" Martin asks feeling Iris soften her resistance.

"Fuck you." Iris says with hurt in her whispered tone. *Why would James not tell me? Worse yet why would he put me in the hands of a sadist like Martin?* Iris contemplates while biting her lip to hold the tears back.

"James did not betray you. It was not important for you to know who I was." Martin says releasing Iris' wrist but making no effort to move back to let her go.

"You are telling me James knows what you are doing to me right now?" Iris asks with her voice on the verge of breaking. Martin runs his fingers softly down Iris' cheek and leans his forehead on her shoulder.

"He knows what you are like and how I am. None of this would be a surprise." Martin whispers in her ear. Iris clenches her jaw and closes her eyes in frustration.

"So, I was sold out as some piece of meat to be wrapped up in a nice little deal and labeled for the boss's brother to do with at his whim? After all can't you find a woman yourself or is that too much work? Not man enough to get your own pussy? James does that too?" Iris spews out in resentment for what they are doing to me.

Martin grabs the back of Iris' neck and holds it firmly. He pulls her from the wall and sits down bringing her over his lap before Iris can comprehend what is taking place. Martin pins his right leg over the back of Iris' thighs so Iris is trapped. Iris feels Martin grab her wrists behind her back before she can think to move.

The air moved quickly with Martin's right hand as Iris felt the first sting of a paddle hitting her ass. The sting was disturbing. First a searing burn across her skin then an itch set in as if blisters were rising instantaneously. Another whack had her screaming. It was no use as swat after swat followed. No matter what Iris said or what she threatened it only encouraged Martin to continue his spanking.

Iris lost count after the 30th swat. Exhausted from crying she finally broke down and begged for mercy. It was then that Martin then stopped and put down the paddle.

Frozen in pain Iris felt Martin's hand slide up her skirt and rip open the seam on the side. Slowly like a child opening a wrapped gift Iris could hear Martin's fulfilled sigh at the treasure he longed to see...her ass covered in welts turning purple from his own hand.

Martin's hand strokes lovingly across both sides of Iris' tender ass. Iris feels the sting subside and the warmth of his hand soothes her to relax. Tears drip from her cheeks and Iris feels as though she is strangely about to succumb to a long awaited deep sleep.

"Yes, you know this is what you need. What you want. Because you didn't ask for it initially doesn't make it wrong. You just didn't know where to find it. It is meant to be. James brought you here to me out of love for both of us, Iris. Search your heart and you will find it is true. No one deceived you. I knew you were the one the first time he mentioned you. He knew it would be hard for you. James knows you so well. Knew what it was that he could not provide for you. He asked me to provide that out of trust and out of love for you. I need it as much as you do." Martin finishes saying while softly stroking Iris' skin.

"Please, I cannot take anymore. I need...." Iris can't finish. Either her mind or her speech fails and nothing comes out.

"As do I, Iris." Martin says then effortlessly stands scooping Iris up and carrying her through a door in the wall Iris did not realize was even there.

Iris feels as if she should surrender. Whatever madness is taking place has her feeling the she should just let it take over. Iris had earned it. Her life passes through her mind. Iris feels redemption for some of the moments and yet a residual guilt for others. *What is this man capable of? Why did James put me here? Is there a grain of reality left in the life that I had known before now?* Iris feels panic set in at the thought that she may just be suffering some sort of break down. In the darkness that greets both of them in the adjoining room Iris finds the courage to speak.

"Hold on! Stop!" Iris demands grabbing furiously at his arms and fighting out of his hold. Iris rolls to the ground with a thud.

"Martin, James was wrong about me and whatever crazy ideas you have ...Well, they are wrong too." Iris says softly as she vows pull herself together.

Iris dusts off her bare ass and tries to gather what is left of the dress as she comes to stand. Iris settles for holding it together with her hand and looks into his eyes. Iris tries to find the sanity she feels he must possess. Either that or he just beat it out her. All Iris is aware of is that it must be lying around somewhere between them. If he thinks he is claiming it after all the hell Iris has had to go through to earn it he is absolutely fucking nuts. That confirms that he and James must be related.

"Martin, really this ends right here. I have to admit that you make it interesting in a painful sort of way. Hell, I am not sure what to think anymore." I say bending down to dust off my knees.

Martin looks at his sleeves and attempts to dust them off unsuccessfully. With an irritated movement he soon has the jacket off. The glitter catches their eyes as a cuff link falls to the ground.

Hoping that they are back to some sort of normalcy, Iris bends over to retrieve it wincing as she comes back up to stand. Martin smiles and retrieves the link from her open hand. Iris smiles back and shake her hair hoping that too will find some respectable shape.

"I am going to forget this happened, okay? I know it is a huge misunderstanding and after I kill James things will be forgiven. Seattle will carry your account and you will be taken care of. Again, after I kill James I will feel much better. I hope you were not too found of him...the son of a bitch!" Iris finishes with harshness in her tone.

Iris turns around and decides this is where she learns to run stairs in stilettos and call it a night. She walks back towards the play room and gets to the opening when it suddenly slams shut almost hitting her in the face. Iris pushes her hands against the door and expects it to give. It doesn't and a sharp chill races up her spine.

"You aren't going to make this easy are you? It was somewhat expected but I must give you credit...I didn't think you would be this difficult." Martin says walking away from her into the darkness. Iris feels like she must be in some awful nightmare and it is about to get worse.

"What the fuck do you think you are doing?" Iris yells

out walking towards the direction of his footsteps.

"You will change that vocabulary if it is the last thing I ever accomplish with you. I will not tolerate it much longer." Martin says from a greater distance than Iris thought he was.

Iris can hear him strike a match on stone and soon the room appears before her eyes. Iris swallows hard at what she sees.

Martin was standing in a far corner of an amazingly large bedroom. Void of windows this room looked like a rustic cellar. Defying its original purpose was a large bed approximately the size of two king size beds. Red velvet covered the bed and black leather made up the head board. A swing dangled from the ceiling with various chains and restraints. Iris took a deep breath in. She bravely proceeded towards the middle of the room.

Martin's gaze warms her as she scans the room for an exit door. Iris feels her pulse race as none are to be found. Her palms get clammy and she rubs them together without realizing all the messages she is giving Martin.

Iris looks up at the unique height of the ceiling. It is as if a middle level of the mansion was eliminated to get the effect. The swing is dangling from an elaborate suspension device and it is up so high Iris gasps.

"Afraid of heights, Iris?" Martin asks as he proceeds to light candelabras on the wall next to him.

Iris walks back towards the area she entered the room at. Before Iris turns she catches Martin pushing something next to the last candle on the wall and can hear the wall close up the space.

Iris walks quickly to where she thought the opening should be and runs her hands over it expecting to find a crack or seam where it should be. Nothing is revealed except, of course, Martin's pleasure that Iris is on the defense and losing ground quickly once again.

Iris gathers her thoughts. She knows this is going to be her game to lose if she doesn't play it right. It is all about strategy.

Iris closes her eyes and leaves her hands on the wall. Every sharp thorn that protrudes from the stone taunts her to fight. Iris knows she can do anything she chooses. Making it through this is just another test. Iris will not fail. It is not in her. Iris has nothing to fear except failure.

Iris plays the affirmations over in her mind. *I must take control...set the limits. Maintain my composure. That is what unsettles him most. Keep Martin on his guard.* Iris' eyes open with a determination the twinkles at him as she turns around.

Martin stands comfortably a few feet from Iris with his hands resting his pockets. The candles have been lit and the room sparkles. Iris looks at him and stares into his eyes. He knows she is ready to fight and win.

Again, the smile spreads across Martin's lips. Iris keeps expressionless. She decides that it is time to see what he has in mind.

"You never answered me, Iris." Martin reminds her as Iris walks past him to look at the book shelf against the wall to her right.

"No I didn't." Iris responds skimming the titles of various literature classics. His taste is impressive...or maybe it is Kira's.

"And?" Martin persists. Iris sees his need to know her fears for useful leverage or bargaining chips. Oldest strategy in the business world. He should know she is smarter than that.

"And I didn't tell you." Iris says flatly and disinterested as she pulls out a copy of Shakespeare's Sonnets.

Martin looks at Iris with a smile that exudes confidence yet soothes any fear of ill mannered intention. Iris looks at his face as he walks toward her.

Martin is so sensual in his expressions. It is also

185

something he is quite aware of. It catches every woman off guard. Another of his tactics to get what he wants.

Iris takes in the sight of him approaching her with all the confidence in the world. His dark hair is complimented by the silver richness of a distinguished gentleman. His eyes are so deep and passionate when he sets his gaze upon her she feels obligated to look downward but refrains from doing so.

This man can see into the deepest and most intimate corners of Iris' soul. It is then that an unexpected shiver inches its way up her spine. Iris inhales then exhales deeply without realizing it.

"You didn't have to." Martin says softly breaking the silence. Iris looks up at him because she knows she insults both of them if she doesn't.

"This is just not going to happen. Whatever you have planned or James thought I was or whatever I led you to think or…" Iris pauses and tries to organize a rational sentence. Iris takes in another breath hoping a world of strength and courage come with it.

"Trust me; I am so not this way." Iris says with little conviction in her tone.

Martin reaches out and takes her fingertips into his hand. With the other hand he covers them tenderly.

"I am listening." Martin assures her while looking down at their hands.

"I hate being told what to do. I am not one to sit and wait for anything. I am certainly not going to be anything more than some rich man's chew toy or pocket pussy when he has limited time for a real relationship!" Iris says raising her voice out of frustration and denial.

Martin's hands press together quickly causing Iris to attempt to take her hand back but she can't. Iris raises her free hand to strike him and his speed in retaining is consistent once again. Iris raises her other hand to pull it from his grasp and she scratches the left side of his face in the attempt.

Iris sees Martin's jaw clench and the fire rise in his eyes as he looks down at her. Iris slaps Martin's face quickly and the sound echoes in the room. Martin closes his eyes in a meditative second then looks down at Iris.

"Get the fuck away from me!" Iris hisses up at him.

Iris kicks Martin in the shin and breaks her heel in the attempt to impale his toes with the three inch spike as it comes down.

"Classical, now!" Martin yells as he bends down to what Iris assumed was a good shot from her.

Iris thinks of how odd that sounds to yell "classical" when someone kicks you in the shin. She begins to laugh at the unexpected reaction when she feels her body rising into the air. At the same moment Chopin fills the room.

Iris thinks it must be Nocturne in B flat minor when she is tossed over his shoulder with a force that nearly knocks the wind out of her. Before Iris can dig her nails deep into his back Martin grabs back and takes her wrists roughly into his grip. Trying to kick him proves ineffective when he grabs into the backs of her thighs with fingers that feel like daggers. Iris yelps and Martin only squeezes harder.

Iris watches as the bookcase quickly fades away while Martin carries her to the bed. In the blink of her eyes, Iris finds herself once again over his lap restrained to perfection. Iris tries to bite his leg but Martin is prepared and grabs her hair and pulling her face to lie sideways looking out at the room. It is then that Iris notices a mirror resting against a chair on the floor. Iris blinks to see what is reflected.

Iris sees Martin looking at me in the mirror.

"You are not this way? Interesting." Martin says firmly. "Then how do explain yourself, Iris? I see you lying over my lap. Your bare skin wearing my marks. Your face is red at the thought of wanting more but afraid to ask. I even feel your heart beating to the tempo that moves above us. It is all purely natural."

Iris looks at herself exposed over Martin's lap. His eyes meet hers in the mirror. She watches as he pins her legs under his right thigh while he uses his right hand and rips the remainder of her dress from her body without even moving her. Martin calls out for a left light and soon Iris feels a spot light above her heat her bare skin. Iris squints to focus and the reflection of the two of them on the bed appears.

Martin leans and slides open a drawer. Iris squirms as he pulls out a leather paddle with holes in it. He holds it up and rotates it for her to appreciate.

"When I get up I am gonna kick your ass!" Iris snaps and wiggles to get free.

"You like that one? I consider it a favorite." Martin says with a smirk.

"Fuck you!" Iris yells so loud that she can feel the veins in her neck bulge.

"I do think that there is one that you will like and it is perfect for this special occasion." He says ignoring her attempt to anger him.

Martin slides Iris' body back and pins her arms under his left leg while quickly using his hands to put something in front of her face. In the quick movement Iris almost misses what he has in his hands. It is a leather strap with a rubber ball in the middle.

Iris is witness to her baffled expression disappearing as Martin shoves the ball into her mouth and buckles the strap in the back of her head. Iris immediately tries to push the ball out from her bite with her tongue but it is futile. In seconds Martin has leaned over twice more and her wrists are cuffed together. Iris can't help but look at her predicament facing her in the mirror. Naked, lying across Martin's lap, gagged and her wrists tightly cuffed together. For some reason Iris feels the disturbing warmth between her legs build.

Iris watches in the mirror as she tries everything to communicate with her body not to deceive her. Her nipples harden at the warmth of his thighs under them.

It is then that Martin moves his legs slightly farther apart and discovers what Iris wanted to hide. His hand slides under and finds its way between his stomach and her left side. His bare hand cups her left breast and Iris closes her eyes to flee his expression. Iris peeks out and can see his eyes studying the two of them together.

Martin pinches Iris' nipple causing her eyes to roll back. He smiles as his right hand makes its way over her lower back and rest upon her ass. Iris tries to wiggle but only gives Martin the opportunity to slide his left hand under to reach her pussy.

Iris moans and whimpers despite the gag and even shakes her head. With a lightening quick movement her ass is displaying a red impression with white dots from the paddle. Iris tries to move off Martin's lap and is suddenly aware his fingers are anchoring down her pussy.

Iris' eyes widen and Martin probes his fingers deeper licking his lips as he waits for her reaction. Again her skin sears in pain and another mark appears. Iris feels electricity speed through her nerve endings and her mind begins floating between pain and pleasure.

Each swat shifts Iris' level of consciousness. Martin leans his face down and blows softly across her ass. Iris feels his thumb rub her clit and she moans deep. Another swat rams his fingers deeper and soon his pinky finds her tight ass. Iris feels everything become unimportant but the movement of his fingers.

Iris waits counting the seconds for the next swat. She watches intently in the mirror. Her eyes beg for another. He refuses with his. Iris feel Martin's cock start to tap at her belly as his hands move in her. Iris arches her back to curl against him so her tits come to view.

Iris watches as Martin's left hand works her cunt and his skilled thumb plays her clit like a miniature drum. He unfastens the gag and tosses it to the side.

"Oh please... Martin." Iris moans out loud at feeling consumed by his hands. Iris feels like she is going to explode and leave nothing behind.

"Ask for permission to cum." Martin hisses in her ear as Iris moves erratically on his hand. He pulls her hair to get her attention.

"Please, Martin, fuck me." Iris whines as Martin stops all movement of his hands in protest.

"Ask for permission to cum." Martin says impatiently as he begins his stimulating assault upon her clit.

"Please, can I have permission to cum?" Iris begs as she grinds into his hand.

"Yes, you may." Martin permits as he slides a second finger in Iris' ass and pushes hard on her clit.

"Ohhh God!" Iris calls out feeling the release is near. Martin grabs Iris' hair pulling her to look at him.

Look at me when you cum." Martin demands then leans over and bites her nipple painfully causing her to scream out in mind bending pleasure.

Iris feels Martin's hands pull harder at her hair and it is all she can take. Her body is ready to surrender to his hands.

Iris arches her back and in the farthest reaches of her senses Iris can hear Martin calling her name to look at him. With all the strength Iris can find to obey, she works to focus on his eyes. The wave's crash through her body slamming every nerve ending against her wall of doubt and denial breaking her free from the prison within her.

Martin's fingers tear at Iris inside and she shakes and convulses around them in release. With Chopin serenading in the background he holds her face still as she surrenders into his

190

eyes. Iris begins crying in abandon as Martin leans his face down so his mouth lovingly covers hers. It is then that Iris tastes his need with her own and accepts the longing within her to meet it.

It took a lifetime to arrive to this point. Two in fact Martin notes quietly while looking out the window of his private study. The waiting for the moment to present itself was one of the hardest things he has to do. All that time waiting in a distance while everything fell into place.

Martin wonders if Iris will ever know what this means to him. Will she accept what he knows is there or will she run? He can't keep her prisoner forever. To have her completely he must have her willingly.

Martin changes his focus to admiring his beautiful gardens. Such a contrast from the desert is the elaborate multi-level pool complete with a water fall. He remembers the difficulty in finding the one who is responsible for maintaining it as well as the exotic plants he brought back from various business trips overseas.

While stopping in a deli in Manhattan for a last minute attempt at lunch Martin happened into a conversation involving a hostess and a gray haired man. The gentleman spoke with a heavy French accent and was quite animated with his hands as he explained how to prune a rose bush just right. What was lost in his pronunciation was communicated clearly in his fingers dancing in the air.

A glance over to the greenhouse has Martin receiving a wave up from the slow moving Claude making his way to the main house for the night. Martin returns the gesture and silently bids him a goodnight.

Martin turns to face his desk and as soon his eyes fall upon the phone it rings. Looking at his watch he realizes he was expecting the call earlier. Martin clicks on the intercom connection and sits back in his chair.

"I know it's later than you expected but the dinner party took longer than I thought. Is she still there?" The tired voice asks in a whisper.

"Yes, sleeping right now actually." Martin says with relief.

"Safe to ask if she has calmed down?" James asks nervously lighting his cigarette.

"Yes, for now. I am waiting for that to change again. She is going to take some work, seriously. I am going to have fun trying to explain the scratches on my face next week when I go to the meeting in Denver." Martin says touching his cheek and wincing when the salt stings from his fingertips.

"Somehow that does not surprise me. She can be so obstinate I would like to take her over my knee myself! I don't think that will ever change." James says taking a long drag from his cigarette.

"It will change. Her tenacity is strength but her lack of discipline is in great need." Martin says purposefully. "I want this to be clear. What if this back fires? It could get very ugly. If we did make an error in judgment in this we could both be losing everything. She is not stupid." James says nervously and taking another inhale of an unsatisfying habit.

"Relax, James, she definitely came here thinking she had the upper hand even down to ignoring the chosen clothing. I sent her back to change and she did. She could have walked out but she chose to stay and return wearing what I had ready on her bed." Martin says positively.

"That says something alright. She wouldn't be afraid to tell you to fuck yourself and shove the account that is for sure." James agrees feeling relieved to know she responded as they counted on.

"Actually Iris did say that and more, but good thing I don't take no for an answer very often. The fact she tested the waters with Kira and it was reported that the pool was warm and inviting to the touch was not exactly what I planned on." Martin adds with frustration.

"What? Iris and Kira? She met Kira? Tell me Kira was in street clothes." James says sounded more worried.

"Of course not. Listen, Iris needs to see the reality of things from the beginning. How am I going to have her take things seriously if they are hidden?" Martin asks James matter of fact manner.

"True. Kira just can be quite a lot to take in." James comments remembering Kari meeting her for the first time.

A very tense meeting and the playtime intended for the two women proved less than compatible.

"I happen to favor her formal approach to service. True Kari has an elegance all her own but I wish to have the same presentation from Iris that I trained Kira with." Martin responds respectfully.

"She serves you well. No one can argue that." James agrees putting out his cigarette.

"Yes, Kira does." Martin confirms thoughtfully.

"With that mentioned, Martin, we need to be clear about something." James speaks firmly in a business like tone.

"I am listening." Martin says knowing the tone in James' voice means that he is making a point.

"Iris is not just anyone. Kari and I are concerned if this will be permanent. Kari almost booked a flight out of here tonight to see her. It was not fun trying to reassure her that you were genuine. You know we love her and ..." James pauses thinking of how much he means what he is about to say.

"She *is* special, Martin. Kari loves you but she knows that this is not your average arrangement and her best friend is in the middle. Iris needs permanence. Not for the moment. Forever and ever Amen. Don't offer what you cannot fulfill. That is all I will say and let you go from there." James says with directness that catches Martin's attention.

"Tell Kari to get some rest. You too. Iris has found herself a home. I may need body armor but irregardless of that, Iris is home. I could think of nothing less than sharing a lifetime with her. Only her." Martin says as he shifts in his chair. He knows that with her in the house he should be ready for anything.

"Message sent and received. We will be there Sunday. I have taken Kari's suggestion and sent Jessi on a frequent flyer mile trip to London to organize the office there. She has been told that Iris went to Mexico and will return in a week or two." James informs Martin.

"Good idea. This will take some time." Martin comments and stands up. He can hear Kira walking towards his study.

"Sounds like you have company." James says quickly hearing someone entering the room Martin is in.

"I do. Iris has asked for me. See you Sunday." Martin says ending the call.

Martin turns off the light and walks toward the staircase leading back to the Master bedroom. His thoughts focus on her. How she needs to be challenged. Taking her is not an option. It will have to be when she asks...even begs for it from him. Before he enters the door he takes a moment to prepare himself for whatever waits behind the door. Assuring himself he must be patient, composed and on guard he takes a deep breath and enters.

Iris walks out of the adjacent restroom wet from showering naked and absent of inhibition. Noting that her guard is coming down he feels small gains of his goal.

Iris tosses her hair back and forth running her fingers through them in a casual manner. Looking up at Martin she smiles sarcastically and walks over to the book case. Focusing on the lower shelf titles she pulls out the one she seems to be looking for. Tossing it to Martin she winks and slips into the chair next to the collection of books.

"So, is this what you have in mind?" Iris asks nodding to the book in his hand. He knows she is holding *The Story of O* without looking at it.

"What part?" Martin asks as he puts the book back in its place.

"Keeping me against my will. Let's see, pawning me off to some pathetic bastard who needs to tie someone up and gag them to get off because his cock can't get hard without humiliating some sorry bitch." Iris says with disgust at the idea.

"I'm not going to pawn you off to anyone, Iris. Quite the contrary." Martin answers and goes to where she is sitting.

"Aren't you fucking noble!" Iris snaps standing and pushing herself past Martin. Marching over to the bed she wraps up in one of the sheets and then begins yanking all the bedding to the floor.

"What in the hell are you doing?" Martin yells as he walks over to her.

"Fuck you. Go read a book!" Iris yells in his face. Martin just smirks at her to her irritation. Once again her hand raises and he is ready.

"I will not tolerate your language, tone of voice and most certainly not tolerate you acting like a child and raising a hand to me!" Martin hisses grabbing her hand pinning it behind her back and having her over his lap in the blink of her eyes.

"I will not tell you again. You will learn your place in my presence if that is the only thing you get out of this!" Martin growls grabbing Iris' hair and facing her yet again to look in the mirror.

"Let me go now!" Iris yells trying to get out of his hold.

"When I am finished you will be permitted to leave." Martin hisses in her ear.
"Fuck you!" Iris screams as Martin starts paddling her ass with his hand.

"That is a privilege that you have hardly earned yet."

Martin says calmly as he squeezes her ass with his right hand painfully.

"I will go to hell first!" Iris spits through her tears.

"You will feel like it that is for sure. I guess you will learn the hard way." Martin says grabbing her petite wrists roughly in his right hand holding them high in the middle of her back.

With his left hand Martin grabs Iris' hair and wraps it tight in his fist and pulls her to stand in front of him.

"Okay! I am sorry. Next time I will count. I will make the bed. Whatever it takes." Iris says grasping verbally at any option but the pain she feels in her scalp and arms.

"Instead of feeling guilty or regret for your actions I am holding you accountable and with your skin you shall make amends. From that discomfort that you will appreciate another's that you thoughtlessly or willfully created. This will be your first lesson, Iris." Martin responds leading her roughly to a dangling chain in the middle of the room.

Before Martin releases Iris' hands he takes a small wrist in each of his and raises them quickly upward causing her to stand on her tiptoes. When she becomes aware it is too late.

Iris whines pathetically when she realizes the cuffs have claimed her again. While she stands on her toes Martin looks at the chain giving it a firm tug to assure himself all is secure. It is when her hand indirectly brushes his that the electricity through both of them. Still holding the chain he feels her fingertips wrap around his. Martin looks down and receives the message she longs for him to hear. Have no mercy. Martin pulls his hand from hers. He knows it is time to begin.

"I want you to know that you are my focus. You are safe. I will not pass you on to another at anytime nor expose you in anyway beyond what we agree upon. After we complete the initial training period we will then choose what we will define our relationship as and our future life together. Before any of the above will be topic for conversation we will first address what just took place moments ago." Martin says holding his arm around her.

Sizing up Iris' tapered waist Martin pinches her right nipple with his left hand. Iris yelps and he feels the blood run to his cock as he stands behind her. Slipping it in and taking her would be so easy. The feel of her skin smooth and flawless under his hand sends an abundance of possibilities through his sadistic mind.

Martin steps back and knows that this isn't just any masochist over for playtime. It is the one... it is Iris. Every detail must be perfect.

"My rules are simple. I expect you to follow them in or out of my presence from this moment forward. Be it business, pleasure or otherwise I will expect you to at all times demonstrate a knowledge and discipline that they require. It is because of what we will share and possess together that I will expect nothing but complete obedience in following them." Martin paused cupping her left breast and tilting her chin to look at him.

"I can't..." Iris begins to say but the blow to ass with his bare hand knocks all confusion out of her.

"Ask permission to speak and only..." Martin pauses to swat her numbingly hard to enforce his point. "When I am finished!" ending with a confirming swing of a belt that appears in his right hand.

"Oh fuck!" Iris exclaims dancing on her toes like an uncoordinated nude ballerina with her ass on fire. Martin smirks at the sight.

"Now that you bring it up." Martin comments landing another stinging blow to her skin bringing yet another welt to surface across her firm ass. "I will not tolerate profanity emitted from your lips except with prior permission from me." Martin says swinging yet another strap mark across her crimson ass.

He soon is witness to the "X" complete its pattern across her bottom and it is then that he is pleased.

Iris thinks of screaming but bites her bottom lip instead. The rush of pain trickles from her skin and it is replaces with a disturbing pleasure. A small whip begins to nip her pussy and she looks into Martin's eyes.

Iris realizes she has never felt so alive and completely uninhibited. With the next lashing across her bare tits she feels released. Iris looks up at the ceiling she fears nothing. Nothing that is but the chance that he will not touch her again.

It is from Martin's ceiling that Iris connects with the truth. The knowing that she hungers to be the source of his pleasure the source of easing his pain. In a meditative state Iris focuses on his words to embed the lesson to every part of her. Eternity passes till his whipping stops and he slides his hand across her welted body to soothe her.

"Tell me what you have learned so far, Iris." Martin asks softly stroking her soft cheek.

As he holds her chin and strokes her bottom lip with his thumb he imagines the taste of her...all of her.

"Not counting your swats." Iris whispers tired and subconsciously licking at his thumb.

"Very good. What is the second? Martin asks kissing her neck and sliding his hand tenderly over her raw welted ass. Iris moans instead of answering promptly causing Martin to squeeze so hard she squeals.

"Ask permission to speak and not interrupt you." Iris says painfully.

"Mmm...So pleasing to hear you respond correctly, Iris. Please continue." Martin whispers roughly in her ear stroking her tight body.

Iris imagines Martin standing there behind her without clothing. Erect and firmly built he is while Iris closes her eyes to discontinue the wild thought. Yes, she admits silently that she could worship that part of him alone. Envisioning the taste of him releasing in her mouth leaves her ravenous for him alone. Martin's painful pinch of her nipples sends her further into the pool of need.

"Focus Iris. Answer me now. Rewards for consistency are imaginable." Martin calls her back with a command.

"Not to use profanity." Iris finishes closing her eyes to will the wetness between her legs to stop.

"Very good, Iris," Martin says softly looking into her eyes so deeply that it as if he is truly seeing her for the first time.

"I want you more than words can possibly express. Consuming you…every last part would still be reserving the depths of my need to have you. I have never felt this way in my life. When I walked into the room and you were there that longing I have always carried was absent as soon as I realized you were finally there." Martin says stroking her cheek with a single fingertip. "Now I will have to live through moments of ache, passion, sorrow and joy because you have become a part of my life that I cannot ever do without." He finishes studying her lips thinking of the heaven they could create wrapped around him, feeding from him.

Iris wonders if this is really happening. Could Martin be genuine in his intentions? This life he speaks of that involves her could this be some type of dark and erotic twist of all of her favorite childhood fairy tales in one? Was this the Beast who knew what she needed? Was she to be whisked away from an unappreciative life to live in a haunted castle? A place in which she in turn brings light to and he eventually evolves into a prince from the strength of her love? Will she suddenly feel the complete awakening within with a mere kiss from his lips?

Iris looks into Martin's eyes deeper than she dared to before. She can see it is true. Her Prince Charming has arrived and he intends to grant all of her wishes with the swing of his paddle. Iris looks down knowing that this is the beginning of their ever after.

"Speak freely, Iris, please say whatever you have been refraining from expressing." Martin gently commands Iris knowing there is so much within her that has yet to said.

"I have never conceived this type of relationship. It goes against what I am about. I am everything but submissive, Martin. Ask anyone who knows me." Iris says subtly rubbing her face to her right shoulder to remove a strand of hair near her eye.

Attentively Martin moves it with a delicate sweep of his fingers. Iris smiles appreciatively.

"I am listening. Please continue." Martin prompts her as he stands firmly focused on only her.

"I hate rules. I will bend them and do whatever it takes to be the exception if they stand in my way. I leave relationships for that very reason. I am not content with monotony. I find that is the common result of a permanent commitment. I resent being held back by responsibility. I don't know if James was clear with you on what type of person I am. I can't keep a plant because by the end of the week it needs water. I can be too selfish to even give that." Iris pauses for a moment to see if he wants to add a comment.

Instead of saying anything Martin smiles knowingly.

"You are better off with someone else. Really, as much as this is stimulating I can't see myself living like this all the time. I can't be secluded from my life and my work. I can't wait for someone to return and tell me what is out there. I am the one who needs to find out firsthand. I am not a weak and submissive person, Martin. If you know anything about my professional career that would give you a far different picture than being a woman that allows someone to walk all over her and enjoy it." Iris finishes looking at him regretfully.

Before Iris stands a mesmerizing man strong enough to

be the cortex of her life but Martin instead longs for what she believes she will never be. Once more he smiles with complete understanding of what she has yet to comprehend. Taking her face in his strong hands he studies her.

"I think that you misunderstand the meaning of submissive in the context of this situation, Iris." Martin says letting go of her face.

Iris watches intently as Martin walks over to the wall to her right and kneels down to pick up what she had missed before now. Martin stands and in turning to face Iris the object chosen is revealed. In his hands is an elaborate black leather whip. Not any kind of whip but a bull whip much like the one she watched being demonstrated by an artist on a trip to Spain. Knowing its power and accuracy sends a cold chill of anticipation down Iris' back.

"Does it take a weak person to stand naked with their hands bound in the air to a chain dangling from a ceiling? Is it the timid that look into the eyes of the one holding the instrument intended to make a symphony out of their flesh and their soul demanding nothing less than a chorus of sound from their lips?" Martin steps back slowly distancing himself appropriately from Iris' welted body.

A sigh escapes Martin's lips in appreciation of her flawless beauty before him. The sound seeps through Iris warming her.

"Is it the fearful that embrace the desire to experience the searing sensation of this whip across their body either for pleasure of the one they call Master? Is it a feebleness that brings them to a height of sexual arousal that leaves them begging for another stroke of pain to release the tsunami of ecstasy within?" Martin asks firmly swinging the whip before Iris' feet like a snake taunting her before striking.

"Iris! Answer me now!" Martin barks startling her.

"No!" Iris reacts still watching the bull whip at her feet.

"Exactly. Keep in mind that such a relationship of submission and Dominance is consensual. The submission is an expression of strength and a self awareness few truly obtain. That strength is in every fiber of which you are, Iris. You are fully aware of its presence and yet you are terrified to release it. It is requiring focus and management to be productive and reach it's potential. That is the responsibility I will take in your life." Martin says snapping the whip in the air within inches of her left breast.

Iris feels her nipples instantly become erect in attention. This response confirms he is right and she knows it.

"I..." Iris begins to speak without permission but the crack of the whip millimeters from making contact with her hip halts her words.

"Think for a moment of how it felt to be taken over my knee and paddled for disobedience. The burn of accountability relieving the guilt of inappropriate behavior. I imagine there was a certain sense in pride at taking the punishment. The redemption that followed when the paddle ceased its attack. Difficult to admit you need anything let alone physical discipline as an adult. The self restraint you have exhibited in refraining from speaking unless permitted must be rewarding to you, Iris. I imagine it is a first among many others recently introduced to you." Martin pauses swinging the whip over her head snapping at the chain the keeps her still. "Have you known of these pleasures before?" Martin asks letting the whip settle to the floor.

Iris looks at Martin and he smiles giving her permission to speak freely with a knowing nod of his head her direction.

"I have not." Iris responds admitting that he is not wrong in what he is proposing.

"There is nothing more beautiful than this vision of you before me. Your eyes wild, your body willing, your mind commanding your senses to receive all that I have to offer. Take the time now to reflect and confirm or reject what I have said. True submission is complete. Not a place you visit when you are feeling adventurous, Iris." Martin says as he settles into a relaxed stand with the whip respectful curled at his feet on the ground.

Iris relives the rush of strength from taking Martin's first swats knowing she could endure whatever he chose to do to her. She remembers the ache of him stopping and not bending her over and forcing his cock into virgin ass. The rejection she felt when she was not in accordance of his chosen clothing has her swallow hard.

Tears start forming in her eyes when the realization hits that it is deep in this room she felt invincible. She could walk away and conquer the world. Never has Iris felt as safe as she does bound to the chain in his ceiling.

It is there that Iris realizes that she can smell the flowers in Martin's garden hundreds of yards above outside. She can taste the droplets of water in the air misting from the waterfall above the garden pool. Her senses explode and she knows that he is responsible for the awakening taking place.

"Freely please, Iris." Martin asks her to respond.

"What would it be like if I wanted this too? I have a job. It is everything I dreamed of. I worked my ass off to get where I am in the company. Another thing… I can't share. I am not going to let you beat my ass then take another while I am hanging here watching. I am not going to walk around wondering who you are tying up to the hotel shower rod when you are away for extended periods. I guess I am trying to figure out what you are expecting before I consent or whatever it is." Iris asks shifting on her feet for comfort.

"It is submission, Iris, complete and irreversible submission. You will become mine. Legally, intimately and without restriction of any kind. I will own you because you will submit to me everything about you. To ease your fear of others in my life sexually I will tell you now that I will be monogamous within every sense of your definition. I will be committed to maintaining your comfort, your needs, your growth, your love and your respect. You are to work and travel as you would have before professionally related to business. Any vacation or destinations for pleasure will be with me and of our choosing. You will reside here and this will be our home. You will have freedom to change whatever you want to make it comfortable and personal as long as you ask me first. You will be monogamous as well and not permitted to have sexual contact with others. I know this will be far more difficult for you since Kira will be a constant temptation to you." Martin pauses knowing that Iris will react to his comment.

"What? Listen..." Iris stumbles nervously trying to explain away what she hopes he didn't see.

"Kira is neither bisexual nor interested in me or another man for that matter. I assume you understand what I am saying...Kira is drawn only to women. This arrangement could prove to be interesting on many levels but that is to be addressed at a later time when I have given it more thought and we all can discuss it further together. Kira is very enamored with you, Iris. I will not deny the enjoyment that I felt in watching you with her. I know that it excited you to know I was watching every hot uninhibited moment between the two of you." Martin explains watching Iris blush in embarrassment. "Did you imagine her mouth going down on you? Did you think of what it would feel like if I walked in and dropped my pants and took you from behind? The burn of that tight ass holding my cock inside. So tight it is painful for me to move back out only to push deeper than you thought possible? Iris... did you think of fucking both of us? Is that what you thought about as you came all over Kira's long fingers?" Martin asks coming closer as he finishes he questioning of what Iris was thinking while fucking Kira's hand.

"I was…" Iris says dryly knowing he knew everything that she thought while he watched them play.

"Want to know what I was thinking, Iris? Want to know what I was doing while Kira was working on you?" Martin asks with an assertive tone. He smiles at her restraint to speak.

Slowly rubbing the handle of the bullwhip across Iris' swollen breasts, Martin taunts her skin. She winces in a last effort to hide her reaction to his enjoyment in her liaison with Kira.

Martin knows where to find the truth in every part of Iris and this time is no different. With firm determined fingers he slides two roughly across her clit. Iris moans and Martin pinches it between his fingers causing her to gasp. Savoring her sounds he blows soft warm air into her ear. His strong arm reaches around her and makes its way to her ass. As Martin's fingers lubricate themselves in her wet pussy he continues to speak.

"I stood in the room adjacent to the one you returned to change in. I took slow sips of a favorite chilled Zinfandel thinking that it would be exciting to watch you change. Exciting to both of us because you enjoy thinking that someone is watching you. You finger yourself and climax harder when you fantasize about someone watching you cum. Don't you, Iris?" Martin purrs in her ear and proceeds to tease the opening of her undiscovered ass.

Iris bites her bottom lip hard to contain the squeal of pain building inside.

"I watched only expecting to see your tits or the ass that I planned to use later. As much as that unsettles you to know I planned on having you from the start how about this… the surprise of Kira positioning herself like a cat preparing to attack its prey was only half the treat. Your response was enough to have me put my glass down and lock the door. As Kira squeezed your tits and played with your bare pussy I unfastened my pants. I slid my hand to my cock and…" Martin pauses pulling Iris in tighter to his body. "I wrapped my right hand around it tight. I squeezed it and stroked my hand slowly down to its tip. As I watched Kira lick your juices off her fingers and then share them with you I began pumping my cock hard and fast. I imagined your ass ready like it is now." Martin growls in her ear and sends his fingers painfully into her ass causing her to buck against him to get away from their destination. "Yes, that is how you would react as I slip it in. I constricted my grip to fit the vision of your ass wrapped around it. I thought of Kira getting down on her knees and putting her mouth to your bare pussy. She would be hungry eating you without restraint. I imagined holding your tits in my hands while taking your ass while Kira worked the front of you. I had to brace my hand against the wall while I fucked my hand. Watching you lean back against Kira and cum in spasms had me slamming my cock into my hand against the wall. That knock that separated you two was me jerking off and exploding three feet from where you two were." Martin finishes sending his fingers deeper into her ass. Iris squeaks as he quickly pulls his fingers back out. "Just to let you know it would be your job should you choose this life with me to offer your mouth to clean up or deposit myself in." Martin comments as he steps back from her at a swinging distance. Dripping juices down her thigh say everything to Martin.

"We will begin with two weeks of training and conditioning. You have been put on a working vacation here with me. Your work will be done from here or while traveling with me should I need to fly out for meetings. Jessi has been sent on a two week business trip to Europe to get our London office organized. Nothing will be interrupted and in fact you will find things improve dramatically for you. Anything you need will be acquired and your comfort will be my first priority. James and Kari will arrive on Sunday with your belongings. Don't know if you are aware but this lifestyle is not unique to James. James and Kari represent all that I hope to achieve with you." Martin pauses and swings the whip to bite her feet. Iris jumps and her large breasts are so swollen with excitement they scarcely move.

"I am proposing a lifestyle beyond kink, marriage, Sunday lunches in the garden and a house full of kids. I am offering the idea of ownership and property. Total power exchange in every facet of our lives." Martin looks at her and can see her eyes widen. "Look, I could take you to the movies and pretend a dress fits you perfectly when we both know it makes you look hideously plump. I can wait for several dates before touching your hand. What makes this different is that we know that none of that compares to the sound of your breathing anticipating what will come next. The thrill of searching for that response that sets your skin on fire and has your heart beating for more. I know what I need and you know what I am asking. Sharing life with you and living as one is what I propose with a lifetime journey of discovery, adventure, passion and a serenity that only two lives such as our joining could bring. This is the choice you must make as I can only accept complete submission. I will wait as long as it takes. That is how certain I am of you being the only one for me." Martin ends with a swing of the whip at her hip playfully.

Iris looks down and remains quiet to the point Martin begins to feel concerned.

"Speak freely please, Iris." Martin says hoping that he has not scared her away with too much too soon.

Sensing the moment of truth is about to present itself Martin quickly walks up to Iris and releases the restraints on her wrists. As she looks at him tears swell in her eyes. In nervousness he steps back.

"Could you love me unconditionally even if I fail more often than succeed?" Iris asks softly rolling her shoulders to ease the tight muscles from hanging.

"I have loved you in such a way long before I laid my eyes upon you. I knew you were somewhere and it was only a matter of time." Martin says tenderly watching her tears make their way down her cheeks.

"That is the way I feel as well, Martin." Iris agrees.

Martin walks over to the key pad on the wall and enters the code causing the door to open.

"There is no turning back, Iris." Martin comments walking back to face her. "This will be permanent." Martin ends with a nod to the open doorway.

Iris leans her ear to one shoulder then the same movement to stretch the other side of her neck. She looks at the doorway and hears early morning chatter of workers getting breakfast started. Iris shakes her arms as if she is preparing for a world record sprint time.

Martin feels his heart begin to sink slowly. It is after Iris hears the whispered prayer under his breath that she slowly squats down. As he expects her to run he turns so he doesn't have to face the reality he can't accept… life without her.

With the grace of a cat grabbing for the ribbon dangled above her, Iris leaps into the air and claims the chain with enthusiasm. The rattle of her wrapping her hands in it causes Martin to spin around. There before him she dangles by choice with the door wide open in the background.

"I have only one question." Iris says with a smirk.

"What is that?" Martin asks squeezing the handle of the bullwhip confidently in his right hand.

"Do you really know how to use that thing or it is something you want me to teach you? I have been to Spain. Took a couple lessons." Iris says playfully taunting Martin.

"Secure!" Martins commands the door to close.

"I guess I will have to remember that one." Iris says

playfully.

"Tell me what you want, Iris." Martin asks looking at her with passion.

"To be taken, to be claimed and consumed as yours. Completely and without reservation." Iris responds shifting her weight to be more comfortable gripping the chains.

"Are you offering your submission, Iris?" Martin asks looking in her eyes.

"I am. Now if you don't mind I am starving and haven't had anything to eat since yesterday. This seems pointless to watch a guy pretend he knows what to do with a bullwhip." Iris chides Martin knowing he will not tolerate it.

Martin feels his blood race to his hands and begins swinging the whip gradually getting height as it sweeps the air beneath her toes.

"I accept." Martin says with an energy Iris never imagined in a man.

With the sound of air splitting around Iris even her intuitiveness was not enough to warn her that he knew exactly what he was doing. The slice of leather finding the second layer of her skin confirmed the lesson and christened the moment of Iris submitting herself to Martin's ownership.

# Service Call

It couldn't get any hotter. That is what the two girls thought as they listened to the air conditioner sputter as it started to die. Samantha looked across the room at Melanie.

"Shit, I think its dead." she said, slowly getting up and heading for the kitchen.

"Are you going for some more ice?" Melanie asked, unable to move from her spot on the couch.

"I'll just bring the cooler in here." Samantha said, dragging the large cooler full of beer and ice into the living room. She adjusted the fan so it would blow on the couch and sat down next to her room mate. It had been a hot week, and the girls had called two days ago for service on their air conditioner. They were told they would be put on the list, but that with the extreme heat it would be a while. Samantha sat down next to Melanie and handed her a beer. Some ice that clung to the can dropped onto Melanie and landed on her chest, dripping down between her breasts.

"Ohhh." Melanie moaned with delight.

"Like that?" Samantha asked, grinning. Melanie responded by scooping up an ice cube and running it over Samantha's neck and down her chest. Samantha shivered as the cold water dripped down into her tank top. Melanie reached for another ice cube from the cooler, but was interrupted by the sound of her cell phone ringing.

"I hope this is good news." she said, answering the phone.

"This is Paul from A-1 Heating and Cooling. I'm about one block from your house."

"We thought you would never make it!" Melanie purred into the phone. She hung up and told Samantha that help was on the way.

"I don't believe it." Samantha said. "Just get me another ice cube."

Melanie took a dripping cube and giggled as she ran it up her friend's leg and under her shorts. Samantha jumped and shivered. She grabbed a hand full of ice and water and dumped it down Melanie's shirt. Melanie jumped up and grinned at her friend. She slowly pulled off her tank top, revealing her firm breasts and rubbed the cold water over her nipples. She took her shorts off and was soon naked standing in front of Samantha. She got on her knees and pulled at Samantha's shorts. She slid them of while Samantha pulled her shirt off. Melanie took another ice cube and slides it up between Samantha's legs, rubbing it on her pussy. Samantha squirmed as Melanie slid the cube into her wet pussy. She spread her legs apart and pulled Melanie's head into her. Melanie started licking as Samantha ran her hands through her hair, pulling her deeper into her wetness.

"Lick harder. God, that feels so good!" Samantha screamed. Melanie responded with muffled moans as she licked furiously. Soon Samantha was cumming hard, soaking her friends face. She pushed Melanie onto the carpet, and climbed over her, with her pussy directly over Melanie's face. Samantha started licking Melanie's pussy. She felt her ass being pulled down and soon felt a tongue licking her again. She felt goose bumps all over her body and her nipples were hard. It occurred to her that there was cold air blowing on them from the vent in the wall.

"Excuse me." A man's voice said. "No one answered so I came in to adjust the thermostat.

Melanie and Samantha both turned their heads to see the young service tech standing there in a tight t-shirt, covered in sweat from working in the heat all day. Neither girl knew quite what to say.

"Hi, I'm Paul." he said, grinning. "Looks like you too are in a little trouble." He started walking towards the girls. He swatted Samantha on the ass hard, causing her to shriek.

"You'd better get busy." Paul said. He grabbed her hair and pushed her face down into Melanie's pussy again. Samantha started licking again, and Melanie watched as Paul undressed, revealing a tight body and a large hard cock. Paul moved in behind Samantha and got on his knees. Melanie lifted her head to lick his balls. He guided his cock into her mouth and she sucked hungrily. He pulled it out and suddenly shoved it into Samantha's pussy. She jumped and moaned into Melanie's wet cunt. He started fucking her hard, while Melanie licked his balls. Soon the three of them were fucking in unison, all sweating despite the cold air now pouring into the room.

"Ohhh….fuuuuck!" Melanie started to scream as she felt the waves of an orgasm building. This made Samantha lick harder, pushing her friend over the edge. Melanie started shaking from the orgasm hitting her. Paul was not far behind, and the sounds of Melanie beneath him soon had him shooting into Samantha. He held her hips as he pushed into her. Exhausted, he slowly pulled out.

"Hey, what about me?" Samantha asked, looking back at him. Paul pulled her down onto Melanie's face.

"Start licking." He said to Melanie. "I'm going to fuck you now."

Paul watched as Samantha started grinding on Melanie's face. His cum was dripping from her pussy, and Melanie was licking it up as fast as she could. He moved around between her legs, stroking his cock. Watching the girls, it didn't take long for him to be hard enough to fuck again. He slid into Melanie's pussy and started slowly fucking her, while kissing Samantha. She continued to grind her pussy on Melanie's face and was soon cumming.

"Fuck! That is so good. Keep licking bitch!" Samantha screamed. When the orgasm subsided she slid off so she could watch Paul fucking Melanie. Paul leaned down and soon her tongue was darting in his mouth. He could taste Samantha's juices in her mouth, as well as his own cum. Soon he was shooting again as he sucked on her tongue. He pulled out and walked over to Samantha, who was sitting on the couch. He grabbed her head and pulled it onto his cock.

"Lick it clean." he said, and she readily obeyed. When she was done, he pulled her onto the floor. He pushed her face between Melanie's legs.

"Now, clean her pussy too." he ordered, slapping her on the ass. She jumped, then started licking the cum from Melanie's pussy.

Paul got dressed and picked up his tool belt. He smiled as he watched the too girls squirming on the floor. Melanie had her eyes closed, moaning softly while Samantha worked on her again. She opened her eyes when she heard a door close.

"Sam, he's gone." she said, pushing herself up onto her elbows.

"Damn, that's too bad." Samantha said, looking up at Melanie. "That was the best service we've ever gotten."

# The Gift

The phone rang and Jen ran to get it. It was Julie, a close friend who she and her husband simply called "Madame".

"Jen, I just got the gift that you and Tom sent. It is absolutely wonderful! I really can't believe you found a first edition copy!" Madame said cheerfully.

"It was Tom's idea. He is always looking through your book collection when we are at your house." Jen said.

"Come over this evening around seven. I have something for the two of you." Madame said.

Madame was a lifestyle mistress. She was a wicked dominant who was skilled with a whip. Tom and Jen were also both dominants. They were unusual in that they were happy together, even though they were not exactly compatible in certain aspects. Tom and Jen spent many hours with Madame at her lavish house. She allowed them to use her submissives, and taught them many things about being a proper Mistress and Master. They had become skilled in erotic torture, and did sometimes top each other, but they longed to find someone they could own.

"Tom, Madame wants us to come over at seven." Jen said to her husband who was just getting out of the shower. She was tempted to push him back in and join him, but they didn't have much time so she got ready. She put on her favorite corset, leather skirt and black stiletto heels. When they were ready they headed to Madame's house. They knocked on her door and she greeted both with a kiss.

"Welcome and thank you both again for the wonderful present." She said, leading them into the main room. "I got you something absolutely delicious and thought tonight might be the perfect night to give it to you."

214

"You don't have to get us anything." Tom said.

"Oh, but you will like this, I promise." Madame said with an evil grin.

They went and sat down and were served wine by one of her girls. The petite blonde dressed properly in a maids uniform served them then bowed before she left the room. Jen remembered the last time they were here she had that girl bent over and screaming while she whipped her. The three of them made small talk for a few minutes, enjoying the wine and the warmth from the fireplace. Finally Madame stood up.

"Come with me. Time for you to get your gift." She said, motioning for them to join her. She walked down the hall to her "playroom" as she called it, although it looked more like a medieval dungeon. She unlocked the door and led them in. The room was lit with only candles and a small fire in the fireplace. Tom and Jen saw a brunette lying on the floor. She was naked, gagged, and her wrists and ankles were chained together. She had a big red bow wrapped around her.

"This is your gift. I hope you enjoy it." Madame said. She walked over to the woman on the floor and knelt down next to her. She removed the gag from her mouth.

"You are my slave. I own you. You are my property to do with as I please." She said to her.

"Yes Mistress." The bound woman replied.

"You have no objections to this arrangement?" Madame asked her. "Speak freely girl!"

"Ma'am, I am only your property. I will always be a slave. I am yours to do with as you wish." The captive woman spoke.

Madame replaces the gag and went to sit in her chair by the wall.

"Do what you want with this slave. I am just going to sit and watch you enjoy your gift." Madame said to them, smiling.

Tom and Jen smiled at each other. They walked over to

the woman tied on the floor. Jen pulled the ribbon off while Tom started taking his clothes off. Tom kneeled down next to her and unchained her ankles, but left her wrists behind her back. His hands ran over her body and she shivered from his touch. Jen was now standing there in only her corset and heels. She took one of the candles and held it over the woman that Tom was holding. He held her thighs so her legs were spread apart. Jen started letting the wax drip, first on her chest, then her nipples. The captive slave jumped as the hot wax hit her. Jen moved it so the wax was on her stomach. She brought it closer so the wax would be hotter when it hit her. She dripped it close to her pussy. The woman writhed in pain and moaned around her gag. Jen smiled and dripped wax on the shaved pussy that was glistening in the candlelight. The slave jumped as it hit her tender pussy.

"Let's fuck her." Jen said.

Tom took some cushions and arranged them on the floor. He lay back on them and watched as Jen helped the slave to her feet. Her wrists were still bound, and the gag was tight in her mouth. Jen positioned her over Tom and slowly pushed her down. Tom guided his large cock into the dripping cunt.

"Oh, that's tight." He said, sliding in.

"I have not allowed that cunt to be fucked. I was saving her for you." Madame said from her chair.

"I want to fuck her too." Jen said, strapping on a large dildo. She took some lube and stroked her rubber cock. Tom had his hands on the slave's shoulders, moving her on his cock. Jen got behind her and slid a finger in the slave's tight ass. She jumped when Jen invaded her there. Jen got down on her knees and positioned herself behind her. She pushed the large rubber cock against the slave's tight hole and pushed in. She screamed around her gag as Jen penetrated her. Soon Tom and Jen were fucking her in rhythm. Madame watched and slid her hand under her dress. Soon she was fingering herself while she

216

watched her friends use the bound slave.

"What a nasty little slut." Jen said, ramming into her ass. She looked at Tom and could tell he was about to cum. He thrust up hard and filled the pussy he was fucking. Jen stopped and undid the strap on cock and left it in the slave's ass. She pulled her back and undid her gag.

"Clean Master." She barked at her.

"Yes Mistress." The slave answered. Jen guided her mouth onto Tom's still hard cock that was covered with her juices and his cum. She sucked and licked him clean. When she was done, Jen took Tom's place on the cushions. She pulled the slaves face to her cunt and had her lick her to orgasm.

"What do you think?" Madame asked Tom, who was standing by her watching his wife moan.

"Very nice. Thank you." He said, picking up a flogger.

"Now, save something for later. You have plenty of time to whip her when you get her home." Madame said, grinning.

"Home?" Tom asked her.

"This is your gift. Not just to use tonight, but to keep. I am giving this little slut to you. I have worked hard training her for you and Jen." Madame said to him. "I will send her cage along when you leave."

Jen was cumming in waves, and screaming at the slave that was eating her pussy. She collapsed and pushed the bound woman away.

"If you are ready, we can proceed." Madame said, standing up. "Let's make this official."

Madame turned on a dim light which revealed her large St. Andrews cross. She took the slave and led her to it. She released her wrists long enough to chain them to the cross. She did the same with her ankles, and then replaced the ball gag in her mouth. When she was satisfied the slave was tightly secured, she walked over to a cabinet and opened it. She pulled out a long thin metal shaft with a handle and something on the end. The slave moaned when she saw it. She knew exactly what it was. Madame took it and placed one end in the fireplace.

"I had the iron made just for you." She said to Tom and Jen.

"You are going to brand her for us?" Jen asked, smiling.

"Of course. Your property should be marked." Madame said, getting things ready. She prepared the inner thigh of the bound slave. The slave shook with fear. She had heard from others of the pain of being branded. Tom and Jen sat and watched while Madame went and got the hot iron. Madame was an expert at branding, and did many ceremonies for other dominants.

"Come place your hands on your property while I mark her so you can feel her squirm." Madame said, getting ready to put the brand on her. Tom and Jen stood up and walked over to the cross. They held her shaking body, smiling at each other. The iron was inches from her flesh and the slave started screaming around her gag.

"Hold her!" Madame shouted. The hot iron hit her skin. She held it there for just an instant then pulled it away. She immediately put something over it. The slave was shaking and crying.

"All done. I will give you instructions on how to care for her brand so it heals properly." Madame said, putting things away. The slave was still moaning from the pain as she was released. Madame hooked a leash to her collar and handed it to Jen.

"You can pick up her cage tomorrow, but for now you can use these." Madame said, handing some cuffs and chains to Tom. They led their slave out to their car and put her in the backseat. They thanked their friend again for the gift and headed home. Jen looked in the back of the car to see their shackled and branded gift.

They arrived home and took her into the house. She was

still naked, except for the collar around her neck and the cuffs that chained her wrists and ankles together. She was led to their bedroom. Tom undid the chains long enough to attach her wrist cuffs and ankle cuffs. Jen was undressing while Tom secured their slave. Soon Tom had joined her on the bed and they were wrapped around each other. Tom had his head between Jens legs and his cock was deep in her mouth. The bound woman on the floor watched and squirmed, wishing she was in the middle of them. She watched as Tom started to jerk and moan. He filled Jens mouth and Jen shook over him as she tasted his cum. She crawled off of Tom and onto the floor. She ran her fingers through the slave's hair and pulled her mouth to hers. She kissed her and let Tom's cum flow into the slave's waiting mouth. The bound slave sucked and licked to get every drop from Jen. Jen stood up and looked down at her. She was chained, branded and had cum dripping from her lips.

What a perfect gift she thought to herself as she climbed back into bed next to Tom.

# Rachel

A late night run through the park after work had Rachel out in the grounds routinely five nights a week. She sat on the grass letting the cool night breeze soothe her. It was far more peaceful than listening to pages turn and Chris bitch about the lack of content in the midterm reports from his students.

It didn't take long for something to catch Rachel's eye. There was a model apartment that the property manager showed prospective tenants that had its lights on. Initially Rachel was thinking someone forgot to shut them off and thought nothing of it until she spotted shadows walking into the model bedroom. In the dark Rachel was not able to be seen so she thought it was worth keeping an eye out to see what would transpire. Besides, Chris wouldn't be done with the students papers till well after midnight.

Inside Rachel clearly saw the two people emerge into full view of the bedroom French doors. A woman with black long hair walked in pulling a tank top over her head at the same time as a man followed behind. Rachel scooted over a little to the right of the tree trunk to get a better view. It was then that she recognized the man as the lead maintenance man for the complex.

About 40 with a toned body, the guy and his California surfer looks was a female tenant's fantasy. Rachel couldn't believe it when he followed the voluptuous black haired woman's lead by pulling off his shirt and literally jumping out of his pants. They began to kiss as Rachel sat under the tree speechless. She swallowed hard as her heart started racing. She couldn't believe what she was seeing and what she knew she shouldn't be watching. It certainly was more exciting than watching Chris correct papers.

Rachel was just about to crawl away out of guilt when the black haired woman pulled away from the maintenance man and pushed down on his shoulders, sending him to his knees in front of her. As the woman licked her full lips and tossed her head back Rachel made a choice to stay put. She never was into voyeurism or even watching porn, but this whole scene involving two beautiful people had her intrigued.

The man slid his hands up the raven haired beauty's thighs until his fingers reached her smooth center. Her hands slid over her firm belly and up to her large heavy breasts. Rachel's mouth was dry and she swallowed in anticipation of what would happen next.

Without wasting time the guy spread apart her pink folds and started working her opening like a flavorful portion of juicy ripe fruit. With his left hand he pulled her right leg over his shoulder. Soon he was sucking and nibbling his way from her delicate bud to her tender backside. Rachel watched her with fascination as the woman pulled and twisted her pink peaks with her right hand. Her left hand kept his head busy with a hand full of his hair as she grinded her pelvis into his face harder and faster setting her own tempo. Rachel was in awe of this woman's assertive approach with her lover.

Rachel felt her own body start reacting each time the woman dipped her hips into his face. In slow strokes she rode taking her time to hold still when he would focus on her swelling pearl of pink flesh. The raven haired woman leaned back and jerked involuntarily when he nibbled her bud out of the protection of its hood.

Rachel licked her lips slowly imagining how sweet the woman's silky folds must taste in his mouth. She could can almost feel the top of his ambitious tongue poking deep inside her. Her own juices started to seep between her legs. The dark haired woman picks up her pace and grinds roughly into his open mouth. His chin glistens from her sliding across his jaw while he takes a moment to smile at his effect on the woman above him. Rachel's hand instinctively found its way between her own thighs when it became too much to just watch.

Chris looked up from the paper to take a break from the opinions of another journalism major. Two thirds of the papers he has reviewed wouldn't make the local high school bulletin. Chris tosses the papers down, covers his face and moans out in sheer boredom. Nights like this had him cursing his choice of professions.

Rubbing his eyes with his large hands, Chris wonders how long Rachel will run this time. It's dark and it's late but that never stopped her. She knows how much it irritates him that she waits until late evening to do it. Chris sighs knowing that the papers in front of him and the frustration it stirs within him during midterms is the reason she does it. He didn't blame her at all.

Walking through the dimly lit grounds Chris makes his way past the pool area and can see the mailbox wall in the distance. Noticing all the apartment lights off or a flickering blue light from a television left on, Chris wonders where the hell she is so damn late at night. Some nights he is afraid to know.

Scanning the grounds quickly for a sign on Rachel, Chris spots the model apartment's lights on and the movement of people inside catches his eye. Looking down at his watch he realizes it is nearly 11 p.m. Probably some painters he dismisses moving quietly along the sidewalk towards the mailboxes. Thinking of Rachel he looks back towards the model apartment and that is when he first hears the sound.

It is soft but familiar as Chris walks slowly towards its direction. Stepping back towards the hedges that run outside the property line Chris gets a closer look at where the sound is coming from under a tree that stands alone in the dark. Chris rubs his eyes to see what is the source of the shadow moving on the ground below it. Creeping a little closer to finally make out the shadow clearly Chris is stunned. It is Rachel.

Just as Chris is about to make a move to come to her rescue he realizes she is perfectly fine except that one hand is in her shorts and the other is fondling her bare breasts since her tank top is hiked up over her chest to give her easier access. Chris swallows hard shocked at what is a matter of three yards in front of him. His wife was playing with herself right out in the open. Hell, he had never even seen her do it in the privacy of their own bedroom. *So, is this how she gets her exercise?*

Rachel with her legs spread open is obviously playing with her clit between her legs. Her left hand is pinching and squeezing her nipples so rough Chris winces at what she is doing. Trying to digest just what Rachel is doing on the lawn late at night would be enough but Chris soon realizes why she is getting herself off.

Looking over at the window of the model apartment, he can make out clearly that there is a couple. He is sitting on the corner edge of the bed and she is straddling him, riding him as if she just may win the Kentucky Derby if she bounces a little faster. The lucky bastard takes a mouthful of her gorgeous mounds and sucks so hard that she tries to pull his head away. Chris looks over at Rachel and her hand works faster in her shorts.

Confused at how the whole idea of his wife masturbating while being a voyeur excites him he looks nervously around at who else is watching. Not seeing another soul Chris returns his attention to what is going on in front of him. *Is this what is going while he corrects papers?*

Looking back and forth at the couple and his recently, unpredictable wife causes Chris to reach down and squeeze the growing bulge in his shorts. *Everyone else was having fun, why not join in?* Chris proceeds to grab a nice handful of his own flesh without a second thought.

Roughly, the muscular man spins the voluptuous woman off his lap and plants her on the bed on all fours. Chris watches intently as the man bends down and out of view then comes back up. As the man brings his arm up, he rams his long member back into her. His hand flies in the air landing the end of a belt buckle on her bottom. Chris slides his hand down his own length appreciating the effect his wife getting off while watching the couple has on him. The sight of the beautiful woman bouncing in pain on all fours was making it all the more exciting.

Wrapping her long dark hair around his hand, the man grips it tightly in his closed fist like reins on an unbroken thoroughbred. With a sharp tug, her head lifts up and her back arches to attention. As a wild mare being broken, he swings the leather belt like a riding crop against her hip causing her to buck and yelp in excitement. The man rides her harder and faster.

It is enough that Chris has to watch the couple but now his wife seemed to be into it just as the two in the apartment. The sounds coming from Rachel were fierce and wild. Her hips gyrating the grass blades under her fingers was enough to have Chris drop the waistband of his sweatpants to get a firm grip on something Rachel obviously has forgotten is alive and missing her considerably at that moment. As Chris' hand wraps around his hard flesh his eyes close softly enjoying the much-needed sensation.

"Take her hard!" a soft growl commands from Rachel's own lips. Hearing his nice little wife talk like that has Chris pump his hand harder up and down.

Chris swallows hard as a sweat breaks out over his brow. It takes all his strength to not take Rachel like an animal right there. Instead, he works his hand harder feeling the slick drops moisten his skin around the head. Cursing Rachel for doing this to him, he lets his left arm support him as he leans forward to pump away in the darkness.

"Ah, yes…" Rachel thrusts up in long deep movements like a dancer on a pole. "Take me, baby." She calls out.

Chris speeds up knowing his wife will have some explaining to do when she gets home. The last time she talked like that was on their sixth date backstage in the dressing room of the warm up band for the BonJovi concert. Rachel's cousin was lead singer and introduced her to the band that was warming up. Rachel had smoked a little too much of the high quality grass and was out of her mind obsessed about riding Chris hard and didn't care who heard them. Taking her into the empty dressing room was all he could do to get her to shut up. She even asked him to leave the door open so someone would stop and watch. Chris knew at that moment he was going to marry her…after he fucked her silly lying on a back up speaker.

"Yes!" Rachel hisses as she grinds frantically leaning forward splaying her legs behind her leaning on her left hand allowing her to slam against her fingers.

Chris watches Rachel pound the ground as a man woman. Over and over her ass tightened and moved downward like he used to do to her back in college on the ramp in back of the apartments. He would ride her so hard that the manager had to finally tell them one afternoon that the metal banging on the rain gutters was pissing off the single students up late studying. Rachel cared less. She would wrap her legs around him while his toes dug into the ground and rode her rough calling out his name at the top of her lungs until all the windows slammed shut and a select few stepped out on the balcony to cheer good old Chris on. Back then it was all night and a quickie was never possible. Rachel and Chris were known to fuck during lectures if you offered them enough booze or money.

Chris moaned deeply muttering about what a little slut Rachel was making him hard like this. His cock was so tight he was going to explode painfully. Rachel looked up as the man moved the dark haired beauty for a side view. Those huge tits were bouncing up all over hell as he pumped her silly. Dropping the belt, the man the grabbed under her arm and over her shoulder to hold her into position. His other hand moved over her other shoulder and wrapped loosely across her throat. Her hands grabbed at his fingers positioned around her throat for extra leverage. Soon her lips spread into a smile confirming she liked it that way.

"Oh, yes!" Rachel said quivering in slow thrusts on her hand.

The man kept one hand on the dark beauty's neck and the other dived down to her shiny bare slit. His muscles worked quickly as the woman slammed back against him tossing her head and closing her eyes. He kept tempo with her racing toward the finish line.

In unison, the mouths of all opened as the waves started crashing through them. The black beauty crumbled against the man submitting beneath him. He slammed her down into the bed lifting her hips high to remind her he was far from finished. His hips pumped into her with three quick thrusts as he yelled out to the heavens above him.

Rachel started to shake and fall forward as the moonlight revealed she had literally shoved her hand inside her pussy. That was more than enough for Chris to pump like a whore's mouth on his cock. God yes, it was so good. That was the wicked Rachel he fell in love with. She still could make him come any place and anytime with the way her body quivered. When Rachel came it was always like an explosion set off right around your cock. Sometimes he felt like her pussy could bite him in two the way it clamped around him like a vice grip.

"Ahhhh…."Chris cried as he shook down into the ground behind the shrubs out of Rachel's view.

Startled by the unexpected but familiar sound, Rachel

grabbed her top back down and her shorts up. Running like a spotted rabbit, she bolted to the apartment. Chris looked up and smirked.

"So, that is how she wants it? Even after all this time." Chris mumbled as he cleaned himself off before getting up. He was not going to deny her anything when it came down to how she truly liked it. Wild, steaming hot, rough and wickedly mind bending. She was going to get it and he was damn ready to finally give it to her good.

It took seconds for Chris to come into the apartment behind her. Her clothes were flying out of the shower onto the bedroom floor when he caught up with her.

"I'll shower after you so we can spend some time together." Chris called to her.

"Actually, I am tired and going to sleep." Rachel answered. "Maybe, we can meet up during spring break."

"Just because life is a bitch doesn't mean you have to be a bitter one, sweetness." Chris called out knowing it really pissed her when he said it.

"Instead of going running tomorrow night I think I may just camp outside for the whole weekend. God knows I get very little to come back for anymore, Chris!" Rachel screamed to let him know if he ever thought he had a chance between her legs during the night he just lost it.

Chris smiled and went off to the other bathroom. Now Rachel was in just the mood he wanted. It wouldn't be fair if he didn't give her the chance to be fighting mad.

When Chris returned she was already sound asleep. Of course she was tired. *After she fingered herself to a mind numbing state watching Debbie doing Sir Dallas she should be exhausted, the poor baby.* Chris thought as an evil sadistic grin lifted the corners of his creative mouth. Perfect. She will not see it coming. He retreated to the kitchen and retrieved just what he needed. Next, he scored the silk ties from his top drawer. *Ready or not, Rachel, here comes Chris!*

Pulling Rachel by her ankles out of the bed onto the floor stunned her enough to allow seconds for Chris to bind her wrists together and to the bed frame. Taking her pink lace panties in a fast tug he wrapped them in a round ball and shoved them in her mouth as she began to scream. With another silk tie, he gagged her silent as her eyes widened in horror that her sweet adoring husband just tied her to their bed.

*"Yes, he is so going to get his ass kicked when I get off the floor."* She promised with all the confidence of a woman who ran daily to drain her frustration over the way her sex life had hit a grinding halt.

"Sorry, baby, did I wake you?" Chris stood above her naked and quite obviously aroused.

Rachel's eyes were glazed over in wide shock at being swatted teeth rattling hard right across the ass while she slept in her panties with nothing covering her. She could barely focus on Chris being the source of her burning ass with his naked state stunning her even more. *Had he lost his god damned mind?*

"I have something to give you long over due." Chris said, spinning their pizza dough paddle in his hand.

Flipping Rachel over face down into the carpet like a champion cattle roper, Chris began paddling her sweet ass with unadulterated joy. He swatted her like he was trying to put out a fire on her ass instead of start one. Chris, of course, did just as she never thought possible. Her skin puckered up and showed he was not playing around either.

"Yes, my dear you needed it." Chris said with excitement as if he had just won the lottery exhaling at the vision of a job well done. "And guess what? I think I am going to finally fix that leaky faucet you have been bitching about." Chris said with a grin grabbing shorts and a t-shirt to put on leaving Rachel to writhe and wince in pain on the harsh carpet she took pride in caring for. Oh, yes. She was fucking pissed off now.

Loud knocking caught Rachel's attention after a half hour of laying there in the dark. She heard faint voices in the front of the apartment. Quickly she wrestled to get free from the bed frame. A male laugh was coming closer and it sure as hell was not Chris! What was he doing bringing people into their bedroom? Was he out of his damn mind? The leaking faucet was in the master bedroom bathroom! Rachel closed her eyes praying the door would not open. Praying didn't seem to work this time.

"Well, there she is. Thanks for coming on such short notice." Chris' voice sounds as he walks in.

"Oh damn!" A female voice says in surprise followed by a giggle.

"Amy!" The male voice said firmly as a reprimand.

"Sorry, Sir." Amy said softly biting her lip.

"So, Nick, you think she has potential?" Chris asks looking down at Rachel with the same neutral tone as if she is the rare body of an antique car he found at an auction and Nick is an automotive restorer coming to give an honest bid.

"Of course." Nick replied, looking down at a very hot looking woman that takes pride in her tight athletic body all the way down to her perfect French pedicure. "She has more than potential, Chris. I think you are on the right track with your wife."

Rachel opens her eyes slowly thinking by some stroke of luck that they are oblivious to her lying on the floor nude, mouth gagged and tied to the bed frame with a bright red ass.

Maybe, this is all a huge dream and she will roll over, open her eyes and find Chris poking her for a sympathy screw to make amends for ignoring her so long. No such luck. There were enough people standing over her to have a Tupperware party. At least with four guests you get free cup coasters. What she was looking at was enough to make her nipples tighten into fleshy knots out of fear.

Chris kneels down to Rachel's side and begins to pull off the gag. Looking down at her, he decides it would make more sense if she were a little more relaxed before removing it. Who knows what she is ready to do in the mood she is in right now. Chris knows that would be hard to explain to the police let alone the school should this all backfire because she screamed bloody murder as soon as the gag leaves her mouth.

"Amy, I think it is time you and Rachel get acquainted if it is alright with Chris." Nick says looking over to Chris.

"I was just thinking the same thing." Chris said with a grateful smile. Anything to loosen Rachel up before he loosened up the silk around her wrists.

Chris rubbed his chin searching for whatever he could to break the ice. He never thought of being in such a situation and certainly was glad to say he didn't have a formal way to address everyone under the circumstances. Rachel stretched his limits and he loved her all the more for it. He just hoped he wouldn't have to post bail before the night was over because of it.

"I think you and Rachel have some common interests." Chris comments tapping the dough paddle with his foot on the floor next to Rachel to get Amy's attention away from his naked wife lying tied to the bottom of their bed. "It is not hard to look at either one of you girls to start with."

"A new submissive?" Amy asks Chris as she kneels down at Rachel's side.

"Well, I am not sure what all that means." Chris says looking over at Nick. "I do know she really seems to enjoy the fact that I grabbed her by the ankles while she was sleeping and yanked her out of bed, spanked her a several times with that paddle and tied her up and gagged her." Chris says with a nervous laugh running his hand through his hair surprised at what he has gotten into in the last couple of hours. "She won't admit she liked it but if you knew about what we did in college…what you two enjoy is like playing patty-cake. No offense."

"None taken, man." Nick says surprised at Chris' directness. "Can I ask why you have her on the floor tied to the bed if she is so cool with all this?"

"Yes. I guess you could say I was disappointed at the way she was behaving tonight. I watched her getting off watching you two and thought about the all times she put me down for doing it." Chris laughs when he realizes what he said sounds bad. "Not watching you two…just getting off alone."

All three minus Rachel laughed at his humorous honesty. Chris was at the end of his rope and was a man to be admired from what Nick could see. This man wanted his woman back. He wanted to make her burn all night like he used to and who could fault him for that? Certainly not Nick.

"Anyways, she seemed to turn into a woman I haven't seen in a long time as things between you two escalated. The rougher you were with each other the more excited she became. I haven't heard the sounds and words come from her mouth as I did earlier tonight in quite a long time. I guess I decided I would try to take things from there to get out of a boring many year rut. Long story short, I love Rachel and I want to discover and enjoy the woman I saw out on the lawn earlier. The one I haven't seen a hell of a long time" Chris says with a sigh.

"Wow. I hear you Chris. Well, she watched us and all that and was excited?" Nick asks Chris shrugging his shoulders and smirking at Amy.

"She was laying there cheering you on with Amy. After she started tearing my ass apart for neglecting her…Well, I decided she maybe needed something from me like what she enjoyed watching." Chris says then clears his throat as he looks down at Rachel who is glaring at him. If she could get her hands on him, he is sure she would serve time after she was done with him.

"So, you were excited watching?" Amy says running her fingertip along Rachel's side. Rachel pulls her hands away from the bed frame but fails to get free.

"Amy, I think one of you girls is not dressed appropriately and I doubt highly it is Rachel." Nick says firmly winking at Chris when Amy looks down at Rachel. "Time to introduce Rachel to what Chris started."

"I can get you a chair." Chris says looking down at Amy.

"No, Chris, Amy is right where she is most comfortable. Aren't you girl?" Nick says with a firm tone.

"Yes, Sir." Amy answers respectfully. With a smile up at Nick Amy pulls off her tank top revealing those amazing tits they watched earlier. Chris stood speechless as Amy skillfully slid her shorts off without leaving her knees. There kneeling naked at Rachel's side was a very voluptuous sweet smelling Amy. Lord have mercy. "Thank you for the offer."

Nick smiles softly and walks around looking down at Rachel lying on the floor and Amy sitting still at her side. How could anything be more beautiful? A seasoned submissive and the prospect of breaking in a new one.

Nick kneels down looking at Rachel to focus on her eyes. Rachel first looks at Nick with contempt but after a few quiet moments, her body softens and Nick smiles as she closes her eyes. After standing back up, he looks at Chris with a confidence that would take most men 20 years with a woman to develop.

"I want Amy to warm her up first." Nick says nodding to Amy to get comfortable with Rachel.

"Ok." Chris says in agreement. He might as well make the most of the situation.

Gently Amy leans over Rachel and traces the line of her face with her finger. Stopping at her chin and leaning forward, Amy kisses Rachel's cheek. Barely moving her lips from Rachel, Amy kisses her chin and her neck. Rachel moans softly under the gag.

Chris watches Amy slide down to lay beside Rachel with his mouth open. He never imagined seeing his wife with another person and especially not a female that looks like Amy. Amy leans over Rachel allowing her tits to rest on top of Rachel's warm chest. Stroking Rachel's right side with her left hand, Amy starts nibbling and sucking on Rachel's neck. It does not take long for Nick to bend down and untie the scarf around Rachel's ankles. As if it was her cue to climb aboard, Amy moves on top of Rachel and wedges her thigh between Rachel's legs to open them. Amy settles between her legs and leans over to whisper in Rachel's ear.

"You smell so good Rachel." Amy says softly, stopping to suck on Rachel's earlobe. "You have such a hot little body." Amy says using the tip of her tongue to tease Rachel's mouth. "I haven't had a woman in a long. I will try to be gentle." Amy says squeezing Rachel's ass tightly in her hand and rubbing her pelvis down into Rachel's. "I want to taste you. Does that make you nervous to know, Rachel? Is it okay that you make me so hot right now that I want to eat you, torture you and fuck you all at once?" Amy asks stopping to slip her tongue around the gag and inside Rachel's lips to taste her, finishing with a firm nip on her bottom lip. "Did you get wet when he was beating my ass with the belt? Because if you did you are going to enjoy what he does to me after I get done doing all those things to you." Amy says sliding her right hand under Rachel's firm ass pulling her up so Amy could thrust a couple times against Rachel's pussy and tapping her clit as she moved down into her.

Rachel feels Amy's soft flesh between her thighs grinding into her pussy. Her mind deceives her and she replays the whole scene of Amy riding her pussy into Nick's face. Rachel opens her eyes in an attempt to block out what she saw only to find Amy looking into her eyes with her mouth open moaning as she dry fucks Rachel slow and deep. Rachel feels her eyes roll back as she sinks deeper into the feeling of Amy on top of her.

Chris swallows dryly as he sits down to get a better view on the floor. Amy's huge tits spill out with Rachel's to each side as Amy slides both hands under Rachel's ass to grind harder into her. Chris feels his dick start to tighten up when Rachel finally spreads her legs wider allowing Amy to finally have full access to her wet pussy and firm clit.

"Yes, Baby, that is better. You want me to fuck you don't you? I love how you feel all wet and ready under me. You are going to be fun to take." Amy purrs in her neck in between warm heavy exhales.

Nick sighs deep at what is beginning in front of him then decides sitting on the floor will offer the best view of the show. As Nick sits down on the floor Amy coyly looks over to him. Reading her mind, Nick leans over putting his mouth to Amy's own. Chris watches Rachel's eyes widen at the two coming together over her. A deep slow kiss begins over Rachel and she has no choice but to watch and feel this gorgeous woman slide her slippery sweet pussy up and down against hers. Watching their tongues dance and explore Rachel thinks of how beautiful his mouth was on Amy's cunt. Without thinking, Rachel's hips rise up to grind into Amy's body. Amy pinches Rachel's right nipple roughly between her fingers while still sucking on Nick's tongue. Harder Amy rides Rachel's body moaning between Nicks parted lips. Rising up Nick unzips his jeans and pulls out his cock. Rachel tries to protest at the sight of Nick's length.

Reaching down to untie the gag on Rachel, Chris pulls out the lace panties and quickly covers her mouth with his. Rachel is able to see Amy open her mouth wide and Nick sliding in his cock over Chris. Feeling Amy grinding into her clit while sucking Nick's cock causes Rachel to melt softly into the heat of Chris' mouth.

Nick knows this is the perfect time to slide the double-headed thick v-shaped vibrator into Amy. The toy was created just for such an occasion complete with a middle probe that was set to a lightening fast speed to torture the girl's clits.

Pushing the button in the middle sends Amy moaning loudly over his cock and Nick's eyes rolling back in delight. Holding the back of Amy's head, he works his way down her throat.

Chris looks up wondering if Amy will choke on Nick's abnormally long tool. Like a baby bird, Amy slowly and carefully swallows its entire length down while not missing a beat at fucking Rachel. Nick comes out of the fog Amy's mouth always puts him in and fights to focus on the task at hand. Twisting the toy to buzz against Amy's clit has her raise up and suck harder on his cock. Nick knows he had better pull off his shirt and get the other end of the toy in place quick. Amy can only hold on for so long.

Rachel watches Nick's chest flex as he fucks Amy's face for a few moments. Looking up at Chris, she realizes he is rubbing his cock. Somewhere along the way he had removed his clothes. Without thinking, she opens her mouth to catch one of Amy's huge tits that are brushing back and forth against her face while she grinds harder into Rachel. Sucking hard then pinching one of her nipples in her teeth, Rachel can feel Amy buck against her as she gags on his swelling cock. At that moment, Nick slips the other tip of the toy into Rachel's wet pussy taking the liberty of letting one of his fingers move in with it. Rachel's eyes widen as she realizes that Nick is fingering her and looks over at Chris. Chris has his left hand on his cock stroking and his right in the back of Amy's head pulling her hair. Suddenly, Amy's mouth moves off Nick's cock and down to Rachel's mouth as the buzzing meets her clit.

For the first time Rachel is kissing a woman. Nick leans over and unties Rachel's hands, which go right to Amy's gorgeous tits. Squeezing and pinching Rachel pulls at Amy roughly. Amy moans as Rachel grabs Amy's ass and pushes her down into her. Chris leans down and starts chewing on Rachel's tit sending her hips up into Amy. Rachel pulls Chris' mouth away from her tit and pushes up to kneel. Grabbing Amy's hair and pulling hard she realizes Nick's fingers slipping into her unused ass. Rachel's eyes roll back to close and she howls in shock. As the first burn starts to become an itch, she now has to satisfy, Rachel growls.

"More!" Rachel calls out lifting her hips up raising Amy off the floor with her.

"That's right. I have more for you." Nick moans pulling out his two fingers from Rachel's ass and sliding his pants off and scooting to sit under Rachel's hips before she comes back down.

"Show me how a slut sucks!" Rachel commands Amy with a painful tug of her hair.

Not missing a second Chris slides his wide thickheaded cock into Amy's mouth causing her to stretch her mouth far wider than ever before. Rachel brings up her head and begins biting at Amy's huge tits. Each time Chris moans at Amy's skilled sucking, Rachel bites harder causing Amy to bounce against her clit. Nick rubs the juices from both of drenched pussies in front of him on his cock. Taking a second, he leans his face into Amy's ass and nibbles her tight hole. Amy moans so deeply that Chris feels her tonsils dance and tap at the right spot on his cock. Chris grabs a hold of Amy's head and begins fucking her face like no one else is there.

"You are such a nasty little bitch. You seem to enjoy my wife maybe you would enjoy this." Chris says pumping with no regard to her teeth scraping his tight skin. Repeatedly his balls slap back and forth as he pounds his cock down Amy's throat. "Oh, yes, suck me. I want to feel you choke." Chris grunts screwing Amy's beautiful mouth. "Suck it harder!" Chris says moaning when Amy groans louder.

Nick knows it will only take a few seconds in a tight little back end to squeeze his cock to the breaking point. Licking his left thumb, he sends it forcefully into Amy's ass. Amy howls around Chris's cock bouncing harder on the vibrator buried between hers and Rachel's pussy. Nick rams his thumb in and out of Amy's ass while lining up his aim for Rachel. Rachel lifts up feeling the buzzing hit just the right spot.

"Fuck yes! Fuck me hard." Rachel says watching Chris toss his head back with beads of sweat racing down his neck.

"Oh, fuck yes. God, yes!" Chris pounds into Amy's mouth three times shooting his fluid all over her mouth. Rachel feels the waves coming for her next as she grabs Amy's tits hard biting them alternately.

"Lift just a little higher." Nick says lifting up Rachel's hips before using his thumb in Amy's ass to guide the women back down into his spread lap.

Amy milks the last of the juice out of Chris before he finally pulls out of her mouth screaming in pain. Looking down at Rachel, she grabs her tits and covers Rachel's mouth with hers. Rachel's eyes open as the thick silky fluid that is both salty and sweet seeps past Amy's lips down her throat. Amy's tongue follows its path and Rachel feels like she is about to crash against every wave as Amy grinds the vibrator into her clit. Rachel's legs wrap around Amy in a last effort to hold on. Seeing the target in full view Nick rises up and pushes down on Amy's ass settling Rachel's ass on top of Nick's long cock. Rachel tries to wiggle away but Chris looks down at her.

"You are going to take it and you will like it. Fuck her hard Amy." Chris says watching the expression on Rachel's face as she realizes it is not Nick's finger stretching the outer skin of her ass.

"This is going to be so fucking good." Nick comments as he pokes at the delicate spot in Rachel's ass.

"Take it Nick." Chris commands.

"There is more than enough for both of us." Nick says laying back enough to position for the ride.

Chris feels his cock and finds it is ready for another round. Pulling off his pajama bottoms, he smirks as he stands bending over Amy's ass. The chance to watch Chris fuck Amy hard excites Rachel more than she dreamed it would. Feeling Amy grinding to avoid the same waves chasing Rachel, she picks up rhythm squeezing Amy's ass painfully in her hands. Chris spits on his palm and bites his bottom lip. Nick looks up and can see Chris position himself right over Amy's ass. In unison, both men make their way into the tightest fit a man could ever find. Heaven in the sweetest form of flesh soon tightened around their cocks.

Rachel screams out and Amy covers Rachel's mouth with her own. Faster Amy rides Rachel. The burn settles and Rachel feels an incredible tickle begin deep. Nick pumps painfully slow all the way in. Lying back, he watches Chris' fat cock screwing into Amy's ass. The sounds of his balls slapping against her ass make Nick anchor on tight to Rachel's hips. Pumping harder and harder the men ride the waves in. Their voices calling out how damn good the women felt only seemed to encourage them to grind the toy between them faster in sloppy

"Oh, fuck yes!" Chris moans reaching over to knead Amy's tits. Feeling his wife's pointed nipples brushing against the top of his hand makes Chris completely aware he is fucking two women. Chris pumps wildly pushing Amy deeper into Rachel. Nick feels the spasms of Rachel's ass as the waves come for her squeeze without mercy around his cock.
"Fuck her!" Chris calls out knocking so hard up into Amy that he sets her off.

"Take it!" Rachel says looking at Amy's contorted face as she cries out.

Rachel slaps Amy's tits sadistically. Amy bounces up and down with the motion of Chris' cock in her ass down into the vibrator in Rachel spearing her repeatedly.

"You slut!" Rachel screams as Nick grabs at her hips to hold her still.

Nick drills his entire length in Rachel like a jackhammer. Nick is making everyone move with the way he is tearing up Rachel's ass. Chris holds on for his life as he feels Amy cum again.

"Oh, God! Please …"Amy growls slamming down into Rachel.

In one fast sadistic thrust of his hips Nick pierces the deepest part Rachel has sending the waves to swallow her whole.

"Oh, fuck!" Nick says as he explodes watching the orgy on top of him. Chris' cock sliding back and forth in Amy's ass sends his cock spitting into Rachel.

"Oh…" Rachel cries arching painfully up as if she is about to give birth. The wave arrives just as Nick sends his spear up into her ass one more time. "Oh, yes!" Rachel gasps. Amy covers Rachel's mouth with hers and the rest of the scream is a loud moan through Amy.

Laying in a sticky mess the foursome slowly untangle from each other. Rachel looks up lying on the floor. Exhausted, she does not have the energy to move after being at the bottom of the pile.

"As for the slump we have had, sweetness, I would assume you know it is over." Chris said looking down at Rachel lying at their feet. "Amy is going to spend evenings with you while I am finishing up the papers. The plan is to expose you to a few things you have yet to learn."

"I will think about it." Rachel said trying to reach for a sheet on the bed to cover her bare body. "I have things to do besides be babysat, thank you."

"Well, Chris seems she has other plans besides yours." Nick laughs in surprise at Rachel's continuing boldness even after the three of them just had their way with her. "I am impressed."

"Impressed?" Chris says with half a laugh. "I will impress the hell out of all of you!"

Chris reaches down and extends a hand to Rachel to get up. Once she is on her feet, he takes her to the bed and tosses her on her back roughly.

"What the hell?" Rachel protests trying to sit up.

"You two tie her up good." Chris directs tossing the silk ties to Nick and Amy.

"I think she has a hard time understanding that she has no options except those I choose to allow her." Chris says with a tone unlike one he has ever used with her before.

"C'mon, Chris." Rachel taunts him with a tone of amusement at her professor hubby getting all dominant on her in front of others. "You think you are actually going to keep up this charade? You have got to be kidding."

"Uh, Rachel, I don't think you understand." Amy tries to intervene and warn Rachel that Chris may not be kidding around.

"Understand?" Rachel asks in disbelief at how odd it feels to be discussing her sexual relationship with two strangers up until two hours ago. "Sweetie, you may like it rough, but I hate to tell you my Chris is not the type to keep up the bad ass role 24/7. Takes too much time and energy. He finds it hard to give a student an "F" instead of the sympathetic "D". Besides, he has to play teacher before he can get hard and appease his wife these days."

"Is that so?" Nick says irritated at Rachel's demeaning tone towards the man who loved her enough to initiate such an intervention to better their marriage.

"Listen, Nick, I would appreciate it if you and Amy

showed yourselves out." Rachel suggests with a smug smile. "You served your purpose. I am suddenly getting bored of the whole swapping idea."

"She is really something, Chris." Nick laughs not moving a muscle to leave. "I could almost take her seriously."

"Well, that makes only one of us then. I know exactly what she wants. Took me long enough to figure it out but I know now. It is gonna be my pleasure to give it to her." Chris says with a wicked glimmer in his eyes as he turned out of the room leaving her restrained to the bed and looking at Nick and Amy.

"Mind if I watch?" Nick called out as he smirked at Rachel frozen in silence on the bed.

"I could care less." Chris answers passing Nick and Amy with a riding crop in his hand. "Haven't seen this in a while, Rachel. Let's see if it still works." Chris grins waving it back and forth above her body spread out on the bed.

"Are you twisted? That is not even funny." Rachel exclaims struggling to free herself from the ties.

"My point exactly. Now I think we are getting somewhere. Time to discuss a few little rules that I plan to enforce." Chris grins savoring her reaction. "Number one…"

# The Wine Cellar

Cynthia pulled out of the small airport rental car lot and headed for the highway. She looked again at her directions and turned onto the road. She wondered why anyone would have a wine collection out in the middle of corn fields and dairy farms were beyond her. She had flown all around the world doing appraisals of wines and even at her young age was considered one of the leading experts on wine. She wouldn't have come out here except this client was special. Julian.

It had been nine months since she first met him in California. It had been at an invitation only party for a major vineyard there introducing a new wine. There was the tour where he caught her eye.

Cynthia had flirted with Julian all over the vineyard, but didn't get to talk with him. That night at the vineyards dinner at the hotel she was seated across the room from him. She couldn't remember what had been served that night, only that she was wishing it was him.

There was a very formal dance that night with a big band right out of the 40's, complete with the crooner. The only reason she attended was that she hoped to see Julian there. She was there for two hours, making small talk with several people in the wine business and was getting ready to go back to her room and call it a night. It was then that she felt someone grab her by the wrist. She looked up to see him standing there.

Julian didn't speak, but pulled Cynthia up to him and onto the dance floor. They danced for several slow songs, her body pressing up against his, never saying a word to each other. When they finally took a seat and Julian introduced himself.

Julian lived on his family farm, although he was far from your average farmer. The fact was that he owned many businesses, but rented the farm out to a neighbor. His house and office was still there.

Cynthia remembers telling him what she did, and his response was to quote reviews she had done of several wines in the latest issues of *Food and Wine*. He invited her to come see his collection sometime, got up, leaned down and gave her the most passionate kiss that she had every experienced. He excused himself and she had not heard from him since, until he called two days earlier.

"Arrogant ass." She said out loud, trying to convince herself that she had only come to see the wine. In her stomach she felt weak, wondering if he was still as wonderful as she remembered.

After 70 miles, she pulled off to look at the directions. No one could live out this far from civilization. She got out of the car and stood on the desolate highway.

"Damn, I can't believe it. This really is a road to nowhere." She said, laughing. She stretched her legs and got back in the car. She wished she would have dressed down and worn jeans instead of a skirt and heels. She pulled back onto the road and within a couple miles she saw a sign with an arrow. It had the name of his company on it and below it said 20 miles.

"This had better be the best damn wine in the world." She said to herself. "I could have been in Venice this week."

Cynthia spotted several large buildings in a grove of trees and hoped she was finally there. She pulled into the large drive and approached an old refurbished house. It was much bigger than she ever expected to find on an Illinois farm.

As she approached the big white barn across from the house she saw huge glass doors, which revealed it was a showroom garage, filled with beautiful classic cars.

She hit the brakes on her cheap rental car when she spotted an Aston Martin Vanquish sitting out front. She had seen one before and knew they cost around a quarter of a million dollars.

She pulled up in front of the house in a well marked parking spot. It definitely looked more like a corporate headquarters now than the farm she expected. She strolled over to the barn and walked past the Aston Martin. She could see several expensive cars through the huge glass doors.

The tall brick corn silo appeared to be offices now, with little windows in it making it look like a tiny sky scrapper. She walked back over to the large house and went up to the front door.

She looked at the classic farm porch, complete with a porch swing. She opened the door and walked into a very normal looking house, except for the desk with the gorgeous blonde sitting at it.

"Hi, you must be Cynthia." She said standing and extending her hand. "I'm Samantha. Have a seat. Emma will be back in a couple minutes."

"Emma?" Cynthia asked.

"Julian's personal assistant." Samantha said. Cynthia sat down on a big couch and looked around the room.

There were very expensive paintings on the walls. Two large swords that looked like they dated back to the civil war were displayed under a glass case. There was even something that looked like one of Jimi Hendrix's guitars up on the wall. She stood up to get a closer look. Samantha saw her inspecting the instrument.

"He played that one at Woodstock." Samantha said.

"He certainly has some interesting collections." Cynthia said, wondering if Samantha was part of one too.

The door opened and a red haired woman walked in.

"Cynthia?" She said, extending her hand. "I'm Emma, Julian's personal assistant. He is detained for a bit. You might as well get settled. Your bags have been taken up to your room."

"My room?" Cynthia inquired.

"There isn't a decent hotel within 100 miles of here, if that. Julian always takes care of everything." Emma told her. "Did Samantha offer you a drink, coffee or tea?"

"Some coffee would be great." Cynthia replied.

"Samantha, you didn't offer her anything?" Emma said, glaring at Samantha. She jumped up from her desk.

"No, Ma'am. Sorry. I'll get it for you Cynthia." She said, heading to a room around the corner.

"Samantha will show you to your room so you can freshen up if you like." Emma told her. "I have to go take care of some business, so if you will excuse me."

"Of course." Cynthia said, wondering how this Scottish beauty ended up on a farm in the Midwest.

Cynthia barely got to her room when the phone rang. She immediately recognized the voice and melted at its sound.

"Cynthia, I'm so glad you could make it." Julian said. "Come back down to the front office and Samantha will bring you to me."

"It will be good to see you again." Cynthia said, trying to hide the excitement in her voice.

She ran a brush through her hair, sprayed on some perfume and slipped her heels back on as she headed out the door. She went down the large stairs and was back at Samantha's desk.

Samantha led Cynthia through a large dinning room to the back of the house. She opened the door to an office and Cynthia saw Julian sitting there. He stood up extended his arms.

She walked over and embraced the most exciting man she had ever met, even though he had disappeared that night before she could see just how exciting he really was.

"It's so good to see you again." He said, lightly kissing her check.

"You too. I wondered what happened to you that night

we met." Cynthia responded, trying to coax a reason out of him for vanishing.

"I had to be on a plane at eleven that night." he replied. "Besides, it was not yet our time."

*Not yet our time? What the hell was that supposed to mean?* Cynthia brushed the comment off and was just glad she was seeing him again.

"Do you want to go see some of the wine now?" Julian asked. "You can pick out a bottle for dinner."

"The wine?" Cynthia said, almost forgetting the reason she was supposed to be there. "Of course."

"I'll just show you the first cellar." Julian said, taking her hand and leading her out of the office. "I'll save the best for last."

"That's what I was hoping for." Cynthia said in a flirty tone. She felt Julian squeeze her hand and she got goose bumps.

They went through some more rooms and she wondered just how big this farm house mansion was. They went down some stairs and there was a long hallway. It looked as though it went for at least 100 feet. It was well lit and had more artwork hanging on it.

They came up to a large gate blocking the hallway. Julian produced a key and opened it. There was another wood door that went down more steps. Cynthia realized Julian must have spent millions renovating the house and adding the underground addition. At the bottom of the staircase were several doors. He unlocked the first one and opened it into a beautiful wine cellar. She was amazed at the collection.

"This is part one." Julian said letting go of her hand. "I'll show you the rest after dinner."

"I never imagined. This is quite impressive." she said, running her hand over the racks, inspecting the bottles and vintages.

"I'm full of surprises." He said.

She walked back to him and looked into his eyes. "I can't wait."

The moment was rudely interrupted by his cell phone ringing. Julian looked at it and answered.

"Yes?" he said. "What? Just a minute, I'll call you right back."

"What is it?" Cynthia asked.

"I can't use this thing down here." He said, shaking the cell phone in the air. "I'll be back in 15 minutes. Just look around for a bit."

Cynthia watched him disappear up the stairs. She looked around at the bottles for a bit, the wondered if she could get a peek at the rest.

She walked out of the room and looked at the other doors. She started trying them but most were locked tight. Finally she tried one and it opened.

What she found inside was not what she expected. She walked into what looked like a medieval dungeon and torture chamber. There were chains hanging from the ceiling, and several devices that looked like they were meant to hold a person tightly in place for whatever torture was in store.

She assumed it was just another collection and reached up to touch one of the shackles hanging down. It occurred to her that all this looked very new, not hundreds of years old. She stopped and took a deep breath.

"My god." She said, realizing that he used all of this now. She was filled with curiosity more than anything else and reached up for the other chain. She closed her eyes and imagined Julian locking the shackles on her wrists. She let go and walked around the room. Her fingers ran over the equipment as she walked to a wall of whips.

The first thought that entered her mind was if he used these on Emma, or if perhaps Emma used them on Julian. This thought made her giggle.

She turned around and spotted the centerpiece of the room. She walked over to the stocks and lifted the top piece so it was open and ready for a victim. It looked to be made of walnut and was lined with soft leather.

She couldn't resist and leaned down, putting her neck and right wrist in place. With her left hand she lowered it down, and put her left wrist in as it came down softly. She closed her eyes and imagined Julian behind her, taking her roughly, his hands on her ass.

Cynthia went to get up and realized the stocks had latched onto her. She panicked, realizing Julian was going to be back down in a few minutes and she was locked into a piece of bondage equipment. She struggled for a minute, and then realized it was useless. She tried to come up with a good excuse for her predicament, but came up blank. Her heart jumped when she heard steps.

"Cynthia?" Julian said, looking in the wine cellar. She heard his footsteps come out of the room and into the dungeon. She was facing away from the door, and couldn't see him come in.

"Oh my." He said. "What have we here?"

"Julian, I can explain." Cynthia pleaded.

"Explain what. You tripped and locked yourself into the stocks?" He said, laughing.

"I….well….I was looking for…."She stammered.

"I usually only put naughty girls in that." Julian said, his voice getting closer. "It seems as if you qualify now."

"Please, just unlock it and let me up." Cynthia said. She felt his hand on her back. It ran up to the base of her neck. His hand left her back and his fingers went into her hair. She looked to see him bending down to her face. His fingers grabbed her hair and held her head tight.

"Is that what you really want?" He asked her softly.

"I…I…yes…I…I don't know." She said, her voice

shaking. She realized she was more excited than she had ever been. The fact that she was captive to this magnificent man sent her head spinning. He knelt down and got even closer to her face.

"You don't know?" He said repeating her indecision to her. "I told you the first time we met wasn't yet our time." He stood up slowly and walked behind her. Suddenly his hand came down on her ass.

"Fuck!" she yelled.

"Now it is our time." Julian said loudly. He started walking around her. "I knew this was you the minute I saw you. You didn't even know it."

"Know what?" Cynthia said, helpless to do anything. He walked back behind her again.

"I know who you are, and what you are." He said. "I know what you want."

"Want? You think I want to be held captive in a rich man's basement?" She said, trying to sound calm. She felt Julian taking her ankles and locking them in place, her legs spread apart

"You want to be captured, taken, ravished, and owned." He said, leaning down and whispering in her ear. He didn't get a response, so his fingers went back into her hair, pulling her head up sharply.

"Yes!" Cynthia said when he pulled her hair. "Yes, I want it."

"You want to hang on the wall, to be displayed, like my wine collection or a piece of art." Julian continued. "I could tell after watching you at the vineyard. You practically stalked me. You saw what you needed and pursued it. I am giving it to you now."

Cynthia started to speak, but knew he was exactly right. She felt his hands on her, going up under her skirt. She was totally vulnerable to him and it made her wet. His hands went between her legs and slipped into her pussy.

"Tell me it isn't so and I will release you right now." Julian said. He waited for a response.

Cynthia had so many things racing through her mind. Was he going to keep her here for his pleasure? Was she really going to be added to a collection of items in his lavish house? The thought thrilled her and scared her at the same time. Julian took a pair of scissors and cut her panties off.

"What about Emma." Cynthia said. "Is she part of your collection too?"

"What I do with my other slaves is none of your concern." Julian said, holding her panties in front of her face. "Now, these are quite damp. Tell me now what it is you need."

"I want you." Cynthia said softly, the thought of being a slave racing through her mind.

"You want me? Is that all?" Julian said, taunting her.

"I want you to take me. I want to feel you in me, fucking me." She continued.

"And?" Julian asked, waiting in front of her.

"I want to belong to you." Cynthia said.

At this point she didn't really care what he did with Emma or Samantha for that matter. She had to have him and if this was the only way, she would gladly let him do what he wanted.

"You are going to get fucked hard, and then when I am done, you will be put away for the night. Do you understand?" Julian said his face next to hers.

"Yes. Please do it. Fuck me now." She pleaded.

Julian took her soaked panties and pushed them into her mouth. Then he took a leather strap and pulled it around her head, holding the soaked panties in place. She could taste herself on the panties and waited to feel his cock. His hands moved up and down her legs. His hand came down hard on her ass, making her jump. She could feel his now naked body pressing up against her ass. She moaned into her gag and pushed back against him.

"Not so fast." He said, pulling away.

He slid a finger back into her pussy. He rubbed her clit and she started moaning again. It was almost more than she could take. Julian took the head of his cock and rubbed it against her wet pussy. He held her still while he slowly pushed in. She moaned loudly as he filled her up.

Finally she was getting what she had craved for so long. She started cumming almost immediately and Julian could feel her juices running down his leg now.

"You wet little slut. It didn't take much for you." He said, pulling his cock out. He slid a finger in her ass and she tried to pull away. "Every time you fucked a man since we met you pretended it was me, didn't you."

"Uh huh" she confirmed, helpless to him.

"Only you didn't know how good it could be." he continued. Cynthia only made soft noises while his finger explored her ass. She felt his finger pull out, then the head of his cock press against her tight hole.

"Mnnnhhhh" she tried to protest.

"It's all mine now." Julian said, pushing his cock in further. "Do you want me to stop?"

"Huh-uh." She moaned, pushing back against his large cock. He slid into her in one stroke.

"I am going to fuck you harder than you have ever been fucked." He said, starting to pull back.

Julian shoved forward and Cynthia screamed into the gag. He increased his tempo and she felt like she was being split apart. She could feel his cock swelling in her and suddenly he exploded in her ass. She pushed back hard, trying to milk his cock with her tight hole.

Julian rested on Cynthia for a minute, and then slowly pulled out. He left her there while he left to clean up. He returned a few minutes later to find her still breathing heavy and covered with sweat.

"I am going to release you for a moment. I expect you to behave." Julian said to her, unlocking the stocks.

He helped her stand up. He took the rest of her clothes off and immediately put shackles on her wrists. He locked them behind her back. He did the same to her ankles and chained them to her wrists. He led her to the door. She was still gagged and could barely walk with her ankles chained. She couldn't believe she came here to look at wine and ended up being wildly fucked in a dungeon. He opened the door and took her out to the other doors. He unlocked one and revealed what looked like a closet. He pushed her into it and locked the chains to the wall.

"I am putting you away for a while." He said. "You need to know what it feels like to be a piece of property." He undid her gag.

"You are coming back for me?" Cynthia asked. "Don't leave me in here."

"I will do what I wish with you." He said. "Emma told me she would love to fuck you. I may send her down in a while to play with you."

"Emma?" Cynthia said, stunned.

"Do you want to leave?" Julian asked her again. "Just tell me and I will release you. You will walk out the door and we will never see each other again."

"No, I want to stay." Cynthia said. She couldn't let this man get away ever again, even if it meant staying locked in a cage, waiting for him.

"I think the girls are going to enjoy you." He said, closing the door. She sat down on the small stool, and realized her pussy was still dripping.

# A Little Discipline Never Hurts

Jerrad was tired when he tossed his keys on the counter after a long day at work. His boss had recently pushed two of the largest cases in the law firm on him and his wife's birthday dinner two nights ago was his first no call, no show in thirteen years of knowing each other. Alex was absolutely pissed off. For the last two days, he had not laid eyes on her. Just as well, with the way she handled things, he would have to take an hour on Sunday to get back over to the mall and replace all the china from the cabinet if they met up now.

Jerrad had enough to deal with in preparing for the two upcoming trials. Drugs and murder kept him working and the $1.5 million dollar home over his professor wife's head. He was alerted to her presence since her Benz was double parked taking up all the room he used to tuck his Jaguar neatly inside. It was her way of telling him to fuck off without having to speak to him and he knew it all too well.

A laugh came from Jerrad's mouth when he opened the fridge and it was empty, void of anything that would save a starving man. Only the cork from his treasured bottle of wine was perched on the counter to greet him. No doubt it was sweet, smooth and long fucking gone. Only his sweet Alex could be callous enough to swallow a thousand dollars worth of wine and leave the cork as a reminder that he had the day from hell.

Jerrad shook his head at the perfect ending to a perfectly shitty day while he moved through the first floor of the house quietly. Last thing he wanted was to wake Sleeping Beauty in her drunken state. He would be better off walking into the lion's cage at the zoo with a slab of raw prime rib tied to his neck.

Relief began to fill his tired body as he walked through the hallway to the guest suite. Alex was always polite enough to move his clothing and belongings in there when she was ready to declare war and he was sure that is where she would not be sleeping. He had the doorway in sight when he passed her office and the computer screen caught his eye. A blinking message box on the bottom flashed calling for his attention. He rolled his eyes and walked around the desk and sat down.

"Once I have my hands on you, beautiful, I shall refuse to let you go. Between now and Friday I have a task for you…to make sure you are truly ready. Once we are together there will be no turning back. You will be mine and mine alone." Jerrad's eyes scanned the message slowly. He rubbed his eyes and swallowed dryly as he took another look at the message.

It was there. The message was really there. Jerrad felt his heart kick back into the ready to kick some ass mode. His veins filled with a rush of heated endorphins. What the hell was she thinking? He worked his ass off to take care of her and she was already stepping outside the lines of reasonable behavior by moving him out of his own damn bedroom every time she broke a nail picking up the dry cleaning in her tricked out Mercedes. He knew he put up with far too much already and she ended up spoiled. But planning to meet a stranger for sex? Now that was the kick in the nuts he just did not expect, even from Alex. Hell, this was nothing like the woman he married. She had to have lost her damned mind!

The box continued to blink taunting him. Each word burned through him, stabbing and twisting like an unclean, sharpened knife being advanced slowly into his gut. He went back over the message studying each word. He counted it blinking 20 times before he finally accepted it was there.

Jerrad sat back and massaged his fingertips across his

chin. His wife's latest whim seems to be entertaining the idea of hooking up and having sex with some stranger she met on the internet. His jaw clenched at the idea of some thick headed small cocked asshole spreading his wife wide open in an hourly motel room like a two cent pervert.

Jerrad's face twisted in disgust at the thoughts coming to his mind. He could just imagine the man's greasy face shoving between her thighs while poorly comparing her to a beautiful rose. He had to swallow back the nausea. His nostrils flared at some prick knowing what his wife smelled like and the sounds she made when she came. The idea of another man getting her off sent a pang of ache to his heart. It made him catch his breath unexpectedly and lean forward toward the keyboard.

"Are we clear where we are meeting? I want to make sure." Jerrad typed quickly hoping that Alex wouldn't wake up and look for him.

"Yes, you wanted it to be 7 pm, Friday at the Toy Chest." The message responded. "Am I right?"

"Good. Just checking. What will should I expect?" Jerrad asked hoping to get a glimpse into the mind of a man who wants his wife for dinner and breakfast the following day.

"For starters…you will get the birthday spanking you deserve." The message blinked seconds later.

"What else?" Jerrad's fingers snapped hard on the keys.

"That fantasy about being used and abused in public will no longer be only a fantasy, baby." The message returned in a flash.

Jerrad's hands wanted to twist the keyboard around Alex's neck until she choked out the reasons she was acting like such a slut behind his tired ass. He caught himself before pushing away from the desk in anger.

"That would make my birthday wish come true." Jerrad typed. She was going to be abused alright. Especially if he had anything to say about it.

"Friday 7 p.m. The Toy Chest." The return message flashed.

"Yes." Jerrad sent back before closing out the dialog box and deleting the history of the conversation.

He was just about to purge all the information he could find to confront her with out of her computer when he heard Alex stumbling towards the bathroom. He shut down the computer with a click of the power button. He knew he would find out what he needed to know Friday night at The Toy Chest. Until then she would be lucky if he didn't give her that spanking to set her ass straight just to make himself feel better. With the mood he was in presently he would wait until morning before running into her. Chances are a couple swats on her ass would hardly satisfy what he wanted to put her through after what he has just experienced.

The following morning Jerrad ran into Alex just as she was going to leave for work. She smelled good, whistling a cheerful tune and dressed rather hot in a white pantsuit that hugged her curves so tight that any man would envy the fabric around her voluptuous shape. She definitely wasn't hurting any after consuming his expensive bottle wine the night before. Jerrad's eyebrow rose speculatively as he watched his wife pour a cup of coffee to go.

"Taking off early aren't you?" Jerrad asked as she grabbed her briefcase and slipped on her sunglasses.

"Didn't know it was a crime." Alex answered with a curl of her lips that said anything but love was happening between them at the moment.

"Maybe not, but being a smart ass after gargling with my bottle of wine is in my book." Jerrad said tossing down his briefcase on the counter and resting with both hands on the top.

"Lick me, Jerrad. It is half mine and the other half went to a good cause." Alex grabbed her travel mug and walked toward the garage door entry.

"Licking is hard when you're sleeping in the guess room. Let me guess the cause…" Jerrad walks after her. "It's too hard to choose which credit card to use so I will drink until the answer comes to me cause?"

"Fuck you." Alex hissed as she slid into the driver seat of her Mercedes.

"All you have to do is step out of the car and bend over and I can give you the ride of your life, precious." Jerrad winked with his arms bracing him inside the doorway.

"Listen, Jerrad, I don't have two minutes to waste on humoring your bruised ego by moaning till you are satisfied and I am bored…again." Alex said turning on the car. "Besides, I already have a ride."

Jerrad felt his ears burn and his chest swell in anger. He wanted to rip her right out of the car and drag her inside by the hair. He was just about to step into the garage when the garage door opened and she was squealing her tires in reverse down the driveway narrowly missing his car.

Jerrad's temples were pounding and his jaw was clenched as the fresh air from outside rolled in across his face. His cell phone in his pocket vibrated and caught his attention.

"Yes?" Jerrad answered with a hiss.

"I won't be home tonight. Do whatever you want for dinner. I will be staying at my sister's after a dinner meeting." Alex said before swearing at a driver that cut her off in a lane change.

"I thought you were having a meeting Friday night." Jerrad growled in the phone as he walked back into the house.

"I am, Jerrad." Alex moaned in irritation. "Today is Friday. Maybe you would know that if you were around more often."

"Kiss my ass." Jerrad snapped his phone closed and slammed the entry door to the garage. "Son of a bitch!"

So it was Friday after all, Jerrad thought to himself. Thankful for small miracles, he ran back upstairs and retrieved a few things before taking off for the office.

Over the course of the day Jerrad was distracted by closing up one of the cases, plea bargaining with another clients lawyer and trying not to think about what in the hell his wife was up to while he sweated it out waiting for 7 p.m. to roll around.

"Jerrad, are you going to be going home tonight?" His secretary asked as he dropped off a file on his desk. "I mean its Friday night, you have a wife and you need to get out of this office."

"Thanks for reminding me…" Jerrad stood up and closed up the file he was working on and handed it over. "I was going to be meeting her tonight."

"Glad to hear that." He smiled walking out and closing Jerrad's office door behind him.

Jerrad looked at his watch and found he had two hours to get ready and across town to The Toy Chest, which happened to be the seediest club in the city and known for being a hard core alternative play arena for those into the BDSM scene. He also knew he would only have one way to get in there without being recognized. He picked up his phone and called in a favor.

"That's right, T.J. I want access through the back, no questions and I want to call all the shots in regards to one woman." Jerrad spoke with assertion as he spun his silver pen in his hand.

Jerrad laughed at the owner's response.

"I know I am married. I believe she will too by the time I finish with her tonight." He said dropping the pen on the desk. "Got a private room with a few willing but trustworthy participants to provide their time as an audience?"

A big grin moved to Jerrad's face. "No, she isn't into that

deep of trouble....yet. How about a little entertainment on the side just in case things aren't going well?"

Jerrad laughed at his response once again. He always had a way of putting things that hit Jerrad funny. No frills and to the point of being crude. He had to hold back more than once in court to keep from laughing at T.J.'s antagonizing the presiding judges.

"Yes and there is supposed to be some smooth talking asshole showing up thinking he is going to be Master of all that he sees when it comes to my wife." Jerrad informed as he stood up and loaded his briefcase. "I would like him to be kept around to enjoy the show as well."

Jerrad's eyes widened at the owner's response.

"No, man, no body damage. Just his pride is all, thank you." Jerrad laughed hanging up the phone.

The stop at the cleaners and a quick change over at the house on the way gave him time to confirm she had stopped by the house earlier.

It appears she spent time getting ready and left her scent of a new perfume all the way from the upstairs to the garage to announce she was in fact going somewhere very special.

Jerrad went upstairs long enough to move all of his clothes and belongings back into the master bedroom closet, stretch out a belt across the length of the bottom of their bed and grab a few items that may be of some relief to both of them later should things work as he planned.

Arriving at the club an hour later, Jerrad took a last look in the rear view mirror to make sure he was looking alright. He wore her favorite suit she bought him for Christmas two years ago by Dolce & Gabbana. Dark shirt and jacket with dark pants that left his light blue eyes dancing in the beauty of his dark olive skin. She called it "hot" and a "power trip" look. He called it a way to tell her she was in a hell of a lot of trouble and power was about to have more than she could imagine to do with it.

"Hey there, Sir. What's up with you this fine evening?" The giant of a man in a suit greeted Jerrad at the back private entrance pulling him into a friendly guy hug and patting him firmly on the back.

"Hopefully nothing before I arrived?" Jerrad laughed confidently taking the drink from the owner's hand that he extended with a smile.

"You kidding, man? I am not gonna let anything happen to you and yours. I got your back, brother." The tall salt and pepper long haired and bearded goliath laughed and patted Jerrad firmly on the shoulder.

Keeping his huge hand firmly in place on as if finding a long lost friend, T.J. led the way through to the private room smiling proudly as he walked side by side with Jerrad. Parting the crowds like Moses through the sea, he soon had Jerrad at the double door entrance to the reserved playroom for the night.

"She is inside." The owner stopped patting Jerrad who was distracted looking at all the groups of patrons in various leather, chains, and fishnet stockings.

Silver hoops and barbells dripped from every imaginable body part as it passed by. One chick strutted by to the rhythm of jingling bells and Jerrad literally coughed up his drink when he realized it was her bare tits making the music as they swayed back and forth and up and down with her model like catwalk.

"She has lots of company right now. Looking pretty hot, too, I have to say. You didn't tell me she was so damn fine, Jerrad. Holding back on us, huh?" T.J. laughed when Jerrad finally looked up at him.

"Not a chance…just didn't want you stealing her from me. She likes her men big and long." He winks then laughs while looking up at the huge man in front of him. "Holding back seems to be my wife's latest talent, but tonight I am calling her ass on the carpet, literally."

"Something tells me she is in for a big surprise then." T.J. raises and eyebrow and rubs his chin for effect.

"That my friend is an understatement." Jerrad patted the giant's shoulder to confirm his statement. "No worries. I will keep it clean."

"No shit. I just finished off paying you from my last court dates." T.J. widened his eyes. "I owed you and now you can collect. I have been told she has been fastened into the cuffs and ankle restraints for a complimentary birthday spanking."

Jerrad's eyes widened and he swallowed the last of his drink while looking up at T.J. through the now empty glass.

"Now this I have to see!" Jerrad smirked handing the glass to a passing waitress with an empty tray.

"I will be happy to stand inside or out. Just let me know where you want me." T.J. grinned with his large arms spread wide open.

"Inside. I need as many witness's as possible in case she pulls something." Jerrad nods toward the closed door. "Alex is unpredictable."

"You ain't kidding." T.J. laughed opening the door.

A couple of women approached the doorway trying to get in front of them and T.J.'s huge arm blocked everyone from proceeding.

"No go, guys. This is a private party. You will have to play elsewhere." He moved them back to the rest of the nightclub.

"That sucks." The dark long haired woman says with a pout.

"Maybe you should instead and we all would be happy." T.J. growled much to the surprise of the petite dominatrix looking woman trying to complain while the other stayed silent.

"Bite me!" She snapped while Jerrad's eyebrows rose at the verbal discord taking place with the owner and a guest.

"Listen, bitch, I would be happy to but I have things to take care of and you will have to wait in line like everyone else if it is that important to you." T.J. reached over and grabbed the woman's braid and startled Jerrad enough that he stepped back.

"Yes, Sir." The woman's lip quivered as her eyes opened so wide that her green eyes started glowing. "I will wait for you out here, Sir."

"That is more like it. Don't move." T.J. hissed tossing her braid back out of his reach hitting the silent woman next to her. "Not even to piss. When I return…bite you I will." T.J. snapped his teeth wildly out at the women scaring them half to death as he loudly snapped his jaws shut just an inch from their shocked faces.

"Thank you, Sir." The woman's eyes immediately darted downward.

T.J. shook his head and rolled his eyes before finally wrapping a comforting arm on Jerrad's shoulders to pull him back towards entering the private playroom.

"That one is always trying to top my ass. I swear if she wasn't so frickin' sexy and feisty it would actually piss me off." T.J. smiled as they entered a dark black lit room echoing with slow contemporary music.

"Is she actually going to wait for you?" Jerrad said looking back at her as he stepped inside the room with his hands in his pockets while T.J. closed the door.

"Hell, yes, if she knows what is good for her." T.J. laughs nodding towards the room full of people. "Otherwise I will have to tie her to the end of my bed and let her sleep on the floor tonight. I was actually hoping to sleep with her instead. Unfortunately that is now up to her and depending on if she is waiting there when I get back, now isn't it?"

"Hey…"Jerrad stopped him by holding on to his large forearm and pointing his thumb back towards the woman over his shoulder. "Aren't you married, T.J.?"

"Yes, man, you just saw me grab my wife's hair. What do you take me for?" He laughed a loud jolly rumble at the baffled look on Jerrad's face. "Man, lighten up. She is happier than hell waiting out there. You need to think of this like the WWF and acting improv class. Sure, people are into it but it is also about attitude and a place where you can let it all bust loose. This is your night, your stage. Make a scene. Make a big one. You have no problem showing your balls in court, man. Do the same here. And let me tell you...they are fucking big balls you got. I have seen them. They scared the shit out of me more than once. Something tells me that is what she is looking to see right now."

"My balls?" Jerrad laughed rubbing his chin.

"You are funny, Jerrad. But this is not the night for comedy. Grill her ass well. Or I am sure the other guy will." T.J. laughed raising his eyebrows towards a crowd of people apparently gathered around a stage with the dark curtains closed. "Tonight is yours or it is his. In a place like this only one has the biggest balls. I am willing to bet it is you." T.J. winked and patted Jerrad on the back. "I will get things calmed down here and give you a few moments to get ready."

Jerrad sighed as he looked at the crowd of people loosely placed around the stage in the middle of the large room. As T.J. made his way to the stage several people allowed him to reach his destination. Jerrad rolled his neck slowly to stretch it and soothe his nerves. Sure, he was used to crowds and being the center of attention. When he finally spotted Alex dancing around on her tip toes tied up on the stage he realized what he wasn't used to...beating his wife's ass in public. Hell, he didn't even try it at home.

Jerrad grabbed a passing server and helped himself to a whiskey-coke. Something told him as T.J. turned around to address the crowd of curious on-lookers that he was going to need it.

"Welcome to The Toy Chest's private playroom. I'm T.J.

and own this palace you are visiting. Play nice and mind your manners and you can stay. Piss me off or someone else and I may just send you home. Now for those of you who are newbies or curious, a few friendly words of advice. If you see something you like don't assume it doesn't belong to someone else. Ask first instead of helping yourself. For those new to our establishment enjoy yourselves by respecting one and all. The easiest way to do that is to refrain from assuming anything. This is a place to enjoy and explore. Please do so in a safe, sane and consensual manner. Now if that all has sunk into your skulls I would like to turn down the lights while a very good friend of mine prepares to take the stage and give this naughty birthday girl the spanking she has wished for." T.J. waved for the crowd to step back as he nodded over to a server to turn down the lights to make it virtually pitch black.

Jerrad finished his drink just as T.J. arrived and handed him a soft black velvet mask that would cover his face for the most part.

"This is not our usual practice but I know you don't need anyone recognizing you in here." T.J. explained taking Jerrad's empty drink glass. "She has a blind fold on."

"Thanks. I should have tried that before now. Things would have been much quieter." Jerrad laughed slipping on the velvet mask.

"Was easy to do when she is led to believe it was her idea to begin with." T.J. grins wide. "There is a variety of instruments on the table next to her on the stage. Feel free to use them."

"Thanks." Jerrad says straightening the mask and looking at T.J. "How do I look?"

"Like you are ready to teach your wife a lesson." T.J. smiles patting Jerrad's shoulder for encouragement.

"You got that right." Jerrad said with a grin that warned of what was to come.

Alex danced around on her tip-toes while trying to get used to the rubber ball between her teeth blocking her mouth from fully closing. She heard voices behind her commenting on her nice body, long legs and beautiful skin. One man asked another who she belonged to. A female decided she looked delicious. Alex could feel her heart race when she finally felt a rush of cool air dance across her thighs telling her someone had finally joined her on stage.

Jerrad took a few moments to stand quietly as the lights lifted so that the crowd quieted their whispers and acknowledged him with their full attention. Alex was wearing her chandelier stilettos that drove him insane with thinking of fucking her. She was bare legged with a short soft white skirt that barely covered her tight little ass. She chose a sleeveless silk white top that plunged so far in the front that the swell of her natural and generously endowed cleavage glowed and bounced for all to envy. A diamond tennis bracelet that he gave her for Valentine's Day the year before adorned her left wrist along with her 5 carat wedding set on her left hand. She planned to wear her wedding rings while meeting him? A surge of anger formed a path down his spine. Her french manicured nails glowed as her fingers moved nervously around the chains that were hooked to the cuffs around her wrists. Her full lips sparkled as they quivered while she licked at them. Her medium length brown hair fell softly over her shoulders in wide curls. Even if she was dressed to meet someone else she looked so damn hot that he couldn't help but want her in the most sinful way possible.

Jerrad could smell her sweet natural scent under all that new perfume. She was excited and he could feel it. Something about that alone had his pulse dancing wildly.

He reached a hand out to brush up the back of her thigh. The feeling of her soft skin sent shocks through his fingertips and caused her to gasp loud enough for him to hear. His fingers curled around the bottom of her skirt and he lifted it slowly. He didn't expect to find her ass bare for the crowd to see. A hiss of surprise escaped his lips and reached her ear. Alex's lips curled into a taunting smile as she wiggled her ass slowly and suggestively causing a few guys to whistle.

In the blink of an eye, Jerrad's right hand found a crop off the table beside them and landed across her ass. Alex looked like a beginning ballet student as she hopped up and down as her skin puckered up in a pink welt to mark the spot that he landed the crop. A rush of energy filled him as he watched the effect his swatting her ass had on her. She was whimpering and her body was bouncing. Only watching her cum was hotter than that. He wanted more and he was aroused the more she moved. He didn't waste time waiting for her to stay still. Another firm swat sent the crop across her ass. Alex tossed her head back and she growled in pain. He took the crop and slid it between her knees and ran it up the sleek inside of her thigh.

"Stand still." Jerrad commanded in a tone of voice she would never recognize as his.

Alex stood still while Jerrad moved the crop up and under the skirt to her center. Just as he was playing a slow, sensual song on a violin he played with her, inspiring her to open her mouth and moan at the heavenly strokes the crop was taking across her clit and outer lips.

"Does that excite you?" He whispered in her ear.

"Yes." She answered licking her sweet lips.

"Do you deserve such pleasure?" He asked through clenched teeth as the anger built that the idea a stranger was playing with her excited her.

"Yes, Sir." She answered softly with a shudder that was full of expectation.

He pulled up the skirt higher in the back and tucked the hem into the waist at the small of her back so that her ass was bare for all to see.

"I disagree." Jerrad spoke slowly with firm control as he stood to the side of her looking at the table of toys. "Something tells me you deserve pain to the point you are craving it to extremes."

"No Sir." Alex quickly shook her head back and forth.

"Really? Then why are you standing here waiting for something to happen? Couldn't you find pleasure in your bed?" Jerrad asked with a flash of resentment that he was watching his wife stand in public chained up like a club slut waiting to be used by someone she had never met before.

"Maybe..." Alex smiled softly before a mischievous giggle escaped her lips. "Maybe not."

Jerrad's hand filled itself with thousands of her curls at the back of her head as it lost itself in the silky brown mane. He pulled back and paused a few moments squeezing the hair tighter in his grasp.

"Ungrateful bitch." Jerrad growled in her ear so that only she could hear.

"Hmm..." Alex purred confidently for a woman who was chained to the ceiling and floor in front of a crowd. "Sounds familiar. Almost reminds me of my..." she yawns in a cute manner for emphasis, "Husband."

The crowd laughs and whistles at her comment. Jerrad smirks at the crowd as he reaches for a small thick wooden paddle after putting the crop on the table. With a fast swing as he stood to the side he nearly lifted her off her feet with his first strike. The air jumped out of her lungs and she made no sound as he landed another swat across her ass. After four more he finally took a moment to breathe and that is when the red welts bloomed all across her ass.

Jerrad swallowed hard at the sight of her tenderized skin. His eyes looked up to find T.J. running a hand across his throat to signal stopping where he was at.

"More..." He heard her voice break the silence between

them. "Please."

"What?" Jerrad asked in disbelief that the same woman who would throw a profanity fit if she got a paper cut was asking for more pain.

"I asked for more. Unless of course, you don't have it in you." She taunted him.

Jerrad looked back over at T.J. as shrugged his shoulders to say who would have known she was into that sort of thing. Jerrad shook his head in disbelief as he looked down at his shoes. She was becoming more foreign to him as the time passed. The distance started to increase as he thought of how she was here to share time with a complete stranger. He walked around with his back to the crowd as he placed the paddle back down next to the other toys. Anger filled him and he looked up at her facing him.

"Do you want me to beg for it?" She asked with a sexy purr through her seductive lips.

"Yes." Jerrad hissed growing more resentful as she flirted with him.

"You wish." Alex laughed at him. "Next." She called to the crowd who began to whistle.

Jerrad looked back at the audience and put his hand on the crop and a few booed. He put his hand on the antique silver hair brush and a few more joined in. He looked up at the crowd and smiled as if he finally thought of something clever. Which he had.

Jerrad stepped in close to Alex and reached his hands around and placed each one firmly across each cheek covering the majority of her luscious ass. He pulled her in close so that he could almost taste her lip gloss as his lips brushed across her open mouth. Slowly his hands gripped down into her tender flesh pulling her ass tighter into his hands, squeezing her without mercy. The audience watched hungrily as Jerrad's fingers moved slowly to pull at the wet space between her legs separating her folds. Jerrad could hear her breathe heavy as he looked over her shoulder at the crowd heating up in excitement.

With a smile he sunk one of his fingers up into her juicy pool, stirring the sweetness inside before pulling it back out. Keeping his hand in the crowd's view, he brought it up over her shoulder to his mouth and sucked it with an appreciative smile.

Alex brushed her nose against his neck sending his skin into bumps. He tongue snaked up to his ear as he stood there frozen at how forward his wife was being with a stranger.

"If you break me, you can take me." Alex whispered into his ear.

Jerrad's hands left her red ass and came between them to her chest. Gripping each side of her flimsy top he tore it in half and the crowd cheered. She was braless. His eyes widened in surprise as her tits bounced back and forth at the motion of the fabric leaving in the air to either side.

He reached over to the table and took off what appeared to be nipple clamps with a chain between them. The crowd cheered as he quickly clamped the first one on her left nipple.

"Oh shit!" Alex yelped as she swung her head back and forth to make sense of the burning pain spreading across her chest as Jerrad pulled on the chain to seize the other clamp in his fingers.

Jerrad clamped the other clip in place on her right nipple and slowly wrapped the chain in his hand. He pulled and lifted her heavy tits into the air with her following standing on her tip toes. He watched her shift her weight from one foot to the other until she could accept that the clamps were not moving unless he chose.

"Do you like that?" Jerrad asked as he lifted his hand higher putting the chain in the air above her head.

"Yes." Alex hissed and bit down on her bottom lip.

"You are full of surprises." Jerrad said watching her tits move up and down while he tugged on the chain.

He wanted to bury his face in the soft moisture and warmth of her heavenly tits but he was supposed to be pissed off. With her dangling on a chain and enjoying the pain he found himself strangely aroused and wanting to slide inside her while everyone watched instead of torture her for tramping around behind his back.

"I made a wish." Alex said as he pulled the chain closer to him making her step into him.

"Really?" Jerrad responded feeling the fullness of her curves and hot body press into his.

"Oh yes." She paused with her mouth open searching for his.

He barely dodged her attempts to kiss him when he yanked the chain to pull the clamps and her tits away from each other. She gasped and tossed her head back.

Jerrad couldn't resist tasting a part of her so he decided to bite her neck roughly before sucking in the softest part of skin just in the crook of her neck. He sucked hard and bit down on the flesh between his teeth until she cried out. She moaned and went limp in his arms as he worked his mouth at her neck and pulled her into his body. Wrapping his arms around her body to grab a firm tight hold on her ass, Jerrad showed no mercy as he sucked as if he was hungry.

Alex's body began shaking and her breathing increased as she panted in his ear.

"Yes…" She moaned in his ear. "Don't stop."

Jerrad sucked harder as one of his hands held her ass roughly in his palm and the other twisted the chain sadistically to torment her nipples.

"Ahh…" She gasped and moaned. "Harder."

Jerrad swatted her ass and then shoved a middle finger up inside hooking into the silky wall. He lifted her by pulling hard at the chain and pulling her up with the hand impaling her between her legs.

"Yes…" She moaned as she felt the first spasms begin in her.

Jerrad fucked her with his hand and sucked at her neck.

"Ahh…" Her body convulsed as she came in his hands. "Jerrad, yes!"

Jerrad's mouth left her neck immediately and his hand let the chain go and grabbed her face firmly. He pulled her blindfold off and then his. His eyes moved across her face for an explanation after she caught her breath.

"I set up the chat box in the office. You were chatting with me the whole time. There is no one else. I just wanted you and your undivided attention. I have missed you so much." Alex was about to continue with her explanation until Jerrad's mouth covered hers. The crowd whistled and clapped. Even T.J. had to give them a hand of applause.

"Time to go home and have a talk." Jerrad said letting her back down to stand on her own.

"What about my top?" Alex said trying to snuggle into Jerrad's chest to hide while T.J. released her from the cuffs on her ankles and wrists.

"You will be lucky if you don't leave here on your hands and knees for pulling this stunt." He whispered in her ear as he tugged hard on the chain dangling between her tits.

"Damn…" She gasped at the pain. "Okay, okay."

"I guess we will see you two later." T.J. said as he tossed the cuffs on the table.

"You can count on it." Jerrad said with a wink pulling Alex along by the chain.

*Dark Fantasies*

*Dark Fantasies*